Assault or Attrition
Book Two in the Ar~~~ ~~~~ ~~~~~~

Cover Art by A

Arena Mode Logo by

Arena Mode is Copyright © a

Blake Northcott, Digital Vanguard Inc. and Noösphere Publishing

ArenaMode.com

Written By
Blake Northcott

Editors
Jim Deley, Jeff Geddes & J.D. Hunter
With additional help from Kiri Callaghan
& Mike 'cleverpawn' Stephenson

Illustrations By
John Broglia
with grey tones by Jasen Smith
with additional greys and graphics by Sean Dyer

Character Designs By
Natasha Allegri
Jason Baroody
John Broglia
Comic Book Girl 19
Dave Johnson
Derek Laufman
Steve McNiven
Mark McKenna
Dan Panosian
John 'Roc' Upchurch

PART ONE
TORMENTOR AND SOLACE

CHAPTER ONE

"How did it feel to kill a superhero?" Her words were muffled by a mouthful of spaghetti.

I couldn't help but smile. Coming from a six-year-old girl the question sounded perfectly innocent – almost sweet. I knew my sister would have never allowed her children to watch the Arena Mode tournament, but she couldn't isolate them from the rest of the world. Eventually, some way or another, they were going to discover the truth about their uncle Matt. And once they did, they'd undoubtedly have some questions.

Three months had passed since the summer of 2041, and I was still the most talked-about man on the planet. Simulcasts speculated about every aspect of my life: my physical condition, my whereabouts, and the psychological toll the tournament had taken on me. And whenever the name Matthew Moxon appeared in the media – almost without exception – my unfortunate moniker accompanied it: *The God Slayer.*

The fact that I'd won a dangerous sporting event designed for superhumans made headlines across the globe; the footage had been replayed, discussed and analysed by everyone from anchormen to astrophysicists. The little details about how I competed without a super-power of my own, all while a massive tumor was eating away at my brain – big news as well. But what the press had *really* been obsessing over, day and night, was *who* I'd eliminated en route to crossing the proverbial finish line: Sergei Taktarov. A man who could fly, shoot lasers from his eyes, and was nearly invincible. A man who many believed to be the Second Coming. The same man who was now lying on a slab in the morgue beneath the Kremlin...and all thanks to Uncle Matt.

"Addison!" my sister hissed. It was that special combination of a shout and a whisper that parents use to scold their children without making a scene. "We talked about this."

"It's all right, Liz." I put down my steak knife and dabbed at the corner of my mouth with the edge of a napkin. "Let them get it out of their systems. Better to hear it from me than a kid on the playground."

I'd spent months in seclusion, aggressively avoiding every interview request that came my way, so I suppose I had this coming to me. With my permission, and a reluctant nod from their parents, Addison and her four-year-old brother Austin unleashed a barrage of unfiltered questions:

"Was that guy you killed Superman?" No, but he kinda dressed like him.

"Are you smarter than Lex Luthor?" Yes. *Way* smarter. And I have better hair.

"Are you rich now?" Yes.

"Will you buy us dessert?" Ask your mother.

"Do you have any super powers?" No. There are some things that even money can't buy.

"Did it hurt when the doctors zapped your tumor?" No, I was asleep when it happened.

"Does your brain still work?" Aside from a little bit of short-term memory loss, yes. At least I *think* it does.

"Are you Batman?" No.

"Are you Iron Man?" Nope.

"Are you a Power Ranger?" Yes. Yes I am.

"Who is that girl you came in here with?" My accountant.

Austin squinted at the young redhead sitting at an adjacent table. "Why did your accounter come here with us?"

It was a fair question. The petite, well-dressed businesswoman was becoming my second shadow. Valentina, who was engrossed in a romance novel, must have overheard my nephew; her lips curled at the edges with the onset of a smile, but she didn't reply.

"Yuck," Addison blurted out, before I could offer an explanation. "These fries are gross. Mom, can we go upstairs to the look-out deck?"

My sister let out an exasperated sigh. "No, but if you finish your milk you can be excused from the table, and go look out the window."

The sentence had barely finished before Addison started chugging.

"And take your brother," Gary added. "*And* stay where we can see you."

I could have afforded a much nicer restaurant, but when dining at the top of the CN Tower, food wasn't the main attraction. Like everyone else, we were there for the view. While not nearly as impressive as the megatowers that dominated London, Dubai and New York City, it was still the largest freestanding structure in Canada, and offered an expansive view of downtown Toronto, rotating slowly to allow guests a three-hundred and sixty degree look at the skyline. Even on a cloudy October afternoon you could see halfway across Lake Ontario.

As the children scampered off towards the window Elizabeth's expression immediately hardened. I hadn't spent much time with my sister since we lived together at our parents' house, which was almost fifteen years ago, but I could still read her tells. Liz was never much of a poker player – every emotion spilled out of her eyes like water from Niagara Falls.

"Matthew," she said sternly, sounding even more maternal than usual. "Since Arena Mode ended we've barely heard from you. Gary and I have been worried sick."

My brother-in-law nodded in agreement.

"I'm fine, guys – really. I just needed some time to decompress. Take a breather, you know? My surgery went as well as I could have hoped, and—"

"Not that," she interrupted. "You called us when you came out of surgery. I'm talking about *after*. We haven't heard anything since August. The news is talking about this Red Army coming after you, seeking retribution for killing that Russian man, and then you up and disappeared."

Gary leaned in on his elbows, removing his wire-frame glasses. "We don't let the kids watch the simulcasts, but they *do* hear things, Matt. They've been worried, too. Did you know that the news has been reporting that you might have been captured by these radicals – or worse?"

Spend a little time in Maui and everyone starts losing their minds. After enduring a deathmatch-style fighting tournament *and* major surgery in the same week, you'd think a guy could enjoy a little rest and relaxation without being cross-examined. "I appreciate your concern guys, but it's all good. Most of the freaks who identified themselves as 'Red Army' killed themselves in that big suicide pact when Taktarov was pronounced dead. They were a crazy cult filled with crazy people. The media is running out of things to report since I won't talk to them, so now they're spreading rumors and bullshit theories."

Elizabeth went on to explain that it's not only my physical well-being she was concerned about, it was my state of mind. I had a long history of going into self-imposed exile, and she felt like I might be hurting my chances at a meaningful relationship with Peyton.

I assured her that Peyton – my committed girlfriend – is *totally* fine with our time apart. She knows I need some space now and then, and she knows how I feel about her.

My sister's problem is that she can't imagine that anyone could experience love differently than she does. She'd been married to Gary for over ten years, and they seemed more infatuated with each other than ever. They were one of those annoying couples who wouldn't spend a night apart without chatting in a holo-session for an hour before bed because they couldn't bear the separation. Not everyone needs that. Peyton and I have our own thing, and both of us *know* it's real; it doesn't need to be constantly reinforced by hand-written notes and trails of rose petals and leaving origami birds on each other's pillows.

As I continued to explain my very normal, non-codependent relationship to my overbearing sister, I heard a rattle. My knife. It was chattering as my hand trembled, rapping involuntarily against the edge of my porcelain dinner plate.

"What's that?" Gary asked, scratching at his beard.

"Just a tremor," I replied as casually as possible.

"A *what?*" Liz shouted, much louder than she had intended. She drew the attention of a handful of guests, as well as a waitress who was refilling water glasses at a nearby table.

"A temporary side-effect of the surgery," I explained in a more reasonable tone of voice. "It's *very* common according to Doctor Anderson, and it's nothing to worry about."

I struggled to steady my hand and slice through the remaining piece of tenderloin, but the trembling persisted, and I dropped the knife. It bounced off the table and landed at my feet. Before I could lean over to retrieve the cutlery a friendly waiter intervened, stooping to assist me. "No, please sir," he said in a thick accent that I couldn't quite place. "I will get that for you."

I was in the process of thanking him when the blade slid into my stomach. It penetrated beneath my ribcage; deep, twisting, scraping the bone as he yanked it out. I toppled from my chair. The waiter had time for one more frantic stab, slashing my forearm as I reached up to defend myself, before Gary tackled him to the ground.

Clapping my hands over the blood-soaked wound, it spurted like a faucet through the space between my fingers. Screams echoed throughout the restaurant. My vision blurred and the room spun. I glanced up to see Gary being shoved away by the burly waiter, who started making his way back towards me, determined to finish what he'd started. And that's when he began to drown.

My water cup emptied. The remaining liquid rose from my glass and splashed into his face. As if on command, a ribbon of water traveled through the air in a split second, directly into my attacker's airway, filling his throat and nostrils.

Gasping and hacking, he attempted to expel the water, but his efforts were futile. The waiter's face reddened as he choked, unable to produce more than a few drops from his mouth.

Undeterred, the man lunged towards me; wild-eyed, knife poised above his head; his white dress shirt spattered a dark shade of crimson.

The room dried instantly.

Every drop of liquid in the restaurant – beverages, the humidity in the air, even the moisture from people's eyes and mouths – gathered in front of Valentina. It formed a massive, gyrating ball of water, hovering inches away from her outstretched hands. When she unleashed it, the force struck my attacker's chest like an oversized cannonball.

Engulfed in a tidal wave of water and shattered glass, his body sailed through the window, across the highway and into the distance, disappearing into the dense fog that hung over the lake.

8

Gary called an ambulance while Elizabeth rushed to my side, pressing a wad of napkins into my wound with both hands.

Valentina raced off to secure the perimeter.

"Oh my god," my sister whispered, her voice trembling as tears streamed down her cheeks.

I tried to force a smile. It was the only way I could think to calm Elizabeth's nerves, and convince her that my injuries weren't as bad as they looked. "Don't worry about me," I winced. "It's almost impossible to kill a Power Ranger."

William O'Neill: I'm not condoning violence, Senator. I'm saying that we live in a religious country – a country of folks who take *pride* in their faith and celebrate it. Is that wrong?

Sen. Alex Jenkins (D-N.Y.): I don't see how that—

O'Neill: And look, I'm no theologian. But I *am* a religious man. I have beliefs, and those beliefs won't be trampled by the left-wing media. I'm a practicing Catholic, for cryin' out loud!

Sen. Jenkins: As am I, Mister O'Neill, but that doesn't really—

O'Neill: With all due respect, Senator, *don't* interrupt me. You'll get your turn, all right?

As I was saying, this is very, very simple: it's about justice. 'An eye for an eye.' But the liberal media doesn't see it that way. They're trying to spin this into some kind of a sob story about Matthew Moxon, this billionaire elitist –who is an *atheist*, by the way – did you know that? This atheist gets stabbed in some Canadian restaurant. Like we're all supposed to feel sorry for him now, after what he did?

Sen. Jenkins: The stabbing was reported less than thirty minutes ago. With so few details about the incident I don't think we can form an opinion about—

O'Neill: It turns out he's fine. It was just a *scrape*, and he's in stable condition.

But what *I'm* interested in: he brings a *superhuman* with him for protection! The guy knows he has a target painted on his back for what he did in Arena Mode, so he's surrounding himself with these human weapons.

That's the same as walking into a building with a bazooka. Is that acceptable, Senator? Walking around with a bazooka? Are we going to have new laws in Canada where you can just waltz into a store and say, "Hey, look at me, I want to buy some gum. By the way, I have a bazooka!"

Is *that* the world we're living in?

Sen. Jenkins: First of all, I'm a Senator from the state of New York. I've actually never *been* to Toronto, where this attack took place, so I don't see how discussing their policies—

O'Neill: All right, so Moxon wins this reality show – this 'Arena Mode' deal right here in Manhattan. It's a nightmare. They block the streets, kick us all out of our homes – and for what? To host some no-holds-barred fighting tournament.

Superhumans fighting to the death? What next, Senator? Are we just going to start throwing babies into lion cages so folks can stand around and film it on their camera phones for entertainment?

Sen. Jenkins: Mister O'Neill, with all due respect I thought this was going to be a debate about the proposed minimum wage increase.

O'Neill: This is a live simulcast, Senator. News breaks and we have to make adjustments on the fly. This is what the folks want to see.

Sen. Jenkins: All right, so do you actually have a question for me?

O'Neill: Absolutely. The question is this: how are we supposed to feel sorry for this Matthew Moxon – this billionaire *atheist* who is, I'm sorry, a murderer?

Sen. Jenkins: Who did he murder, exactly?

O'Neill: Sergei Taktarov! In cold blood. And his accomplice – this Brynja What's-her-name who claimed to be a resident of Iceland, conveniently disappears.

Sen. Jenkins: Let me get this straight, Mister O'Neill: Sergei Taktarov backed Matthew Moxon into a corner, where he was hiding in an alley. He slammed Moxon into a dumpster, nearly knocking him unconscious. Then, before he could finish the job, Moxon's partner dropped an acid-filled bullet into his brain, killing him.

O'Neill: Right.

Sen. Jenkins: So the rules and regulations of the tournament aside, wasn't Moxon just defending himself? Taktarov was about to kill *him*.

O'Neill: Possibly – we don't know that.

Sen. Jenkins: Taktarov killed two people earlier in the tourna—

O'Neill: Look, I'm not a criminologist and I'm not going to argue semantics with you, Senator. But this year, a number of evangelical pastors predicted a cataclysmic event. They talked about the End Times. Do you think it's just a coincidence that these predictions come now, in the *exact* same year as Moxon kills Taktarov?

Sen. Jenkins: There have been predictions and prophecies about the end of the world virtually every year. They go back centuries.

O'Neill: I don't keep track of *every* single prophecy – I'm a busy man. All I know is that folks predicted the End Times *this* year, and look what happened?

This is history repeating itself. *Every time* a saviour with supernatural powers comes to earth, promising to usher in a new age of peace and prosperity, he's *killed*.

Sen. Jenkins: As far as I'm aware that only happened once.

O'Neill: And now it's happened again! Are you denying that, Senator? You're just going to sit there, stare me in the face and deny it?

Sen. Jenkins: I'm not s—

O'Neill: Moxon figures out a way to kill this man – a man who appears to be nearly indestructible – and then disappears. He falls off the face of the earth for months. No press release, no comment. He just up and leaves America in some state-of-the-art hover plane.

Then, three months later he shows up in Canada of all places – the guy can't even be bothered to return to America – and in his *first* public appearance he gets stabbed.

Sen. Jenkins: So what are you saying?

O'Neill: I'm saying that this is just the beginning, Senator. The tip of the iceberg. Moxon shows his face for ten seconds in a country where it's practically illegal to be in a bad mood, and he almost gets killed.

He's the most hated man on the planet, and there will be a *lot* more people out there gunning for him, you mark my words.

And on a related note, my new book 'The Beauty of the Status Quo: Life, Liberty and Low Taxes.' will be available tomorrow.

Sen. Jenkins: Wait, how is that a related note? And are we finished? I thou—

O'Neill: Thank you for being here, Senator. And now a word from our sponsor.

CHAPTER TWO

"Are you out of your mind?" the nurse shouted from just beyond the threshold. "Lay down, you'll pop your stitches!"

With my bare feet dangling from the side of the hospital bed, I scanned the room through bleary eyes, tired and stinging from the harsh glare of fluorescent bulbs overhead. I'd forgotten where I was, and how I'd arrived.

By the time the nurse reached me the blood had already seeped through my gown. "Lay back," she instructed, rapidly unfastening the buttons around my abdomen. The gruesome gash beneath my ribcage looked freshly sutured, with a single stitch popped out of place. "It doesn't look too bad. Just take it easy, and I'll find a doctor."

I glanced at the translucent bracelet fastened around my wrist. 'Joseph Brant Memorial Hospital. Burlington, Ontario'. It all came back to me in broken, jagged fragments. Screams. Blood. Flashing lights. And questions – lots of questions. Doctors and nurses asking me if I knew my own name, and what day it was, and if I could count how many fingers were being held up in front of me. Surprisingly simple questions become quite a challenge to answer when you're fading in and out of consciousness, blood streaming from a gaping wound in your body.

I craned my neck in search of clothes and quickly realized I wasn't alone. Valentina was slouched into an angular wooden chair, cradling a paper cup in her lap. Using her ability to manipulate water she was creating a tiny show for herself, forcing the liquid to dance and flow in long, spiralling streams. When she averted her eyes the water fell, splashing back into the cup.

"Good morning, sunshine." Her voice was scratchy and dry from the winter air. The dark circles around her eyes indicated that she hadn't slept in days – possibly since I was admitted. "Do I submit a form for overtime pay, or will the funds show up on my next paycheck?"

"Don't worry about it. You'll be compensated." I squinted at the oversized clock on the far wall, which marked each passing second with an annoying click.

"Sixty-two hours, nineteen minutes," she stated, before I had the chance to ask the question. "They said you can leave as soon as you're able to climb a flight of stairs. You were lucky, Mox. The blade missed every major vein and artery."

I never believed in the absurd notion of luck, but as I continued to cheat death time after time, the concept was slowly growing on me.

As Valentina continued to fill in the blanks of the previous two and a half days, a towering, dark-skinned man strolled into the room with a briefcase in-hand.

"Officer...Dziobak?" I remembered him from Manhattan, when he was hired as private security for Cameron Frost. Even with my memory functioning at a hundred percent, I still had no idea how to pronounce his name.

He chuckled and extended his hand, shaking mine gently. "I told you, Mox – call me Todd. And it's 'detective' now, which is why I lost the blues." He gestured down at his perfectly pressed khaki pants and crisp white shirt. "How are things? Aside from being a human pin cushion?" His eye trailed down to the fresh bloodstain that dotted my hospital gown.

"I've been better," I said flatly. "But they said it'll be *months* before I can break dance again." I motioned to my bodyguard, who scrambled to her feet and attempted to straighten her blazer and skirt. The outfit was rumpled with a coffee stain marking the left arm; after sleeping in her clothes for two consecutive nights, there was no amount of fussing that could have made it appear even remotely presentable. "This is Valentina Garcia."

"I read the reports," Todd replied with an affable smile. "Nice work up there in the tower, Miss Garcia. A little messy, but effective. Is that what they taught you in Central Africa?"

I raised an eyebrow, glancing back at her.

"I see you did your homework on me," she replied, her words frosting over as they spilled from her lips. "Africa was just a job."

The detective had clearly struck a nerve. Valentina's posture stiffened, hands balling into tightly clenched fists. I'd never known her to have a short fuse, so the visceral reaction to the officer's question caught me off-guard.

Before the conversation spiralled out of control I decided to intervene, projecting as much authority as I could while lying prone in a hospital gown. "Can someone please tell me what's going on here?"

"Your bodyguard has quite a resume," Todd explained. "She protected a military dictator for over a year. Quite an evil bastard from what I understand, even by the impressive standards of that region." His eyes flicked back to Valentina. "Not too picky about the clients you work for, I'm guessing."

"The money spends the same as anyone else's," she fired back.

Todd smiled once again, but it didn't reach his eyes. "I'm sure it does, Miss Garcia...once you wash the blood off."

I threw my legs over the side of the bed, forcing myself to stand. The sudden movement caused a burning sensation that stretched from my lower abdomen straight up my spinal column. I swayed. Todd reached out and clasped his hand around my arm, keeping me upright. I made a mental note to ask for some additional pain-killers when the nurse came to re-stitch my stomach.

I thanked the detective for his assistance, and asked Valentina to step outside for a moment so we could speak privately. She agreed, replying with nothing more than a sharp nod.

Todd waited for the heavy wooden door to slam shut behind him before speaking again. "She's a piece of work."

I couldn't argue, but her results speak for themselves. "She has her moments, but I owe her my life."

The detective said nothing, but the look on his face spoke volumes. In his line of work, you survived by putting faith in the people watching your back. When someone takes an oath to protect you – and pulls through in a life-or-death situation – it's hard to pass judgment on their track record, no matter how sketchy the details might seem at the time.

"Should you be walking around?" he asked.

I groaned and leaned back, using the edge of my bed for support. "Probably not, but I need to get out of here sooner than later." I glanced down at his briefcase. "I appreciate the visit, but I assume you're not here for a social call."

He laid the case flat on my bed and unlatched the locks, flipping open the lid. Inside was a tattered manila folder six inches thick. Old school cop, old school filing system, I suppose. I couldn't blame him; given the choice, I still preferred the texture of paper against my fingertips to scanning a lifeless holo-screen.

Riffling through the stack of photographs and hand-written notes, he yanked out a creased eight-by-ten snapshot and held it up for my inspection. "Recognize this beauty?"

It was the waiter who stabbed me; a stocky, unshaven man in his mid-thirties, with closely cropped black hair and a broken nose that looked as if it had been continually deviated from a lifetime of bar fights, and had never been allowed enough time to properly heal between brawls.

"His name is Oleg Vovchanchyn, a Russian who immigrated to Canada three years ago. When the Toronto PD fished his body out of Lake Ontario I gave them a call and asked to see some of the evidence." Todd pulled out a second photo that showed the man's shirtless chest, likely taken just prior to an autopsy.

Tattoos – seventeen of them, to be exact – blanketed his torso, all with distinct meanings. I assumed at one point they were black, but over the years, the symbols and images had faded to a time-worn, muddy blue. A grim reaper stretched around his ribcage, clutching a sickle in one skeletal hand and a newborn baby in the other. Todd explained that, in a Russian prison, a tattoo of the reaper signifies that you've killed before. I didn't want to know what the baby meant.

Vovchanchyn also had a pair of stars that adorned his shoulders, barbed wire wrapped around his midsection, and the Crucifixion of Christ emblazoned across his chest. Although they all meant something different, they had one thing in common: they were old. Nearly ten years, by the looks of the most recent ink – all except for one. A single tattoo was not only in color, but practically glowed like a fresh coat of paint: a bright red hammer and sickle emblem on his left bicep.

"So he's a Russian," I said flatly, tapping the photo. "Aren't they into that Soviet-era stuff?"

"Maybe," he replied. "But Oleg here went out and got inked *recently*. What significant event in this guy's life could have prompted him to get his first tattoo in a decade?"

"He's Red Army. How did he know I would be at the CN Tower?" My first reaction was to assume that I was being followed, or that, however unlikely, someone in my inner circle had leaked my location.

"He didn't," Todd said with a small shake of his head. "His phone records and Emails came up clean. Not to mention he's been working at the 360 Restaurant for the last two years. I think it was a coincidence."

It didn't seem possible. "So someone who wanted me dead just *happened* to be serving a plate of fries at the table next to me? Shit...guess I'm not as lucky as I thought."

"It was going to happen to you sooner or later, because it's been happening all over the world."

"What, people getting attacked by angry Russians with poor hygiene?"

"No," Todd replied gravely. "People getting terminated who look a hell of a lot like you." He leafed through his file folder and produced more than a dozen photographs of dead bodies. All of the victims were around thirty years old with short brown hair, a square jaw line and blue eyes – it was uncanny. The man who got his throat slit in Oslo could have been my twin.

"This file represents the body count that piled up during the three months you've been gone. This is the first killer we've caught thanks to your bodyguard, but after a shooting in Budapest last month I dug up this security footage." He pulled a tablet from the inside pocket of the briefcase and projected a small holo-screen into the air. The soundless video played instantly, displaying a young girl with shoulder–length blond hair, dressed from head-to-toe in black leather. She was circling a corner to duck into an alley, making no attempt to conceal the smoking revolver that she was clutching in her hand. When her back faced the camera, Todd commanded the footage to pause and enhance three-hundred percent. With her hair flowing in mid-stride, the base of her neck was exposed, and it revealed a bright red tattoo. Fresh as a new coat of paint.

I studied the video as it flickered in the sunlight that began to pour through my room's lone window. The pieces came together with terrifying clarity. "How many?" I asked, unable to unglue my eyes from the holo-screen.

"No idea," Todd replied softly. "A hundred? A thousand? Hell, we don't even know *how* the Red Army is communicating. All we know is that there are a *lot* of them, and they're everywhere. And today my theory was confirmed."

"What's that?"

"That the group's objective is pretty simple," he said. "If there's a chance to kill Matthew Moxon, take it – no matter what the cost."

The reason I hired a bodyguard in the first place was because I anticipated the backlash, even before news reports started flooding in about the rise of the Red Army. I just had no idea things would escalate this rapidly, or to this degree.

Despite the deepening economic divide in America and around the world, violent crime had actually decreased across the board. Angered with the disparity between the privileged and the rest of the population, people vented their frustrations online and during the occasional protest – but for the most part, the working poor remained silent. Not because of apathy; at least that's not how I saw it. I think it was simply a case of exhaustion. Over time a grim realization set in: no matter who they voted for, the man or woman in the Oval Office would maintain the status quo. It was unfair, and demoralizing, and it was certainly worth shouting about, but the average person was simply too tired to continue ice skating uphill.

Now, this was something different. In the aftermath of Sergei Taktarov's death, a spark had been ignited that birthed a movement. Russia's Son had embodied everything people wished they could be: he'd been strong, assertive, and powerful beyond measure – and they thought he would be the answer to their prayers. Whether he had the power to carry out his promises and enact massive change was irrelevant, because his followers believed in him. For the first time in generations there'd been hope, and I'd dashed it.

The Red Army's backlash certainly had the potential to escalate, although it seemed unlikely. Movements, violent or otherwise, were always stomped out before they had the opportunity to spread. The Chicago riot of 2030 was the last public protest of any consequence; it erupted when Congress passed a bill to lower the already stagnant minimum wage, and the result was a silent massacre. People took to the streets, only to be met with tear gas, cattle prods and worse. Only a handful of fatalities were reported, but some estimate the real number was closer to a thousand. In the aftermath, anyone wearing a 'Remember Chicago' armband anywhere in America was detained and questioned, being accused of sympathising with domestic terrorists.

By the time the most recent presidential assassination attempt took place in 2035, most of the modern world was already a polarized oligarchy. You were either one of the elite or you weren't – there wasn't much in-between.

Now, the world's most deprived citizens were standing up and taking action, no longer resigned to suffer in silence. Someone – anyone – needed to pay. The government was untouchable, and the upper-class were faceless; a group of random businesspeople who had hoarded most of the world's wealth. I was the easiest person to point a finger at, and until the witch hunt was called off, I was in the Red Army's crosshairs.

I staggered to the window and pressed my palms into either side of the frame, peering down at the parking lot below. Police cars surrounded the building, and a number of blockades were in place to stem the flow of traffic. Visitors and staff members alike were being thoroughly searched before they were permitted to enter the hospital.

"This can't all be for me?" I asked without turning around.

"Every last one of them," Todd replied with a small nod. "You were moved a couple times already in between surgeries; first Mississauga, then Oakville. We're now in Burlington – a city around forty miles west of Toronto."

"Do Peyton and Gavin know I'm here?"

"I called them as soon as I heard," he said. "I sent a bird out for them – they should be here within the hour."

I was still staring out the window when she arrived. From five stories up I spotted a slender girl dressed in black, her pink locks billowing in the frozen wind.

Detective Dziobak went downstairs and ushered her past security with a wave of his badge, leading her towards a pair of sliding doors. Her brother – my best friend Gavin – was nowhere to be seen.

When Peyton walked into my room I rushed towards her, throwing my arms open. The greeting I received was a lightning-fast slap that nearly threw me off-balance when her palm connected with my cheekbone.

Todd walked through the doorway behind her, just in time to catch the show. "Well, that's my cue," he said bluntly. "Mox, nice seeing you again. I'll be in touch about the thing, if anything..."He trailed off momentarily, fumbling for the door handle. "Miss Lockridge, it was a pleasure." And with a quick nod he slammed it shut behind him.

I massaged my aching face with one hand and threw the other to my side. "You can't slap someone who just came out of surgery! And *wow*, have you been working out?"

"*Ass*hole!" Peyton screamed. "If you wanted to break up you could have been a man and told me to my face. I think I deserve at least *that* much."

29

My words lodged in the back of my throat. "Break up? I don't want to...I didn't break—"

"Three months!" She shouted, waving an accusing finger in my face. "You said you needed to blow off some steam, so I figure, 'Okay, well that's just Matty being Matty'. Maybe a night at the bar and a few days huddled in your man cave reading comics – then everything would be back to normal. But you disappeared!"

"You *know* me," I implored. "I'd never leave you."

Her eyes widened. "You packed your stuff and left town...in a jet. I think that's the textbook definition of 'leaving'."

"I've been going through some..." I trailed off and tilted my head back, eyes fixed on the fluorescent bulbs overhead. I didn't know how to explain my state of mind without coming off as a victim – or worse, a mentally unstable whiner who lacked any basic coping skills. "It's my head. My thoughts, my dreams...Arena Mode did things to me that I can't explain. I didn't want to burden anyone, so I left until I could sort it out on my own."

"I know you're new to this whole relationship thing," she said quietly. Her voice lowered in volume, but I could see the anger bubbling behind her eyes. "So maybe I should have bought you a manual, or signed you up for a seminar or something. But *this*," she said sharply, waving her hand back and forth between us several times, "*this* is what it's all about. Talking and stuff – like normal humans tend to do."

I never excelled at communicating with other humans, which I guess was part of the problem. It was why I spent so much time alone in a windowless room engrossed in graphic novels. And it was why I did most of my socializing online, where I could get things off my chest using no more than a few lines of text and an Emoji. Keeping in constant contact with someone was outside of my comfort zone, and I didn't realize how big a part of this whole dating thing that actually was.

Although, in my defense, Peyton knew all of this well before we started dating, so I'm not sure what she was complaining about. I'd been the same since the moment we met.

"So where have you been this entire time?" she asked with a tone that suggested an accusation.

"Maui," I replied swiftly.

"Bullshit. You hate the sun. And water. And basically everything that has to do with being outside."

"I was!" I scanned the room for my belongings, frantically searching for my jeans. "When I find my wallet you can check my passport."

"So you were in Maui...for *three* months?" She folded her arms tightly across her chest and arched her eyebrows, scanning my face intently. "Alone? You didn't go *anywhere* with *anyone* else?"

This was that awkward moment in a lie when a half-truth comes into question. I was technically being honest: yes, I was in Maui – and yes, I was alone. At least 'alone' in the sense that I wasn't hooking up with another girl. But there were a few layovers on my itinerary during the flight home, and I was doing things that I simply couldn't share with Peyton. At least not yet. "Look, I *did* go a couple of other places, but that's not important right now. There's something I need to tell you."

She pressed her lips into a tight line, narrowing her eyes in frustration. "At this point nothing will surprise me."

"I think we should move in together."

Her jaw fell slack. "Okay...I'm surprised."

"And I already have our new place picked out." When I was able to locate my personal belongings (which were folded neatly into the bottom drawer of my nightstand – the last place I bothered to look) I dug my phone from the pocket of my jeans. With a voice command I expanded a small floating holo-screen, displaying a three-hundred and sixty degree, rotating picture my new home: 'Fortress 23'. Located across a remote mountain range in Northern Alberta, the dome-like structure was built directly into the leeward side. Multiple levels, hoverpads and a military-grade hangar spread across more than a hundred acres. It was the most impressive structure I'd ever seen: a futuristic castle roughly the size of The Vatican – and it was all mine.

The fortress was part and parcel in a lawsuit I'd won in the aftermath of Arena Mode. Cameron Frost – the tournament's founder and mastermind – had entered as a participant, concealed inside of a giant mechanical exoskeleton of his own design. The fact that he failed to reveal his identity before entering the game wasn't technically against the rules. What *was* against the rules (and the law) was the way he manipulated the tournament in his favor as it progressed, allowing him a number of unfair advantages.

In 2041, sporting events functioned more or less as they always had, though the stakes were continually raised to keep up with the times. Brain damage, dismemberment, death – these things were incidental in the pursuit of a championship trophy. Within the confines of Arena Mode, you were permitted to disable your opponent by any means necessary; but get caught cheating while you're doing it? That's something the American people simply won't stand for.

Without a will or a family to fight for his estate, it was awarded to me as the last man standing. He'd been responsible for the death of several people during the course of the games, and had put another in a coma. The rest of the participants had died in combat, so by default I was the only one able to wage a legal battle. His companies, stock holdings, and as it turns out his real estate were all being transferred into my name, and the total value was staggering. The ten billion dollar prize I was awarded for actually winning the Arena Mode tournament was pocket change by comparison. Although the lawsuit was resolved relatively quickly, it was taking several months to transfer all the assets. Primarily because Frost had kept so many secrets buried in so many different places, it was taking a while for my lawyers to dig them all up.

I had just discovered that Fortress 23 was now part of my continually-expanding real estate portfolio, and I hadn't had the opportunity to inspect it in person. Although in light of my current situation, the timing couldn't have been better. With the Red Army pursuing me, it was the perfect location to lay low until the movement died out. Far removed from any major cities, the fortress would be nearly impossible to locate, let alone travel to across hundreds of kilometers of rocky terrain. And if anyone from the Red Army *was* able to find me, there was *no way* they were getting in; based on the initial specs I'd reviewed, the fortress was reinforced, top to bottom, with iridium plating – it would take a nuclear blast just to cause a dent.

I explained the impressive list of amenities to Peyton as the floor plans slid by. "It has everything," I said excitedly, swiping over to a photograph of the massive dome, "including an ecosystem generator that can replicate any climate. Even during the coldest months of winter we can swim in a tropical oasis. And the best part is that there are enough resources to sustain us for *decades*. I'll be protected from the Red Army, and we never have to leave."

She shook her head from side to side, eyes reflecting a deep sadness. I'd seen Peyton upset before; I'd seen her drained, defeated and demoralized – I'd been at her side during her worst days. But this was something different. It was as if she was in mourning. "What makes you think I'd want to live there?" she asked.

I stared at her for a moment, puzzled by her question. This was the most logical plan I could imagine, and I've pored over every possible scenario. "You don't get it: you'd *never* have to work again. We'd have everything we need at our fingertips; safety, security, all the money we need. It's perfect."

She glared back at me. "You're unbelievable, you know that?"

"I don't—"

"This is your man cave all over again," she interrupted. "That dusty concrete cube you'd hibernate in when you lived in The Fringe. This is just bigger and has nicer bathrooms."

"But it's *safe*," I assured her.

Peyton brushed the long pink strands from her face and sighed deeply, sagging against the wall. "So is a prison cell, Matt. You don't want to live in this dome to be 'safe' from the Red Army. You want to hide. You want to bury your head in the sand and pretend that life isn't going on around you. I thought – or I *hoped*, at least – that after Arena Mode you'd learned something."

"People *hate me*," I shouted, much louder than I'd intended. "I could get killed at any moment. How can you not get that?"

"There are a lot of unpopular people. People who make hard decisions that affect millions, and *they* don't go into hiding. They go out and live their lives."

"And they're taking a huge risk," I replied.

She took a few steps across my small recovery room and placed a warm hand on either side of my face. Her voice softened and her eyes drew me in. "You *lived*. For the first time in your life you stood up, made a tough decision and fought for something. Arena Mode should have been your wake-up call: live life to the fullest, because it can end when you least expect it. And here you are, ready to throw in the towel."

I pulled her hands off my face and squeezed them gently. "I don't think you understand the gravity of the situation."

"I don't think *you* get it. The more you retreat into your shell – do nothing, say nothing – it's just going to upset people even more. You're a public figure now. Running makes it look like you have something to hide."

I raked my fingers through my hair and exhaled loudly. "I don't *want* to be a public figure. I never *asked* for this."

"And I never asked to be this cute and insightful," Peyton replied with a tiny smile. "We all have our crosses to bear."

I returned the smile, but it quickly faded from my lips. What she was proposing didn't make sense – for any of us. "Look, Fortress 23 is my only option at this point. Maybe, once this Sergei Taktarov thing has died down, in a year or two, I can come back to New York. Then we can start fresh."

"That's kind of the thing about life," she replied with an exasperated sigh. "It *doesn't* die down. Ever. Stuff continues to happen outside your little bubble whether you like it or not."

I knew Peyton was emotional. She was clearly still furious that I'd been out of reach for so long, but she wasn't listening to reason. I needed someone else to help convince her that Northern Alberta was the best course of action. "When Gavin gets here let's all have a talk. Maybe we can come up with a plan, all right?"

"Gavin isn't coming," Peyton said, not much louder than a whisper. "He's back in The Fringe cleaning up what's left of Excelsior."

"What's left?" I asked.

She swallowed hard and stepped away from me. "A mob burnt it down two weeks ago. Molotov cocktails, right through the front window. The police thought it was because they figured *you* were inside. You were at Excelsior, on camera before Arena Mode, so..." She turned her head, blinking a pair of tears from her eyes. "The whole thing is a write-off."

Excelsior Retro Comics was much more than just a store to Gavin; it was the culmination of his life's work. His entire personal *and* professional comic book collection had been reduced to ash, and it was all because I'd retreated into hiding, unwilling to step forward. "I have money now," I said reassuringly. "I can replace everything. That's not a problem."

Peyton shook her head. "Not everything can be fixed by signing a check."

"I can...it's all right – I can help," I stammered. "Look, when things cool down I'll help him rebuild."

"If you really wanted to help you would have been there for Gavin, *and* for me. Months ago. The way we were there for *you* when you needed us most." She took a moment to zip up her fitted black coat and pull on a pair of thermal gloves. "You seem to have your mind made up, so there's nothing left for us to talk about. Enjoy living in your bubble. There are people back in New York who need me, and I want to be there for them."

Peyton abruptly turned towards the exit and I lunged forward, hoping to stop her. A razor-sharp pain sliced across my abdomen when I made the sudden movement, stopping me in my tracks. "Wait," I said through gritted teeth, reaching towards her, "I want to be there for you guys – I do. You can count on me."

Peyton paused for a moment, just an arm's reach from the door. She lingered in a moment of hesitation before reaching for the knob. "I'm sorry," she sighed. "But right now, I don't even trust you."

CHAPTER THREE

"I should have stayed in Sudan," Valentina grumbled.
"Shit was always blowing up, but at least it was warm." She
pulled her jacket tight around her waist, burying her chin
into her collar.

Turning my back to the wind, I yanked my wool toque
down over my ears with both hands. It was an exceedingly
unpleasant October afternoon, even for Ontario; a light
morning snowfall turned to freezing rain, punishing every
square inch of our exposed skin like tiny needles. The
hospital's rooftop hoverpad was open to the elements, with
nowhere to seek shelter from the icy shards.

My jet arrived a moment later and touched down silently,
and the entrance ramp lowered to invite us aboard. The new
G12 with vertical take-off and landing capabilities was the
most expensive aircraft available, and also the fastest; with a
top speed that exceeded Mach 2, I could travel halfway across
Canada in just over an hour. It was the first toy I'd purchased
with my fortune, and the only luxury item I'd really had a
chance to enjoy.

Valentina and I removed our jackets as soon as the door
sealed shut behind us. My pilot, Kirk McBride (who referred
to himself as 'Mac' most of the time – or, depending on
whom he was introducing himself to, 'Big Mac') greeted us
with a beaming grin. "Mister Moxon, Miss Garcia, nice to

have you aboard. Can I offer either of you a beverage this afternoon?"

"Kiss my ass," Valentina hissed. She shoved him aside and stomped to the back of the plane, disappearing into one of the private rooms.

"What's up with red?" Mac asked innocently – or, more accurately, in a tone that was designed to feign innocence. "She seems even more pissed off than usual. Did someone drop a house on her sister?"

"She hasn't slept in three days. Cut her some slack."

Mac smiled again – a crooked, mischievous grin that usually meant he was about to suggest a detour. With two day's worth of beard stubble and a thicket of dark rumpled hair, he perpetually had a dazed look to him, like he'd just rolled out of bed after a night of binge drinking. He was more than just the life of the party – Mac *was* the party. Well into his forties and two decades removed from college, he still celebrated each day as if he lived in a raucous frat house. His abundance of energy baffled me; at twenty-nine years of age I was perpetually exhausted, but Mac had a seemingly bottomless gas tank, fueled by nothing more than alcohol and debauchery.

"*No,*" I said emphatically.

"I didn't say anything," he protested, holding his hand up in surrender.

I pressed my fingertips into my eyelids and let my head sag forward. "Just say it," I insisted. "I know you have something in mind."

"Okay, so have you ever been to Montreal?"

I shook my head. "I *just* had surgery," I grumbled. "We're not going to a strip club."

"How did you know I was going to suggest a...anyway, this isn't just *any* strip club – it's *the* strip club. In Montreal they play by an entirely different set of rules. You know how when you're in a club in the States they have that pesky 'no touching' rule?"

I winced and took a seat, reclining into one of the lounge's white leather chairs. "No, Mac. I did not know that."

"Well," Mac explained, his hands more animated than usual, "in Quebec it's practically the opposite. You can touch the strippers *anywhere* – they almost insist on it. And lap dances only cost—"

"Look," I interrupted, "I know you've been on this jet for nearly three months, and you're going a little crazy, but I need to *rest*. Recover. Groping a nineteen-year-old French girl with daddy issues isn't at the top of my priority list."

"I just figured, you know...after what happened in Argentina. You'd want to get out. Live a little."

"I'm not going to talk about Argentina," I said quietly, careful not to let my words travel throughout the rest of the aircraft. "And neither are you."

"Fine, fine." Mac smiled and returned to the cockpit. He took a seat and pulled a long red lever, bringing the powerful twin engines to life with a soft rumble. "Where are we off to now, 'Mister' Moxon?" He added the 'Mister' ironically, since he knew it bothered me.

"Fortress 23," I instructed. "But first, we need to make a stop in Thunder Bay."

"What's in Thunder Bay?" he asked curiously.

"Another hospital."

Mac glanced over his shoulder. He flashed a set of pearly-white teeth as he extracted a pair of aviator glasses from his jacket. "Mox, you sure how know to party."

It took us just thirty minutes to cross The Great Lakes and arrive at our destination – a small hospital on the outskirts of Thunder Bay, Ontario. The sleepy, overcast city seemed particularly quiet, and the snowfall had accumulated far more than in the Toronto area. We touched down on hospital's small rooftop hoverpad and I stepped out of the jet, landing ankle-deep in crisp white snow.

Valentina zipped up her jacket and followed closely behind, but I insisted she stay onboard and try to get some rest. I was still concerned about security, but a superhuman assassin seemed like overkill for a stroll through a small-town hospital. I had my wrist-com in case of emergency, and she wouldn't be far away if I needed her. She grumbled and argued, but I insisted she stay. A consummate professional, she never let me out of her sight while we were in a public place. Part of me thought Valentina was just *that* dedicated to her job – and a larger part believed she was more concerned about the fact that her final paycheck might not clear if I were killed.

I wandered through the stark white hallways, passing the occasional nurse or janitor on the way. No one gave me a second glance. When I arrived at my friend's room in the recovery ward, he appeared much like he had on the day after Arena Mode; pale, sickly, his breathing shallow and weak. A small rectangular monitor blipped quietly in the deathly silence, tethered to his chest by a series of thin silver wires.

Kenneth Livitski's bleak hospital room was brightened by the abundance of cards, flowers and comic book paraphernalia that surrounded him. His parents and siblings lived nearby and visited on a daily basis, never arriving empty-handed. The private room I'd financed was the largest that the hospital had to offer, but was quickly filling up due to the constant influx of gifts. I might have to rent out the adjacent room just to accommodate his growing collection.

In the three months since he'd been in a coma, I'd come to visit exactly once. Wrapped up in my own bullshit, as per usual, I always came up with excuses why I couldn't make the time. Since Arena Mode ended I had avoided Peyton, walked away from my best friend Gavin, and I'd barely given Kenneth the time of day since he'd landed here.

Living in denial was one of my specialties, but I never lied to myself about why Kenneth was in a coma: he was here because of me. Because I had convinced him, along with the rest of the world, that I was a superhuman before the tournament began. He believed that I'd have his back as much as he had mine, but when the fighting began and a sword pierced Kenneth's abdomen, I panicked – I was sure he was finished, and I was sure that I was next. And I ran.

His family never blamed me for what happened, though I almost wish they had. The last interview I saw with Kenneth's mother was a simulcast on CNN, where she prayed for not only her son's recovery, but for *my* safety as well. When the reporter asked if she harbored any ill will towards me for fleeing when her son was stabbed, she smiled warmly and stated there was nothing that I could have done to help. It was all in God's hands, and we'd have to wait for His plan to unfold. I don't know whether it was innate kindness or just irritatingly powerful positive thinking, but she refused to lash out, and assign blame for something she had no control over. Her son was in a bad place, but she didn't want anyone else to suffer just because he had.

I think the reason I avoided these visits was because I feared running into Kenneth's mother. If she screamed, or slapped me, or cursed my existence I could deal with the sting. But I couldn't bear the guilt if she let me off the hook.

I patted Kenneth on the hand, silently swearing to be a better person. To come visit more often, and keep pursuing every medical alternative to help him come out of this coma. Stem cell replacement and tissue re-gen therapy had kept him biologically alive; had he suffered that much internal damage even ten years ago he would have certainly died. But it was the blow to his head that was the larger issue. When the blade was extracted from Kenneth's torso he fell, cracking the back of his skull on a curb as his body went limp. Medical treatments were advancing at an impressive rate, but there was still nothing available that could improve his condition.

I reached into my jacket pocket and pulled out a small vintage figurine I'd purchased in Japan. It was him. A limited edition Kenneth Livitski toy, complete with his 'Living Eye' costume and removable mask, identical to the one he's worn in Arena Mode. I articulated the arms and posed the legs, carefully standing it on the end table next to his bed. It made me smile to think that if he woke up tomorrow, the first thing he'd see would be a plastic figure of himself staring back at him. For someone who loved comic book culture even more than I did, it would be like waking up in Heaven.

When I turned to leave a cold draft hit the back of my neck. It was powerful, as if someone had inexplicably turned the air conditioning on full-blast during a snow storm. I craned my neck upwards and that's when I saw it – saw *her*. A swirl of blue mist materialized from the aether, touching down at my feet like a funnel cloud during a hurricane. I shouted and scrambled backwards, which was when she took form.

It was Brynja.

CHAPTER FOUR

The porcelain-skinned, blue-haired girl who stood before me was visibly shaken. She looked and sounded exactly how I remembered Brynja; her almond-shaped eyes, waif-like frame, the tattoo of a blue manticore emblazoned across her left arm – every discernible detail was identical. It *was* her...it had to be. I just wasn't sure how it was possible.

She blinked hard and squinted, perplexed as she studied my face. "What the hell...*Mox*? Where's your armor? And why are you wearing those clothes?" It took her a moment to realize that she was in a different time and place – which explained my change of attire. And it took her a moment longer to realize that she wasn't wearing any clothing of her own. "What the *hell!*" Brynja threw her hands across her chest, pulling her knees together. "What did you do to me, you freak?"

"Me?" I stepped back, shielding my eyes with an outstretched hand. "I didn't *do* anything! You died back in Arena Mode – or disappeared, I guess – and this is three months later, and..." I spread my fingers ever so slightly, sneaking one more glance (just to make sure I wasn't hallucinating), "here you are."

She tore the sheets from Kenneth's bed, wrapping them around her torso. "I...*died?*"

"Well," I replied, lowering my hand. "I guess 'died' would be overstating it, considering the fact that you're standing here and stuff. You disappeared after the bolt hit you." As I explained what I'd seen I could almost see the light bulb illuminating over her head: towards the end of the Arena Mode competition I was struggling to disarm a British swordfighter named Winston Ramsley. During the brawl his weapon discharged, firing several thousand volts of electricity into Brynja as she rushed to my aid. A moment later she blinked out of existence, never to be seen again – until now.

She stared at me for what felt like an eternity, carefully studying every detail of my face. It was as if she was trying to figure out if *I* was real – if she was somehow dreaming, or hallucinating this entire experience. Or possibly even still trapped inside The Arena, under the influence of a powerful psychic.

And that's when the door flew open.

Standing in the threshold was a squat, gravel-voiced orderly with a pile of muddy brown hair pulled into a bun. "I'm sorry, sir," she grumbled, "but your escort isn't permitted in here. She'll have to wait downstairs in the lobby."

Brynja cocked her head and raised an eyebrow, suddenly snapped out of her daze by the old woman's accusation. "Wait – did you just call me an escort?"

"Yes I did, ma'am. It's a classier word for 'hooker'."

Brynja actually gasped. *"Hooker?"*

The orderly nodded once again. "That's correct, ma'am. A prostitute. A call girl. A wh—"

"I know what an escort is!" Brynja interrupted. "I'm not an idiot! But why would you think I'm a..." She trailed off momentarily, glancing down at her conspicuous lack of clothing. "Oh, okay – I get it. No, you're confused. See, I *arrived* like this. I appeared here, from New York City where I was fully, totally dressed. And now, my clothes are gone. They were..." She paused for a beat, shrugging her shoulders. "Vaporized?"

The stoic orderly didn't blink. "Of course they were, ma'am. Either way you'll have to wait downstairs. It's hospital policy: no nudity in the visiting rooms. And no fornication in, on, or around the coma patients. Again, hospital policy."

"Fornication?" I repeated, not sure I heard the word correctly.

"It's a classier word for 'sex', sir. Intercourse. Copulation. Fu—"

"Yeah," I said, holding up a hand. "We got it."

The orderly yanked a sleeve away from her swollen wrist, revealing a battered watch that looked older than she was.

"You got five minutes to get cleaned up, and then I want you *both* out of here. Not a second more or I call security."

"Wait," I said as the woman reached for the door handle. "People bring escorts into the hospital so often that you have a policy against it?"

She nodded once more. "You'd be surprised, sir."

I exchanged glances with Brynja and the orderly tapped the face of her watch with her fingernail. "Four minutes, thirty seconds," she warned before slamming the door shut behind her.

"I guess that's our cue," Brynja said. "Maybe when we get out of here you can explain...you know, everything."

Hands clasped tightly around the thin hospital linens, Brynja glanced around the room, apparently unsure of what to do next. She couldn't walk onto a freezing rooftop wrapped in a sheet, so I searched through Kenneth's clothing. His family was continually brining jeans, jackets and shirts to his room, hoping he'd wake to find all of his favorite outfits at his disposal. Judging by the overfilled closet and overstuffed drawers, it looked like they'd spent the last three months migrating his entire wardrobe to his bedside.

Brynja slipped on a black Buffy the Vampire Slayer t-shirt and a pair of oversized jeans, using a belt to cinch the sagging pants around her narrow waist. While slipping on some thermal socks she finally noticed who was lying in the bed. "Holy shit, is that Kenneth?" She raced across the room and embraced him. "I can't believe he made it out of The Arena! This is amazing – and it explains why I'm here."

I stared at her for a moment, creasing my eyebrows together. I wasn't sure what was just explained, or how any of this suddenly made sense.

"His *powers*," she replied, in a condescendingly slow cadence, "you know, that thing where he can create anything he wants?"

My memory had been on the fritz lately, but I don't recall one of Kenneth's powers being the ability to resurrect people from the dead. "All right," I said with a heavy dose of skepticism, "so even if he somehow manifested you out of thin air, despite being in a coma, you'd be a recreation – like a physical representation of who you *were* – not *you* you...right?"

"*No* idea," she replied casually, squeezing him once more. "You're the brains of this team." She pressed her ear to his heart and closed her eyes, smiling broadly as his chest rose and fell.

Kenneth Livitski had suffered trauma to his brain, but technically speaking it was still functioning. Not at a hundred percent, I was told – although evidently it was working well enough to trigger his abilities. Recent studies have concluded that coma patients do have control over their senses to varying degrees, with hearing being the most prominent. It's possible he knew I was here, and that he manifested Brynja for some reason or another – though only one reason made any sense. "Brynja, you can still do that mind reading thing, right?"

"Sure, I can give it a try. Who do you want me to read?"

I glanced down at Kenneth.

"Oh, right. You think he's readable?"

"Well he's not brain dead," I replied. "It's worth a try."

She moved in closer and brushed the chestnut-colored bangs from his forehead, placing a palm flat against his cheek. A moment ticked by and Brynja's eyes widened, pupils dilating until the inky blackness nearly eclipsed the whites. She leaped from the bed and stepped back, clasping a hand over her mouth.

"What?" I shouted.

The color drained from Brynja's face. She stared blankly at Kenneth's body, dazed and unfocused. I offered her a seat but she refused to take it, waving it off absently with one hand.

"What did he say?" I asked again, lowering my voice. "Is he all right?"

"He's just repeating the same words over and over," she said softly. "He wants us to pull the plug."

CHAPTER FIVE

I made my way to the rooftop with Brynja in tow, who was buried beneath one of Kenneth's brightly colored ski jackets. Not the most fashionable choice of attire, but it was a better alternative than catching frostbite. My jet wasn't permitted to remain on the hoverpad since incoming emergency aircraft could arrive at any moment, so Mac circled overhead until I sent him a signal that I required a pick-up. A moment later the jet landed, and the entrance ramp lowered to invite us aboard.

"Moxon!" Mac greeted me with a wide smile and a pat on the back, peering over my shoulder at the blue-haired girl who accompanied me. "The man wanders into a hospital and comes out with some arm candy. I guess this trip wasn't a total waste of time after all." He offered to take Brynja's jacket as he flashed her a grin. "I'm Captain MacBride, but most people call me 'Mac'. What do I call you, sweetheart?"

Valentina, who was resting comfortably in the cabin, glanced over the top of her book – just long enough to roll her eyes at Mac's abrasive first impression.

Brynja shook her head and refused to respond.

"So Mox, is she DTF?" Mac asked, making no attempt to lower his voice. "You gonna introduce her to the mile high club once we take off?"

Brynja's lips curled into a seductive smile and she stepped towards him.

Fearing for what might happen next I stepped in the opposite direction.

She leaned in and placed both hands on his chest. "There *is* a club I'd like *you* to join: it's called the mile down club."

"Sounds hot," he replied without missing a beat, "Tell me about it, Blue."

"Once we get a mile in the air," Brynja breathed, slow and smoky, "you set this bad boy on auto-pilot. Then you and I sneak downstairs...and once we're alone, I smash you in the face and throw you out the cargo door."

Brynja shoved Mac hard against the cabin wall, turned, and stomped towards the seating area, heading directly for the bar. She helped herself to the spiced rum, twisting off the cap and gulping straight from the bottle.

Valentina glanced at me and smiled wider than I'd ever seen. "I like her."

It was less than an hour into the flight and we'd all settled in. Valentina had retired to a private room for a nap, and Brynja, who had borrowed some of her clothes, looked measurably more comfortable. Business casual wasn't her style, but at least the white dress shirt and pleated pants seemed to fit.

I assumed that Brynja would want an opportunity to rest, or at least lie down, but she was unnaturally energized. Sitting at one of the cabin's interactive tables she incessantly opened holo-screens, scanning and scrolling through four windows at once. She read articles, activated video clips, and searched every newsworthy simulcast from the last three months. It was as if she was trying to fill her brain with every bit of data that she'd missed out on, and couldn't consume it fast enough.

My wrist-com blipped to life as I was pouring myself a drink, signalling an incoming call. The name 'Jacob Fitzsimmons' blinked into view and I accepted the transmission. Appearing on the holo-screen was a narrow, thin-haired man with a boldly aquiline face, clad in a meticulously tailored charcoal suit – the only color I'd ever seen him wear. Fitzsimmons was always direct, never one to waste a moment of time; so as per usual, there was very little small talk. My lawyer pointedly asked if I'd 'heard the news', to which I replied 'what news?' So many outlets were covering my every move that I couldn't keep track of them all. I assumed that if something truly significant surfaced, one of my lawyers would call and fill me in on the details.

He notified me that an incoming video was about to play. I darkened the cabin lights and projected a full-size screen into the air, where an image of a beautiful woman appeared. Dressed in a stylish black coat, with her shoulder-length hair tucked behind her ears, the woman stood in front of Moscow's Kremlin; the multicolored onion-dome roofs were clearly visible in the distance. Her expression was hard, colder than the weather surrounding her.

"Playback," I instructed, and the video came to life.

"As I stand here before you," the woman began in a proper English accent, "the world bleeds. Billions of our brothers and sisters toil each day, living well below the poverty line, lacking the basic necessities that should be afforded to us all. Ravaged by war and disease, this wound continues to fester." Her voice was calm and reassuring. She sounded British, though her angular cheekbones and naturally blond hair were distinctly Scandinavian.

"There *was* a man who had the power to heal it," she continued. "A noble man. A beacon of hope in these dark times who brought with him the promise of better days to come...and he lies martyred, murdered, in the building behind me.

"I am here as an emissary. I have spoken extensively with religious leaders, and met with the most prominent spiritual figures from every continent. And while they have differences of opinion when it comes to their faith, one belief they share is undeniable: they agree that Sergei Taktarov – Russia's Son – was brought here for a singular purpose. That purpose was renewal.

"He died at the hands of Matthew Moxon, The God Slayer; an apostate who remains silent, in hiding, remorseless for his actions. This is unacceptable.

"This is not about hatred or revenge. This is about the long-suffering citizens of the world who are owed their recompense. They deserve answers. They deserve the truth. And above all else, they deserve justice.

"Please donate, and give what you can: whether it's one dollar or a thousand – whatever the Lord has blessed you with. These funds will be used to strengthen our movement. Whatever you pledge will be returned to you tenfold once Matthew Moxon has been found, because when the God Slayer has paid for his transgressions, a new age of prosperity will be upon us. It has been foretold, and it shall come to pass.

"The crusade is upon us: we will avenge our loss, destroy the broken system that plagues us, and rebuild in the ashes. May peace and love be with you, my brothers and sisters."

When the video concluded my lawyer's conference call window winked on.

"Where is this from?" Brynja asked. "I've been scanning the news sites and I haven't seen this woman before."

Fitzsimmons paused for a moment and glanced off-camera, riffling through the hand-written notes on his desk. "It's one of those crowd-funding websites...Kashstarter, I believe it's called."

It was beginning to make sense. Crowd-funding websites have been popular since before I was born, but most of them required that the project creator actually offer something in return – a book, a comic, an invention, or some other tangible item.

Kashstarter.com, on the other hand, had no such prerequisite. Sign up for a free account, and five minutes later you can ask people to donate money for virtually anything. I brought up the site and expanded the browser window, revealing some of the other projects that occupied the main page – including a Japanese man who wanted to raise a million dollars so he could have experimental wings surgically attached to his back; and a young woman from Brazil was offering her virginity in exchange for a cherry-red Lamborghini X-900. Amidst this nonsense was the video we'd just seen, entitled 'Justice for The God Slayer'. It was perched in the top slot, with over thirty million dollars having already been raised.

"How long has this thing been live?" I asked. "And how did we not find it before?"

"It's been two hours," Fitzsimmons replied.

I had a hard time believing it.

"How is this shit even legal?" Brynja shouted, banging her fist on the tabletop. "This bitch is threatening to kill Mox right there on camera! I know people raise money for crazy reasons, but you can't collect donations so you can *assassinate* someone...can you?"

My lawyer explained that it's not so simple. The woman from the video – who was later identified as Astrid Neve, a twenty-nine year old translator from Manchester – didn't make any direct threat. She used words like 'justice' and 'crusade', but deftly side-stepped the use of any explicit call-to-action that would involve a physical attack – the language was deliberately ambiguous. You can't pursue legal action based on insinuation, and on the surface that's all this was. What she's planning to do with this money once it's raised is incidental.

"So what if someone attacks Mox after they see this video," Brynja asked. "Would this woman be held responsible? Isn't this hate speech or something?"

"It's a fine line," my lawyer explained delicately. "This woman can just claim that she was speaking in metaphors. It happens on simulcasts all the time: a political commentator will make a vague reference to ridding the world of someone they disagree with, and before long that person turns up dead. There isn't really a legal recourse for this type of rhetoric."

It was a shocking video that had the potential to further incense an already bitter group of Taktarov's followers, including the Red Army. And although this type of talk had already sparked violence, there was surely a limit to how far people would go. Something new would happen – a political scandal, a celebrity wedding, a football game – that would take everyone's mind off of Matthew Moxon, the God Slayer. That's what I kept telling myself until my lawyer opened one final video.

"I know this is a lot to absorb," Fitzsimmons continued, his measured voice etched with a hint of emotion, "but...there's one last thing I need to show you. This happened just twenty minutes ago."

A new window blinked to life and the video began streaming. It was a live New York Chronicle Simulcast, where a camera was fixed on a high-rise which was being devoured by flames. It appeared to be a residential apartment, where a blackened hole was blasted into the mortar, and had taken out several stories. A pillar of ash-colored smoke climbed into the sky, obscuring most of the building's surroundings. It looked like a scene from Africa or the Middle East – some war-torn region where bombings were commonplace. But as the smoke dissipated, the skyline behind the building came into view. I saw the Empire State building, alongside a row of familiar megatowers. It was Manhattan.

"It's your apartment," Fitzsimmons said flatly. "Someone attached an explosive device to you front door."

It took me a moment to process the information. "What...what was the response? Locally, I mean, in The Fringe?"

"Status quo," Fitzsimmons replied. "Blockades, arrests, martial law. The entire city is under curfew. It seems to be contained for the moment – no looting or rioting in the area. But—"

"*Yeah*," I interrupted, massaging my forehead. "I know. 'This is probably just the beginning', right?"

Fitzsimmons shook his head slowly. "That isn't what I was going to say, Mister Moxon. There is no 'probably' about it. This *is* the beginning. And I don't see things calming down anytime soon."

CHAPTER SIX

"That's no moon, Brynja...that's a space station."

She looked at me like I was a complete idiot. "I never said it was a moon. And why the hell would anyone think *that's* a space station?"

I made a mental note to keep the Star Wars references to a minimum as long as Brynja was my guest.

Peering out the window as we made our approach, the structure began to take shape on the horizon. Beyond the snow-capped mountains, encircled by an endless sea of pine trees sat my new home: Fortress 23. The word 'massive' didn't cover it – it was imposing. A shining metallic city built directly into the side of a mountain, it would be impossible to miss if it weren't so isolated; the only sign of life for miles in every direction were migrating birds and the occasional heard of caribou. It was just like Superman's Fortress of Solitude – if his fortress was furnished with several hundred rooms and a staff to clean and maintain it. I definitely had to come up with a better name for it though, or at the very least find out what had happened to the other twenty-two.

Mac circled the jet around to an extended landing strip that led to the hangar, where two enormous, interlocking steel doors guarded the entrance. We hovered in place, awaiting a prompt.

"Please identify yourself," a voice crackled over the com. It echoed through the cockpit and was audible in the cabin.

"This is eleven thirty-eight," Mac said, using his most official-sounding pilot voice, several octaves lower than his usual tone. "I've got Moxon on board and we're knocking on the front door."

"Welcome home, eleven thirty-eight. We're unlocking the deadbolt and turning on the porch lights."

And with those words the metal doors pulled open, gears grinding slowly as sheets of ice cracked and fell from their surface. The hangar slowly came into view. The opening was cavernous. Home to a fleet of twenty aircraft with room for twenty more, the enclosed area was like a small city all its own. Bright lights illuminated in sequence, from front to back, bathing the hangar in a powerful white glow.

The landing gear lowered and the jet touched down so gently that we never felt the tires making contact with the surface. A man in a navy flight suit holding a pair of neon orange batons waved us in, directing our aircraft across the tarmac and into a docking space. We hadn't yet rolled to a stop before the hangar doors closed behind us with a resounding boom.

Brynja and Valentina stepped out of the jet first, staring with wonder at their surroundings.

Mac jogged down the stairs and let out a low whistle. He was practically salivating at the collection of rare and expensive aircraft that filled the hangar. "These are some impressive digs, Moxon. And these birds...can I take one of them out for a spin?"

I assured him there would be time for that as soon as we'd settled in. After the Kashstarter video and what was happening in New York, there was no way I was going to leave the Fortress– at least not any time in the foreseeable future. We were here for the long haul, and he could play with the new toys later.

A whirring sound echoed from across the tarmac. It was a six-wheeled transport; an open air vehicle that looked somewhat like a golf cart, but without a roof. The driver was a small, round man with a tangled beard and a mess of black hair. "Great to finally meet you," he shouted with an eager wave. "I'm Chandler Oswalt, one of the...well, your staff, I guess. Me. I'm part of it. Mister Moxon, sir." His face reddened as his words spilled out in rapid succession, and in no discernible order.

I returned the wave and smiled. "Take it easy, Chandler. No need to be nervous. I'm Matt."

He stood and adjusted his uniform, a navy-blue flight suit with a white 'Frost Corporation' logo embroidered on the chest. "I'm taking bags for...I mean, I've got them. Your bags. Where are they?"

I was more than happy to carry my own things. Having a staff at my disposal was still a relatively new experience, and

I had to admit, at first it was a little exciting. It was how I imagined Hollywood stars or British Royalty living – not having to lift a finger for anything. But over the course of the last three months, the novelty of having my doors opened and my belongings carted around was beginning to wear off. It started to make me feel more like a feeble toddler than a powerful multi-billionaire. "Not a problem, I can handle—"

"Right up the stairs and in the back rooms," Valentina interjected, pointing a thumb behind her.

Without any further instruction Chandler wobbled up the stairs as fast as his stubby legs would carry him.

After loading up the transport and we'd taken our seats, Chandler instructed us to buckle our seatbelts. Valentina protested, but there was no arguing with him – it was regulation. When he was satisfied that we'd followed protocol, he taxied us across the tarmac and into the main lobby; a pristine, marble-floored space that looked more like the set of a science fiction movie than an actual room. Pencil-thin blue lights ran across the stark white walls, intersecting and diverging in intricate patterns. Small robotic cleaning devices chirped and hummed, dusting and polishing every square foot. It was like Frost Tower in Manhattan, and featured much of the same technology, with the exception of a machine I'd never seen or heard about.

"What is *that*?" Brynja shouted. As the transport came to a stop she unbuckled her belt and jumped out of her seat.

She was staring up at the ceiling, where a pair of orange metallic spheres were rotating like a helicopter blade, tethered by a long grey cord. The softball-sized devices made their descent, coming to a stop in mid-air. They were like two oversized, pupil-less eyes, peering at us curiously.

Chandler turned to Brynja and motioned towards her seat. "Sit back...I mean *please*, sit...if you want. In the transport. Don't be alarmed."

"What the hell are these?" Valentina asked, extending her leg. She reached out and tapped one of the floating spheres with the toe of her boot, causing it to bob slightly, but maintain its position.

"*No*, don't do that..." Chandler scrambled from the driver's seat and ran to the device, yanking a rag from his back pocket. He frantically polished and wiped the surface. "This is...it's nothing to be afraid of. She's new. *It's* new...it's not a she, *obviously*, it's a thing – things don't have sexes. Genders, I should have said. That would have sounded less creepy."

"What does it *do*," I asked.

"Oh," Chandler replied, the heat rising in his face as he continued to polish. "Her...*it's* name is London. She's a utility fog. I got to name her. You know, because London is famous for the...everywhere? In the air?" Mac, Brynja and Valentina exchanged glances, but no one replied.

"Anyway," he continued, "it's nanotech, which as you know is *very* cutting edge stuff. Self-reconfigurating, completely modular...think of it like a flying exocortex. But it doesn't attach to you, obviously...it's like neuroinformatics, combined—"

"So what does that mean in *English*," Valentina said curtly.

"It can change shape," I explained. "And it contains data – like a central hub for Fortress 23, am I right?"

Chandler gestured towards me and nodded, breathing heavily. He seemed to have winded himself just attempting to give his explanation.

I approached London and ran a finger along the surface of one of its spheres, amazed by the seamless design.

"Elevated blood pressure, low iron, protein deficiency," it announced in a genial Scottish brogue. The device had a crisp female voice, with a slightly synthesized inflection. *"You also seem to have recently recovered from surgery. Would you like a complete medical analysis, Matthew Moxon?"*

"Okay, keep that thing away from me," Mac said, leaning back in his chair.

"Why?" Valentina chuckled. "Are you worried it might reveal your blood-alcohol levels?"

"How is this possible?" Brynja asked, now approaching curiously, though she was careful not to make physical contact with the spheres.

"I scanned Matthew Moxon's fingerprint," London said, "and I was able to determine his identity. I then took a sample of his DNA and made a surface-level assessment, detailing his primary medical issues."

Chandler gestured for everyone to return to their seats. "I just invited her so she – *it* – could give you guys a tour. Show you around the place and explain it. Things. With words. It's better with the words than I am." He used his rag to dab the perspiration from his forehead before squeezing back behind the wheel of the transport.

Once we were seated and properly buckled, Chandler drove us to the west wing, using a voice command to raise the massive transparent blast door that separated the hall from the main lobby. London followed along, floating and rotating above our heads as it cheerfully guided us through the fortress.

"If you'll look to your left," London chirped, "you'll notice that the exterior walls are reinforced with iridium plating, an alloy which can only be found inside of meteorites. While expensive and incredibly rare, the brilliant Cameron Frost purchased two thousand acres of land here in North-Western Alberta when he discovered that there was an abundance of the material in the area. A large meteor had escaped NASA's detection and fallen into a remote forest region in November of 2033. Mister Frost, in his infinite wisdom, mined the iridium and began construction on this very spot."

"Brilliant?" Brynja scoffed. "Infinite wisdom? Was London dating Cameron Frost at one point?"

"Um, it's old programming," Chandler explained. "Frost was sort of...well, he was very proud of himself and his – what he accomplished. He has the fortress AI include random compliments whenever possible during speaking...speech."

We continued touring the complex level by level. The nine above-ground floors were primarily for living quarters and amenities, each dedicated to a specific purpose: bedrooms on levels one through three, fitness on level four, media and communications on level five, kitchens and dining on level six, and additional storage, equipment and supplies on levels seven through nine. There were accommodations for five hundred people – I suppose Frost was expecting a lot of guests in the future.

We'd periodically pass by a staff member while on our tour. Men and women wearing the same navy blue flight suit with white 'FC' emblem on the chest – identical to Chandler's. They avoided eye contact for the most part, pretending not to notice us as they went about their duties, but a few of them shot me a sidelong glance as we zipped past in our transport. The look was one I was all-too familiar with: disdain. As a middle-class citizen, I'd experienced that icy glare more than my share of times while traveling to Manhattan. Simply walking the streets in a pair of faded jeans and a comic book t-shirt was enough to draw contemptuous glares from the elite – the upper-class who had purchased, renovated and occupied every piece of real estate in the affluent borough. Some of the nicer-dressed Manhattanites even crossed the street to avoid me as I approached. It was as if abject poverty was an airborne disease, and being in close proximity to someone as lowborn as myself could have infected them.

At least while I was in The City I knew exactly *why* people hated me. It was the same reason why they hated every peasant from The Fringe or The Dark Zone. Here, I wasn't sure if Cameron Frost's existing staff despised me because I was now their boss (which was reason enough, I suppose) or if it was because the last time they'd seen their previous employer, it was during Arena Mode...right before I'd blown a sizable hole in his throat with a modified handgun. From their perspective, I'd gunned down their former boss in cold blood, and had looted his bank vault in the wake of his death. This was of course the entire point of Arena Mode, making it a pretty valid perspective to have.

I decided then and there that I'd give each of them a raise whether they deserved it or not; I could afford it. And then, hopefully, I wouldn't have to deal with the discomfort of living with two dozen people who glared at me like I was the antichrist.

The seven sub-levels of the fortress were reserved for research, development and storage. On sub-level five (labelled 'SL5' above the elevator lift) we continued around the perimeter of the massive circular structure and passed the power core – a thorium reactor that acts as a generator for the entire fortress. *"The reactor,"* London explained, *"is powered by liquid salt – far more efficient than uranium reactors of the past. In a stroke of genius, Mister Frost also began developing a new form of solar power for the dome, which, in less than eighteen months, will make Fortress 23 completely self-sustaining."*

After more than an hour navigating through the lower levels of the fortress, it hadn't occurred to anyone that the enormous dome that topped the structure would be part of the tour. We'd spotted it on the flight in, but through the powerful snow squalls we couldn't see inside.

"What's in the dome?" Brynja asked.

"I was going to save it for last," Chandler replied sheepishly. "It was going to be the finale. The big...you know, exit. No, that sounded stupid – finale was better."

"Can we check it out now?" I asked. "We can circle back around so you can finish your tour afterwards, I promise."

Our guide reluctantly agreed, even though it was going against the pre-determined fortress tour schedule. We motored down the long white hallway and through a set of sliding metal doors onto a steel platform; it was an oversized elevator reserved for vehicles and large cargo shipments. The doors slid shut behind us and we sailed to the rooftop level, opening into bright daylight. The dome that capped the top floor was completely transparent. The only way we could detect it's presence from the inside were the flakes of snow landing on its surface, melting away once they made contact.

While the enormity of the dome above was utterly mind-boggling, what surrounded us was even more incredible. It was a tropical paradise. Like stepping out of an elevator into a Hawaiian postcard, we were overwhelmed by the sights and smells of lush palm trees, pastel-colored flowers and natural rock formations, some with waterfalls cascading down their sides into shallow inlets. Tropical birds flew overhead and lizards scattered underfoot. London was chiming in with facts about terraforming and climate engineering experiments, but none of us paid any attention – we were mesmerized.

I smiled, shaking my head in disbelief. For someone who avoided the outdoors at all costs, I could definitely get used to this. "This is incredible," I whispered, not realizing I was saying the words aloud.

"Yeah, it's nice." Chandler grumbled, shuffling his feet.

"What's wrong?" I asked.

"After seeing *this*," he said, kicking at a small rock, "you guys aren't gonna want to check out the desalinization laboratory on sub-level six, will you? I mean it's *exciting*, but, you know...in a different way."

After a few more hours of exploration everyone settled into their rooms on level two. I made a quick trip to the infirmary to have my wound tended to, and was greeted by the resident nurse – a tiny, middle-aged woman with deep creases in her angular face, and a bob of sandy-brown hair. She was polite (or at least was professional enough to feign politeness), offering me a firm handshake and a tight-lipped smile. She quickly instructed me to hop up onto a gurney where she could inspect the incision below my ribcage, which was thankfully free from infection and healing nicely.

As she ran some additional tests I asked her name, and the nurse, oddly, introduced herself as a number: 'Twenty-seven'.

"So did your parents just hate you?" I replied with a grin.

She didn't return the smile. 'Twenty-seven' explained that her name was actually Judy, and she'd been an ER nurse in Phoenix for over two decades. She was laid off due to budget cutbacks, and accepted a position here in Fortress 23 after being recruited by The Frost Corporation. The number was how Frost referred to his 'sub-level' employees, meaning the staff who worked in the subterranean levels of the Fortress – the ones he didn't have to interact with directly. Frost always liked to associate numbers to faces, which he felt make them easier to keep track of. It was demeaning, but by Judy's rationale, for a six-figure salary with full benefits in *this* economy, he could call her whatever the hell he wanted.

Judy ran one additional scan on my abdomen to monitor the internal damage. Like the external scar, it was healing nicely, although I needed to avoid strenuous activity for the next several weeks. Popping a stitch on the incision was one thing – internal bleeding as a result of pushing myself too hard would require another surgical procedure. I thanked the nurse, and assured her that if anyone specialized in taking it easy, it was me.

When my exam was complete I retired to Cameron Frost's private quarters, which were the largest in the fortress. I pulled open the double doors to reveal my new bedroom: stark-white, ultra-modern, and easily ten times the size of my former apartment back in The Fringe. Everything from the carpeting to the linens were pristine, as if they'd never been touched – it looked more like a high-resolution photo from a furniture catalog than a room that had actually been lived in. For all I know Frost had never even slept there. The floor-to-ceiling windows offered a panoramic view of the mountain range to the south, where the dim moonlight bathed the snowy peaks in a pale blue glow.

"Tinting," I said through a drawn-out yawn, and the AI responded by darkening the windows to an inky black. I fell onto the mattress, too exhausted to bother pulling back the covers, and stared up at the ceiling.

My mind raced. Even after Chandler's tour and London's detailed explanations, I had barely scratched the surface of this massive structure. I'm sure it would be weeks before I had the chance to inspect every room. I was overwhelmed by the sheer number of toys I had at my disposal, and couldn't wait to continue exploring – it had barely sunk in that all of this was mine. And I was still trying to process the information about the Kashstarter campaign to finance my destruction...not to mention the naked dead girl who appeared in a swirl of blue mist. Even by my standards it had been a pretty strange day.

But despite the distractions and shiny objects, I couldn't get Peyton out of my mind. I wondered where she was, and what she was thinking. Staring into the darkness, trying to will myself to sleep, I couldn't force her out of my head – and the parting words that spilled from her lips burned in my mind: *'I don't trust you.'* I wasn't sure if she planned that particular part of her speech in advance, or if she knew how painful it would be for me to hear, slicing my insides like a freshly sharpened scalpel. I was a lot of things (many of them I wasn't proud of) but untrustworthy was not one of them. I'd always been there for Gavin and Peyton – at least I *felt* like I always had been – and they never failed to reciprocate.

When I broke the news that a tumor was eating away at my brain they never gave up on me, even after I'd pretty much given up on myself. They pushed and pushed until I had no choice but to feel like there was some sense of hope, and some reason to keep on fighting. If Gavin and Peyton wanted me to live *that* badly, they must have seen something in me; something that I couldn't see myself, no matter how hard I tried. Their faith was what fueled me during the final stages of The Arena. And it was the thought of losing them had given me the drive to defeat Cameron Frost.

An agonizing hour stretched into two. I eventually stopped checking the time, but at some point before dawn my heavy lids fluttered shut, and I drifted off thinking that now, I had everything in the world that I'd ever wanted – except for the only two people I wanted to share it with.

CHAPTER SEVEN

After a few hours of dreamless sleep I awoke feeling more exhausted than when I'd gone to bed. I sat up and winced, gently rubbing my aching stomach. Advanced stem cell therapy had greatly accelerated my healing process, but modern medicine could only do so much.

It was sunrise, and I thought I'd take the opportunity to explore some of the fortress in silence before my staff and guests awoke. The nurse had recommended a little light exercise if I was feeling up for it, and this was as good a time as any.

During our guided tour we hadn't reached the lowest sub-level, so I figured it would be the best place to start exploring. I took an elevator down to SL7 and strolled past an endless row of rooms – laboratories, storage areas, the odd bathroom or maintenance closet – until I reached a large circular door that resembled a bank vault. The polished silver door had a touch-screen keypad off to its side, recessed into an alcove, with two words etched into the steel panel above it: South Tunnel.

Entering my ten-digit access code caused the door to swing open with a gentle hiss, and the long narrow hallway illuminated. It sloped upward, leveling out after a few hundred meters. I must have walked the featureless cylindrical tunnel for a solid half-hour before I reached a second door, which looked identical to the one at the entrance. There was no keypad, and no voice command would open it. If someone had been observing me on a security cam, they must have had a good laugh watching me shout every variation of 'open up!' I could think of to an inanimate object for several minutes.

I turned back, and had reached the main level hallway when my wrist com signaled an incoming message. It was Brynja, screaming frantically. "Mox, you have to come here and see this. It's amazing!"

Her level of energy at seven in the morning was baffling. "What, did you find," I groaned. "The coffee maker?"

"No, you idiot, this is *better* than coffee. I'm on the main level in the lounge. Come quick!" The transmission blipped off before I had a chance to respond.

I was skeptical. It seemed unlikely that Brynja had discovered something more exciting than coffee at this hour. Locating the nearest elevator, I stepped aboard and shot up to the main observation floor, which is where I found her: sitting in an oversized circular room, surrounded by clothing. More coats, sweaters and pants than I could imagine her ever needing in her lifetime. And shoes – my god, the shoes; mountains of boots, high-heels, runners, and original designs that couldn't possibly have had any practical use. "Where did all of this crap come from?" I asked, scratching my head.

"This isn't crap, you dick – it's my new wardrobe. I printed it!" She motioned to the doorway behind her, which lead to what would become my favorite device in the entire fortress: a next generation 3D printer.

"You printed all of this...this morning?"

"No," she said with a laugh. "I never slept. I discovered this room last night after dinner, and I haven't stopped printing since." She paused and looked me up and down, curling her lips into a tiny frown. "You might want to give this thing a go yourself."

I'd been wearing the same clothes since I left the hospital, which were incidentally the same clothes I was wearing at the CN Tower during my stabbing. I wore a dark hoodie to conceal my t-shirt, which was torn and blood-stained. I agreed it was probably best to burn what I was wearing and take a cue from Brynja – why spend hours flying to the nearest mall when I could generate any garment I needed right here?

It was an incredible machine: the next generation model 3D printer could replicate virtually anything, from textiles to machines with moving parts. A few torrent sites had searchable archives, home to literally millions of design files called 'physibles'. It was simple: download the source file, upload the proper materials and feed it to the printer. A few minutes later your desired item would appear in a large metal chamber like magic.

The machine had a single design flaw: you had to ensure you had enough of the correct material loaded into it before printing, or it would default to a random compound – usually whatever had been loaded in previously. My short-term memory issues didn't help with the problem. Forgetting to check the levels of cotton and polyester, one evening I printed everyone a cushy new aluminum pillow for their bedrooms. My running shoes made of chocolate chip cookie dough with licorice shoelaces were another amusing disaster (and provided a surprisingly delicious snack, considering the combination).

As a child my father had purchased one of the very first commercially available 3D printers, which was a relic by today's standards. At the time the technology was mind-boggling, and my family was fascinated with the device. Occasionally my sister and I were allowed to model and produce our own toys under my dad's strict supervision. The first gen 3D printers worked by using hot polycarbonate plastic, which hardened as the design cooled and took shape. Design options were limited, and the printing process seemed to take forever, but one option was all I needed: I wanted to make Lego. Sure, I had toy chests filled with the tiny plastic blocks in my room, but there was something special about inputting a design and printing my own.

With this massive printing monstrosity at my disposal, I became a kid all over again. Over the following month I must have created a thousand things with my new printer: graphene-coated armor suits. Swords. Shields. A customized toaster that looked like the original Nintendo system. Frisbees. A working bicycle. Sniper rifles that could fire marshmallows a thousand feet. And of course, mountains and mountains of Lego. At one point I'd printed so many Lego pieces that a room in the north wing was dedicated solely to my growing collection. The entire compound was littered with pieces until the maintenance staff got tired of stepping on them. Several people threatened to quit if I didn't start cleaning up after myself. I wasn't much of a 'clean up after myself' type of guy, so I hired some additional cleaning staff dedicated solely to the task.

When I wasn't printing Lego or playing video games with Brynja I was reading. After a week of searching I'd located Cameron Frost's hidden library in one of the deep subterranean levels, accessed by pulling a lever in one of the supply closets. It was *epic*. A collection of every book and graphic novel I'd ever heard of, leather-bound and carefully organized in a three-story room with a cathedral ceiling. Retrieving a book from the top shelf required a harrowing journey, climbing up while clinging to a series of sliding wooden ladders. It was three days later before I'd realized that London could hover up and retrieve them for me, but there was a strange sense of satisfaction in risking a broken leg to source out the perfect reading material.

I read one novel after the next, day after day, until I came across a series of hardcover books that were not novels at all: they were Cameron Frost's personal notebooks; filled from cover-to-cover with handwritten notes and crudely-drawn sketches, detailing Frost's plans for the next decade. Beyond his desire to produce violent reality television – which had become the linchpin of his entire financial empire – he had aspirations that ranged from grandiose to the brink of insanity.

His expansion into feature films was the least surprising of his ventures. Frost had worked tirelessly to purchase the film rights to every major movie franchise from the past fifty years; Star Wars, Star Trek, The Lord of the Rings, The Matrix, Indiana Jones, Tron – he had put in bids for every single one of them. Frost was sure that he could reboot these franchises and attract an entirely new generation of fans. And even stranger: he had delusions of writing and directing the movies himself.

Beyond his desire to become the next James Cameron, Frost's passion for robotics was evident. He'd crammed entire volumes with schematics, detailing every moving part of incredibly intricate exoskeletons. A paraplegic as a result of a yachting accident, he'd been obsessed with regaining his ability to walk, and when medical science had failed him, he turned to the next logical option.

The exoskeleton that Frost had worn into The Arena – a heavily armored, Japanese-inspired mech that he'd dubbed 'Fudō-Myōō' – was far too large and impractical for everyday use. It stood nearly seven feet tall and was as bulky as an all-terrain vehicle. It was a juggernaut, but it worked: he could walk, run, swordfight, and even fly for short distances.

Frost's plans, according to his journals, were to create next-generation models of the Fudō armor using his printer, all while making incremental upgrades. First would be waterproofing along with an underwater propulsion system so the units could explore the seas; then advanced flight capabilities, followed by space travel. He'd wanted to be the first person to walk on the surface of Mars, and wanted to arrive there without the aid of NASA or a space shuttle – he was going to do it alone, in his own exoskeleton.

His plans to privately finance space missions were incredible, but his ambitions went far beyond that. Frost had scientists from around the world working on wild, theoretical projects with budgets that ranged into the billions. Desalinization serums that would convert entire oceans into potable water sources. Terraforming machines that could give an otherwise dead planet a living, breathable atmosphere. And a teleportation device that would allow matter to travel from one place to the next, creating a gateway to the other side of the world. I had no idea how far along any of these projects were, or how many scientists and engineers had been receiving paychecks to make them a reality, but I was curious to find out.

His political aspirations were as lofty as his scientific ones. He one day aspired to run for President (which was no surprise) but his short-term goal was to declare Fortress 23, and the surrounding area that I now own in Northern Alberta, it's own country. There were a list of people he'd given 'donations' to in order to make this happen, or at least to grease the proverbial wheels; usually untraceable BitGold transfers that were made to offshore accounts in various amounts, never less than seven figures. Some additional digging revealed page upon page of documents and notes from meetings he'd attended, all in pursuit of being the undisputed ruler of his own sovereign nation.

As I scoured the reams of documents that Frost had taken great care to conceal, for the first time I felt like I'd been taking for granted what the purpose of the Fortress actually *was*. Was it a sanctuary? A retreat? A sandbox where he could build whatever he wanted without interruption – regardless of how experimental or dangerous? Without question it was all of those things. Although I had a suspicion that it's reason for existing was perhaps something else entirely; and somewhere, locked inside this unimaginable castle the size of a small city, was the key.

CHAPTER EIGHT

The following months dragged by. November turned to December, and two weeks prior to Christmas I could feel depression setting in. At first I thought it was seasonal affective disorder, which wasn't uncommon during the winter months in regions with cold climates. I'd spend time in the dome, sun tanning under the glow of an artificial sun each day, but my symptoms only worsened. It wasn't the cold nights and grey Canadian skies that were bumming me out – it was loneliness.

Peyton was ignoring my messages and Gavin was nowhere to be found. Taking time for myself was one thing, because I always had the option to make contact with others when the mood struck. Being isolated with the knowledge that I *couldn't* contact my best friends, even if I wanted to, was completely foreign, and it was taking its toll.

A weekly holo-session with Gary, Elizabeth and the kids was my only real connection to the outside world. It was nice to hear their voices and chat about their days. I'd ask the most mundane questions, like if they'd had a chance to put up their Christmas tree yet, and they'd always respond with amazing enthusiasm and an alarming amount of detail. And during every session, I felt like I needed to thank Gary for saving my life back in Toronto. Without the lunging tackle that slowed down the Russian (buying Valentina enough time to launch him out the window) I might not be alive. "You are the most bad-ass computer programmer in Canada," I once told him. He smiled, and said that he credits his fast reaction time to my sister: years of practice dodging dishes she launched at him during their all-out brawls. His response sent them both into fits of laughter; I don't think they'd ever had an argument in nearly ten years of marriage, let alone a fight.

Although virtual chats staved off my depression, I needed real human interaction to brighten the days when I felt truly alone. The time I spent with Brynja helped a lot. We played games, watched movies, and she was the only person who seemed interested in chatting with me about comics. She didn't know Stan Lee from Bruce Wayne before she arrived at the fortress, but she was a quick learner. In just a few short weeks of reading sessions and movie marathons Brynja was becoming an expert in geek culture, and before long she was making Star Wars references like a pro. One particularly cold evening I caught her referring to Alberta as 'Hoth', and I wanted to embrace her like a proud father.

It wasn't long before she was taking her fandom to the next level without any further prompting or instruction on my part. Brynja began using the 3D printer to make cosplay outfits, dressing as her favorite Marvel and DC superheroes. On any given morning I could have breakfast with a blue-haired Harley Quinn or Wonder Woman, which always elicited a smile from passing staff. One evening we planned a session of Dungeons & Dragons, to which she turned up dressed like a warrior princess, complete with a sword, studded bra and leather loincloth. Her dedication grew to an obsession, rivaled only by my own.

When we weren't pursuing our hobbies we researched. We scoured records of superhuman sightings and phenomena from across the globe, trying to find an instance – even something remotely comparable – to what had happened when she appeared out of thin air that day in the hospital. Hour after hour, day after day we came up blank.

Brynja's powers had also faded since she had reappeared. She read Kenneth's mind just moments after she manifested, but explained that since then she hadn't been able to do it again. She used to read surface thoughts with ease: Brynja could pass by someone and 'see' what they were thinking, or hear their voice in her head as clear as her own. And now, nothing. Her other ability (the one she considered a curse) was being able to pass through objects like a ghost. Now, fully corporeal, she was able to walk and move and interact with objects, remaining completely solid.

Whether we were at work or play it was a great distraction; the time we spent strengthened our friendship. I didn't learn much about Brynja's history though, aside from the fact that she'd once played guitar in a Seattle-based rock band, and that she no longer spoke to anyone in her family. She liked to keep the past in the past, and focus completely on the future. It was admirable, and a character trait that I wish I possessed. While she could move on without looking back, *I* couldn't stop beating myself up over pretty much everything: things I *wish* I'd said to Peyton while I had the chance; all the actions I should have taken once Arena Mode was over; and the things I'd done inside the Arena that I could never undo.

I even regretted killing Cameron Frost in the end. For months following Arena Mode I'd been haunted by visions of his dead body lying at my feet, wheezing his final painful breath into a shallow pool of his own blood. Deep down I knew that I shouldn't blame myself for what'd happened. After all, that was the object of the game: it was me versus him, and he'd wanted me dead – there was no way around it. But in hindsight, part of me wishes I'd thought faster, and come up with an alternative to blasting him in the throat with my modified handgun. He was the first and only person I'd ever been directly responsible for killing with my own hands, and the images still lingered in my mind.

Brynja's outlook on life was considerably more cheerful than my own. Although I was the one stuck with the now-infamous moniker 'The God Slayer', *she* was the one who'd actually done the slaying that day. Sure, it'd been my plan, and my distraction, but it was Brynja's superhuman ability to phase through objects that had allowed her to drop an acid-filled bullet into Sergei Taktarov's head. She didn't regret what she'd done, or take pride in her actions. It was just that she never looked back.

"You cheated death," she told me one night as we laid on a blanket and ate pizza in the dome, staring up at the silky, moonless sky. "*Twice.* You survived a tumor that doctors said would kill you, *and* won a fighting tournament that you had zero chance of winning."

I had never really thought of it that way. The odds of surviving one of those events were astronomical – surviving both could be called a 'miracle' (if I believed in that type of superstitious nonsense.)

"You're *here*," she continued. "You're alive. Whether it's good luck, or beating the odds, or from a freakin' magical spell – it doesn't matter. This is a fresh start, and you don't owe anyone anything."

"There's just so much that I wish I'd done differently. So much bullshit I feel responsible for. And with Kenneth in a coma..." I trailed off, staring up into the void.

"He could come out of it, you know." Her voice was a soft, reassuring purr. "He could wake up one morning, put on one of his stupid t-shirts and call you up out of the blue. Stranger things have happened."

I smiled weakly. "You're starting to sound like Peyton." I didn't recall Brynja being this optimistic during our time together in The Arena. She'd been assertive and forceful, more like a drill sergeant motivating her troops. This new, bubblier version of her was definitely not unwelcome, though. It was exactly what I needed.

We propped ourselves up on our elbows and she leaned in close. "This is my second chance, too," she said. "I came back from the dead, and now I'm with the only person on earth who's as lucky as I am. I was a ghost, remember? Passing right through things. And now..." She reached out and touched my face, gently stroking my cheek with her thumb.

"Not quite as ghosty," I noted.

"Maybe we *can* be," she replied with a warm smile. "Just together this time. No one knows we're here, and we have everything we need. It's not so bad being a ghost under the right conditions." Her hand cupped my cheek, and our lips drew closer. "This is *our* time," she whispered. "Let's enjoy it."

I stared at her for a beat, cocking an eyebrow before saying, "Do you realize how dirty your hands are right now?"

Brynja grimaced, pulling her hand away from my face. She frantically wiped her greasy fingers across her pant leg. "Ugh, I'm so sorry."

"Don't worry," I said apologetically, shaking my head, "It's no big deal."

Her lips stretched into an evil grin. "I was apologizing in advance...for *this*." She rolled on top and pinned me down, knees pressed firmly into my chest. Before I could push her off she grabbed a slice of pizza and began smearing it across my face.

Brynja and I became inseparable, and the friendship continued to grow. She was bright and funny, and gave me a reason to wake up every morning. Before long I'd almost forgotten about the outside world – I even stopped watching simulcasts. The rest of the world had melted away, along with its conflict and complications; this is where I wanted to be, and I was happier than I'd been in a very long time.

But as the days wore on inside the isolated fortress, not everyone was in the same mood for bonding and togetherness.

Valentina locked herself inside of her room, surfacing only for the occasional snack, and to ask about her most recent paycheck. She could verify her account online, of course – as could everyone else on my payroll – although she insisted on a printed, signed statement every two weeks to add to her records. Aside from reading romance novels, bookkeeping seemed to be her only hobby. Our conversations were limited to the bi-weekly arguments about the bonuses she felt that she deserved for overtime pay, and they always ended with her storming off.

Mac's biggest issue was boredom. I never wanted to go anywhere, so for lack of anything to do I'd send him on errands, which were nothing more than random trips across the globe with an assortment of items to purchase. I would ask him to fly to Italy just so he could pick up an authentic Roma pizza, or down to Australia so he could purchase me a hand-carved Aboriginal boomerang in some remote region of the Western Outback. It was meaningless busy work, but it kept him happy and occupied.

And once every few weeks I'd hand him a wad of cash and give him twenty-four hours to spend it, each time with the explicit instructions that, a) he could do whatever he wanted with the money, and b) I didn't want to know what he did with it. There was a method to my madness when it came to the bonuses and vacation time I granted Mac: when he hung around the fortress, he routinely made not-so-subtle advances towards Brynja ('Blue') and Valentina ('Red'), to which he was summarily shot down on each attempt. Crashing and burning never deterred him, which was both admirable and embarrassing to watch. And although Brynja laughed off Mac's tired routine, I feared that if he persisted with Valentina, she would shoot him down for good – and not in the metaphorical sense. Getting him out of the fortress for some actual, physical contact with a woman (whether it required payment or not) was in his best interest, both mentally and physically.

For the most part the staff avoided me. They resented the fact that Frost had kept them locked away, hundreds of kilometers from civilization. They'd been working there for the better part of a year with no vacation time – a policy I'd kept in place without even realizing it. I didn't blame them for being grumpy. I asked Mac to take a transport plane and drop them at home for the holidays, leaving the fortress with a minimal staff: Chandler, Valentina, a maintenance worker, a chef, and Judy, the nurse. They were all guaranteed a generous Christmas bonus and some additional time off when the rest of the staff returned, so everything was in order.

With a skeleton crew came a few inconveniences. As self-sufficient as Fortress 23 was, there was always a computer system that required an upgrade, or a mechanical device that needed a tweak. The elevator that served as the main access point to the dome was under repair, and wouldn't be functioning until later that evening.

I'd wanted to surprise Brynja with a picnic for lunch, so I gathered some blankets and comic books, instead making my way up the spiralling metal staircase that opened to the center of the ecosystem. After stepping out onto the grass I heard footsteps clanging their way up the stairs at my back. It was Chandler, who was sweatier and more frazzled than usual.

"Mister sir, Moxon, I mean...hold on..." He leaned forward on his knees and breathed heavily – something Chandler was prone to doing after any form of physical activity.

"Hey buddy," I said, patting him on the shoulder. "Can you make sure there are a few Dr. Peppers in the fridge? Brynja and I are going to have lunch up here in the dome. Maybe Marten can throw together some club sandwiches, too. The ones with those little—"

"No!" Chandler panted, waving me off with both hands. "You don't understand, you *have* to see this. It's a...you don't know how bad the thing...the situation is. It's bad. Very, very bad."

I didn't ask any more questions. I threw open the doors, sprinted down the stair case and raced into the main lounge, where the primary media hub was illuminated and glowing brightly in the dimmed room. The holo-screen was broadcasting a live simulcast of The Fringe – my former neighborhood – on the outskirts of New York City.

Half of it was gone.

Partial transcript from the CBC Evening Simulcast 'Live from Toronto'
Hosted by George Sokratous, December 2041

Dennis Benoit, Member of Parliament (Liberal): Arena Mode opened a lot of eyes, for sure. I mean, we were all aware of superhumans before the event this past summer. We knew they existed, and that they lived among us. We didn't know how many there were, or what type of powers they possessed, but for the most part we felt comfortable because they weren't a problem.

George Sokratous: They were just like us, more or less. Except they dressed better.

Benoit, MP: You think...is it the spandex, maybe? Is that what you're referring to?

Sokratous: it was a joke. Sarcasm.

Benoit, MP: Ah, I see. Right.

Sokratous: But seriously, they were blending in pretty seamlessly for the better part of a decade, up until now.

Benoit, MP: Right, right. I mean, the *potential* was always there for superhumans to pose a threat, although no more than any other threat.

Like any weapon; a handgun, for instance: it can be used to protect your home from an intruder, or, in the wrong hands, an unstable individual can use it to go on a shooting spree.

Sokratous: Are you calling superhumans 'weapons'? That seems to be an analogy that a lot of politicians and pundits have been floating around since we saw their potential during Arena Mode.

Benoit, MP: No, no, no – not exactly.

I mean, *yes*, some of these people *do* have massive destructive power. We all saw Sergei Taktarov fight Dwayne Lewis during Arena Mode, and they took down half of Manhattan in the process. That was a controlled event in the context of a sport, and Cameron Frost's estate paid for the cost of the damage, but still – it was an eye opener. And now this...

Sokratous: The event in New York.

Benoit, MP: Some people are calling this an isolated incident. And of course, it could be. No one is taking responsibility for this explosion, and no terrorist groups are being linked to the attack.

Sokratous: Although you're not so sure.

Benoit, MP: It definitely seems like this is related to Matthew Moxon in some way. This could be Red Army, although I'm not going to speculate.

Sokratous: So in the wake of the tragic event in New York, which took over four thousand lives that we know of, what is the response here in Canada going to be?

Benoit, MP: The same as in America, the United Kingdom, Australia, Brazil, and every other country that has a reported superhuman population. We will likely be enacting the Emergencies Act. It's not a popular decision, but it's the only think that is going to keep the Canadian people safe.

Sokratous: So this is martial law?

Benoit, MP: No, no, no – we aren't going to be trampling the Charter of Rights and Freedoms. But this measure *is* being reviewed by Parliament as we speak, and we'll see if it's the right course of action.

Sokratous: That's what they said down south about the Patriot Act. "We won't be trampling anyone's freedoms." Now I can't get on a flight to Orlando without a rectal exam.

Benoit, MP: They gave you a...are you serious? Right there in the airport?

Sokratous: No. Again, that was sarcasm.

Benoit, MP: Ah. I see. Very amusing.

Sokratous: This *does* beg the question, though: how is Canada going to succeed in keeping its population safe from superhuman attacks, while at the same time ensuring that the government remains transparent, and doesn't overstep its bounds?

Benoit, MP: I don't really know where the boundaries are anymore, to be honest. After New York, the destructive power of these superhumans has exceeded everything that we predicted. Our worst-case scenarios just got significantly worse.

CHAPTER NINE

It was the event that the government had warned us about for nearly a decade: a catastrophic superhuman attack in a densely populated area.

Homeland Security had, of course, prepared for this type of eventuality, taking precautions for a threat that didn't yet exist – at least in the wealthier areas of the country. Cerebral Dampening Units were the government's most powerful weapon to combat an enemy that they didn't fully understand. The basketball-sized metal spheres could disrupt the brainwaves of a superhuman within a one mile radius, temporarily nullifying their powers. You'd see them mounted atop buildings and stoplights, giving off their invisible, inaudible signal day and night. They were designed to make us feel safer while walking the streets, though up until that day few really feared a superhuman attack.

The CDU's were ubiquitous in the nicer parts of The Fringe, and there were several in the vicinity of the attack. They didn't make any difference. Unfortunately, a few well-placed shotgun blasts were enough to render them useless, which was exactly what happened. With the cerebral dampeners disabled, real horror was about to begin.

The video footage was chilling. After a group of masked terrorists cleared the area and destroyed the CDU's, a man emerged from an unmarked white van. He stepped into the street, tore off his shirt and began to glow. His bizarre and terrifying transformation took only seconds. Pale skin turned to cinder, cracking and peeling, while a copper glow pulsed from beneath the surface. The whites of his eyes burst with lava and his skeleton became visible through flashes of blinding light.

The final sound before the blast wave was a guttural scream – that's when half of The Fringe was annihilated.

At first it looked as if the man had exploded like a biological bomb, with his accomplices standing idly by, making no attempt to escape the blast radius. The satellite weather cams told a much different story. There were no flames, or smoke, or pieces of flying mortar – it all happened in reverse. From a distance it looked like an *im*plosion rather than an *ex*plosion, as if everything had been sucked into a gaping black hole. Like water down an invisible drain, matter ceased to exist at the core – pulling inwards from every direction, caught in the undertow of a swirling amber maelstrom.

It took just a second. A heartbeat passed, and the buildings, cars, and pedestrians were simply gone, culminating with deafening silence. What remained was a crater, impossibly deep, filling from the newly-formed waterfall that flowed in from the Hudson.

While a series of smaller windows across the top of the holo-screen showed replays of the implosion from different angles, the live simulcast feed continued below. First responders were on-hand, but seemed directionless. They were there to put out fires and save lives, but there was nothing left to do but bear witness. There were a few casualties around the perimeter of the crater, where people were lucky enough to have been standing just outside of the blast radius. Everything else had vanished.

The remaining boroughs of New York City were shut down, and the police, which suddenly looked more like the military, took over. The last terrorist attack in the city was fifteen years ago, when a small dirty bomb killed three tourists in the northern half of Manhattan. That was all it took. The massive over-correction in security protocols unleashed an entirely new level of police presence, and the technology followed. As soon as the superhuman detonated, everything changed: eight-wheeled armor tanks rolled through the streets, batons collided with skulls, and boots buried in stomachs. Any onlookers who came within arm's reach of an officer were doused with an experimental new liquid, shocking their nervous system to the point of convulsions.

As I stood perfectly still, staring into the floating screens with horror, my wrist-com chimed. It was an alert from an old website I'd signed up for years ago. 'Hyve Mynd' was the hottest social media tool in 2038 – a place where hipsters could share their thoughts on movies no one had ever heard of, and fashion accessories no one wore. Of course as soon as it went mainstream the core audience abandoned their accounts. My own account, which I'd created for the sole purpose of sending old-school text messages to Gavin and Peyton, had long been abandoned as well – they were the only two followers in my 'colony'. When the novelty wore off they stopped using the service, and I'd forgotten it existed.

I accessed my Private Hive to find a single message blinking, awaiting my response.

HyveMynd

WHERE EVERYONE AGREES THAT
POPULAR STUFF IS TOTALLY LAME

Welcome back, TheRealMox! You have ... one ... new message in your Private Hive.

P!nkM0nst3r: I'm OK.

TheRealMox: holy crap Peyton i nearly had a heart attack when i saw the simulcast, just found out about this 30 seconds ago

P!nkM0nst3r: You should see it here, it's chaos. The looting and riots have already started. I'm hiding out in a friend's apartment.

TheRealMox: DO NOT tell me where you are yet in case this is being traced

P!nkM0nst3r: Thought so. It's why I didn't use my wrist-com. At least this can't be geo located.

TheRealMox: stay put, i'll come pick up you and Gav in the jet

P!nkM0nst3r: Gavin is missing. I haven't seen him in days. I just hope he wasn't in the blast zone.

TheRealMox: WTF?! could he be hiding out somewhere too??

P!nkM0nst3r: Hopefully he's in The Dark Zone. He's been spending a lot of time there since Excelsior burnt down.

TheRealMox: shit

P!nkM0nst3r: I know.

TheRealMox: he's a tough bastard, if anyone survived this it's Gav

P!nkM0nst3r: I would just feel better if I heard from him.

TheRealMox: me too but he'll turn up soon i know it. just lay low and stay inside, don't go near the windows

P!nkM0nst3r: How are you going to pick me up? The streets are filled with cops and looters.

TheRealMox: can you get to the roof of the building you're in?

P!nkM0nst3r: I think so.

TheRealMox: good, i'm getting my pilot and some security, be ready and we'll be there in 90 mins

P!nkM0nst3r: Please hurry <3

Seeing the text-based emoticon at the end of her message made me smile, just for a moment. It had no reason to, but Peyton's signature 'less-than sign followed by a three' heart was a small reminder of how things were before I left. Life's little wrinkles that made me nostalgic for the time before the Red Army wanted my head on a pike, and before I competed inside The Arena. Barely six months had passed, and looking back it seemed like a lifetime.

Mac was nowhere to be found, so I sent Chandler to search for him and pass along a message. We were heading for New York, and wheels needed to be up in ten.

Valentina didn't answer her wrist-com either, and she wasn't in her room. I scoured the fortress. Time was ticking away, and searching her most likely hiding places was taking longer than I'd hoped. I passed the chef while running through the main corridor, who said he'd spotted Valentina heading towards the hangar around an hour ago.

I sprinted down the length of the hangar, past the fleet of aircraft and through the open blast doors. A few flakes of snow drifted in through the opening as I approached, and as I stepped into the morning sunlight I saw her near the end of the runway.

Valentina was in full winter camouflage, dressed head-to-toe in white thermal hunting gear, complete with yellow-tinted shooting glasses. She was peering through the scope of a sniper rifle into the forest below. I jogged towards the end of the runway and shouted as I approached. "Sorry to interrupt your caribou hunting, but we have a problem."

"I'm not shooting caribou," she mumbled without looking away from the eyepiece. "I'm shooting campers."

"What?" I stared out into the distance and saw a small hunting party warming themselves by a fire. From what I could tell there were at least three of them in the camp; they'd pitched a small tent next to an all-terrain vehicle. "Are you out of your fucking mind? You can't just shoot people for fun!"

She turned to me and held up the rifle, cocking an eyebrow. "You don't recognize the piece?"

I squinted at the military-style weapon. I'd never seen it before.

"It's one of *your* sniper rifles, Moxon. The ones you printed last week? It only fires marshmallows, remember? And not even that far, either – I've been shooting at those dicks for an hour and haven't come close to pegging one."

I couldn't believe I'd forgotten. It was time to up my meds, because my short-term memory loss wasn't showing any signs of improvement. "Right, right. Well sorry to interrupt your long-distance food fight, but half of The Fringe just disappeared thanks to a superhuman suicide bomber. New York City is on lockdown."

"I guess the NYPD has their hands full," she said with a half-hearted shrug, reaching into her pocket in search of additional ammunition. She popped a marshmallow into her mouth before feeding a new one into the chamber. "Not our problem," she mumbled as she chewed.

"I have friends in the city," I said, raising my voice, "so it's a pretty goddamned huge problem for me. I need you to come with me and Mac, we're picking them up."

"All right, take it easy," she replied calmly, adjusting the gun's strap before flinging it over her shoulder. "I'm in. A security op beats standing around here firing confectionery at endangered birds."

Great. So in addition to answering for numerous crimes that I wasn't responsible for, I was probably going to start getting angry calls from the Canadian wildlife preservation society.

"But," she added, poking a gloved finger into my chest, "...*you're* not coming along for the ride."

"Why the hell not?" I asked sharply.

"You *know* why the hell not," she fired back. "We *both* know why this happened. It doesn't matter whether this was Red Army or an independent act of aggression: New York is going to pin the blame on someone, and since the bomber died it's going to be *your* stupid ass. You pay me to be your bodyguard, and this is me, guarding your body. Stay here, lay low and keep out of trouble – we'll be back with your girlfriend in a couple hours."

"But—"

"But nothing," she insisted. "You're *not* a superhuman, and you never will be. Acting like one will just get you killed."

She stomped down the runway and into the hangar, already screaming into her wrist-com at Mac to hurry up.

Valentina was blunt, but she was right. The group of suicide bombers parked their van directly across the street from my old apartment, which wasn't far from Excelsior Retro Comics. They knew exactly what they were doing, and there were no other explanations for their attack; The Fringe wasn't a military target, and had no political or social significance outside of the fact that it was my neighborhood. If they weren't there with a plan to vaporize me, then the target they selected was a pretty big coincidence.

Staying behind made sense. There wasn't much I could do to help, and this was a two-person operation. With Valentina as security and Mac piloting, I would just be dead weight. And if they got stopped and searched, however slim the chance, having me on-board could make matters considerably worse. When there is a tragedy of this scale, politics dictate that someone has to shoulder the blame. Logically the Red Army should have the finger pointed in their direction, but in times of crisis, rational thought is rarely the first reaction.

The following hour was torture. Even though I knew the operation was a routine pick-up, waiting for Peyton to arrive drove me into a chest-tightening panic. Mac suggested that he could send me real-time updates, or hook me into the jet's in-cabin video feed so I could be in constant contact. It was a nice thought, though I didn't think it would allay my anxieties. I needed someone real to talk to, and I needed a distraction.

After quickly explaining the situation to Brynja, she did her best to keep me occupied. She suggested popcorn and a movie to keep my mind off of current events. I reluctantly agreed, but twenty minutes in I was fidgeting in my seat, unable to maintain my focus. I wanted to continually check the news feeds, and scour simulcasts in search of any tidbit of information – no matter how small – that New York might be improving. Something that would indicate that Peyton's situation wasn't as grave as I'd feared.

Unable to sit still, I excused myself and left the media center, retreating to my room. I paced the long row of windows that lined the entire length of my chamber, staring out into the mountain range. That's when I detected some unusual movement.

In the distance, down in the forest clearing was a newly erected camp site. More elaborate than the previous one that Valentina had spotted from the runway, this site was large enough to accommodate a hunting party of twenty, possibly more. Several ATVs were parked around the perimeter, as well as a pair of small hover jets. Since I'd been here I hadn't seen a single person anywhere near the fortress, and the staff had always noted that over the course of the last year, there hadn't been anyone in the vicinity – not a single camper, hunter or tourist. This was the second group to set up camp on the edge of my property in less than twenty-four hours, and the timing was suspicious.

Gazing out the window, I was startled by a series of raps at my bedroom door. It was Chandler, accompanied by London floating close behind.

I forced a smile and gestured for him to enter. "Did you notice the campers outside?" I asked, motioning towards the forest clearing.

"I did," he replied, peering out the window. "But not those ones. I mean, I can *see* them, obviously – I'm not blind. But there are more...the other ones. They're here. Knocking."

I raised an eyebrow. "Even for you, that was a *really* weird sentence."

Chandler's pale cheeks glowed a bright shade of crimson. "I'm *so* sorry Mister Moxon, sir. I didn't mean—"

"It's okay," I reassured him. "Just relax. What's going on?"

He asked London to give us a look at Fortress 23's main runway, accessing the micro-cams outside of the hangar's blast doors.

"Absolutely," London replied cheerfully. *"Serving the handsome and talented Matthew Moxon is my genuine pleasure."*

"What was that about?" I laughed.

"Remember when you asked me to stop London...you know, with the Frost compliments? How she...*it* always talked about him? Well I *tried*, but since you're the default owner of the fortress now, it...well, I screwed up."

The two floating orange spheres merged as if they were made of liquid, flattening and expanding into a rectangular screen. The security feed blipped to life.

The screen displayed a young girl standing at the blast doors, rapping her knuckles against the steel surface. The fur-lined hood of her winter coat obscured most of her face, but from what I could tell she was a child who couldn't have been older than twelve. Flanking her was a pair of large men wearing hunting jackets, with military-grade hardware strapped to their shoulders – old AK-47 machine guns, from what I could tell. They were the campers that Valentina was using for target practice earlier, and they looked *pissed*. Something told me the assault rifles they brandished weren't designed to fire marshmallows.

"This is irregular," Chandler mumbled to himself. "This is *highly*...I mean, we don't usually get guests. Or visitors. Not that we're going to invite them in, obviously, that would be up to you because you're the new Frost. I mean, you're not *him*, you're the—"

"*Chandler*," I interrupted, patting him on the shoulder. "I get it, this is strange. Let's just go down and check things out."

Not the best with confrontation, Chandler opted to stay upstairs and observe from a safe distance. He informed me that I could open the massive interlocking doors to the hangar, but leave a transparent blast shield in place. It doesn't offer the same measure of protection as the regular doors, but the micro-alloy could withstand a grenade blast without suffering so much as a scratch, which would provide me with more than enough security. There was no way the visitors were getting past it.

I marched through the hangar to its cavernous opening, and waited patiently as the blast doors inched their way open. A narrow stream of light poured through the crack. It slowly revealed my visitor, standing just an arm's length away, separated by a thin sheet of protective glass.

She was a porcelain doll; beautiful and pristine, her lips a pale shade of pink, cheeks stung red from the arctic air. She pulled her hood back with both hands, revealing a ribbon of golden blond hair and intense crystal-blue eyes. I'd only witnessed a gaze that piercing once in my life. It was in The Arena, right before I watched a man die at my feet.

The girl standing before me was the only living relative of the late Sergei Taktarov – his little sister, Valeriya.

And I knew exactly what she wanted.

CHAPTER TEN

"We have not been introduced, you and I." Her English was clearer since the last time I'd heard her speak, her Russian accent barely perceptible.

The weird thing about coming face to face with an arch-nemesis is that it's rarely the person you expect – at least that's how it happened for me. I'm sure Bruce Wayne didn't anticipate using millions of dollars worth of high-tech equipment to battle a deranged clown; or that Clark Kent, an alien with the powers of a god, would spend most of his time fighting a businessman. And the last person who I expected to come knocking at my door (in the middle of the Canadian wilderness, no less) was a pre-teen girl backed by a group of heavily-armed thugs.

I'd seen Valeriya Taktarov's iTube video that went live shortly after Arena Mode. She threatened me for what I'd done to her brother, and invited the downtrodden to join a new Red Army. Her words were articulate, impassioned, and more than a little bit frightening, especially spilling from the lips of a young child who'd just lost her only living relative. And that was the last I'd seen of her.

Months had drifted by, and there had been no follow-up. Valeriya had disappeared, or so I thought. I assumed she'd gone somewhere to grieve, and would eventually move on with her life. When The Red Army surfaced and the movement gained momentum, I had no idea that she wasn't just the inspiration, or the catalyst – she was the puppeteer, pulling the strings from behind the curtain.

If Valeriya was revealing herself now, it could only mean one thing: her opening act had had drawn to a close. This was the onset of phase two, and whatever she had planned, it was going to be a game-changer. She wanted me in the front row, eyes forward, and she had my full attention.

"No need for introductions," I replied. "I know who you are."

"And you already know why I am here, and what I want." It was a statement, not a question.

"It was you. The Kashstarter campaign."

Her face didn't reveal a single tell. She just stared up at me, unflinching. "What makes you think that?"

"The words that Astrid Neve used in the video, the terms she used...you wrote that speech for her." I'd recognized a similar tone and inflection during Valeriya's powerful speech that she delivered just prior to the Arena Mode tournament, condemning the values of the Western world, and calling out the tyranny of capitalism. Her iTube video following the event was just as biting, and equally eloquent. "Not to mention the clothes." I flicked my eyes to her designer jacket and matching boots.

"The clothes?" She asked.

"I know the Taktarov family background. You're the orphaned daughter of poor farmers. Either you hit the lottery, or you're using some of that Kashstarter money to finance a new wardrobe." Brynja had replicated a number of similar garments using our 3D printer over the last three months. I recognized the designs because I frequently found them scattered around the fortress. I was hardly an expert when it came to fashion, but I could spot the difference between a four-thousand dollar jacket and a cheap knock-off that was stitched together by slave laborers.

"Are you, the richest man in the world, going to lecture *me* about my lifestyle? About excess?" Valeriya's words poured out like venom, although she didn't seem angry, or even annoyed. I couldn't read a single emotion by studying her face.

"So why not just do it yourself?" I asked. "Taktarov's only living relative, asking for revenge? That's strong motivation to rally support."

"Sympathy for a poor little Russian girl who misses her brother?" She nearly laughed at the notion. "That will move a few – some who are easily swayed, with soft hearts. What I required was an army. For that type of commitment I needed a common enemy."

It was a brilliant strategy. Nothing brings people together faster than mutual hatred. I still wasn't buying her reasoning, through. She could have recorded the video herself, and was more than capable of delivering a powerful address. "It seems like being on-camera yourself would have had more impact. Why not just tell everyone that Sergei was The Chosen One and that I was the bad guy?"

Valeriya's tiny lips twitched at the edges, hinting that she was about to crack a knowing smile. She resisted the urge. "I needed someone without an attachment to Sergei. Someone to plant the seeds. The world is angrier than they have ever been, and slowly, they are readying themselves. In a few moments when I release my new video, they will see who I truly am, and they will finally be prepared for what I am about to become."

I folded my arms across my chest and smiled. A calculated smile, wide and condescending. It was in my best interest to keep her talking. The more she said, the more I could learn. I knew Valeriya wouldn't tip her hand, or reveal anything she didn't want me to know until the time was right, although I could sense her opening up. I was hoping for a slip and if I kept pressing, I might be able to rattle her. "And what will you 'become', Valeriya?"

She paused for a moment, as if giving my question some genuine thought. "A messenger. Like Joan of Arc."

"So you're becoming a bipolar egomaniac with a God complex?"

"No," she replied calmly, unfazed by my verbal jab. "I will be an inspiration, just as she was. When Joan of Arc heard the voice of The Almighty and passed on his message, the people listened. She was able to lift the spirits of an entire nation with nothing more than her words. France was losing the war to England, with little hope of turning the tide. She re-energized an army that changed history."

This was getting ridiculous – she *had* to be screwing with me. "People were idiots back then. Some farm girl claimed that god was speaking through her and everyone just blindly accepted it. You think this shit will work *now?*"

"How are things any different?" she asked, without a trace of irony. "Five centuries have passed and *nothing* has changed. People are sad, broken. They are crushed beneath an oppressive leadership that barely allows them basic necessities. Yet they remain credulous and devout, even as their prayers go unanswered." She lowered her voice and stepped forward, pressing her palms flat against the blast door. "They are going to believe me because they *want* to believe me. They needed someone like my brother, and now, with the only person he speaks through, they will have faith once more. Something worth fighting for."

I laughed, loud and caustic. "So *this* is your play? I refuse to come outside, and you leak a video claiming that you speak to your dead brother – a 'god'? Gather as many fanatics as you want, you'll never get to me." She certainly knew her history, but not much about state-of-the-art architecture. This steel and iridium plated fortress could withstand a full assault from an *actual* army – her Red Army, which was no more than a few belligerent idiots armed with pistols and rifles, had no way of breeching my security. Trying to shoot her way in with ancient machine guns would be like trying to dismantle a tank with plastic forks.

"You believe that you are safe inside of Cameron Frost's fortress?" she asked, her eyes narrowing.

I nodded confidently. "Yup. Pretty confident." Even if she released her statement and it inspired more dissidents to gather – which felt like a long shot – it wouldn't have changed the fact that she'd have to get inside the fortress *before* the authorities arrived. She had three hours, max, and then she'd be hauled away in handcuffs, along with her gang of hired thugs.

"Perhaps you *are* safe. For now. But your friends, your family...they are on the outside." She spread her hands and gestured around, to nowhere in particular. "Not quite as safe out here, I would assume."

A painful knot twisted into my stomach. I knew what she was implying, but I couldn't believe she would be willing to go that far. "If you have something to say, just say it." I needed to hear the words out loud.

She glanced over her shoulder towards one of the hunters – a tall, stocky man with a serious looking beard. He jerked the sleeve away from his wrist and tapped his wrist-com, projecting a small holo-screen into the air.

"Would you like to see someone *you* love suffer? See them die, the way my brother died at your hands?" Her icy demeanor was melting away. I could see the fury in her eyes, like crackling embers about to burst into flame. The unnerving transformation set my teeth on edge.

I held up my hands. "Look, I don't know what you're planning, but it's not too late. We can—"

"It *is* too late," she shouted, hammering her palms into the glass. "Much, much too late. For my brother, and for you. Come out here, *right now,* or he dies."

The holo-screen flickered into focus, revealing my brother-in-law, Gary. Bound, gagged, bleeding from a gash across his eyebrow. A masked man stood behind him, holding a syringe to his neck, with his thumb poised to press down on the plunger.

I froze. I wasn't angry, or afraid – at least not in that moment. I just kept rolling the same thought over in my head: this was some kind of a trick. It had to be. A virtual masking program meant to create the illusion that one of the kindest, most selfless people on this dying planet was about to die himself.

"You have nothing to say?" She asked innocently. "Perhaps *he* would like to say something. To beg for his life."

The man standing guard ripped off his gag. Gary let out a hoarse cough, dotting the camera lens with blood. "Don't come out," he shouted. "They'll kill us both. Take care of the kids an—"

His final words were muffled by the gloved hand of his captor, cranking his head back as the syringe plunged into his neck. The jade-colored liquid disappeared from the barrel, filling Gary's bloodstream. The effect was instantaneous. His body convulsed violently, then stiffened. It happened so fast that he didn't even scream. The whites of Gary's eyes turned a sickly shade of green, and two sizzling streams of acid dripped from his tear ducts, running down his cheeks. It was over before his captor could pull the empty syringe from his neck.

"More humane than the way you killed my brother, was it not?" Valeriya waved her henchman off with the flick of her gloved hand. He stepped back obediently, terminating the holo-screen transmission. "It was you, was it not? The one who decided that *this* was the way that Sergei should die?"

I gazed, unblinking, into her crystal eyes. The gravity of the situation was still sinking in.

Valeriya stared back at me, eyes narrowing slightly, as if she was trying to solve a puzzle. "This upsets you, but it is not the type of pain I was hoping for. You are *concerned*, for your sister and her children, perhaps. Sad for their loss." She shook her head, as if disappointed by my reaction. "It will take more to convince you to give yourself up. I see this now. Maybe whoever is coming back in your jet."

Her words snapped me out of my daze.

Peyton, Valentina and Mac. They were on their way here. Right now.

"I can see the gears moving," she said calmly. "It is written all over your face. Do you leave your family and friends out in the world, exposed, and hope they can hide from us? Maybe, but I do not think so. You are calculated and require control. You want them here where you can watch them, protect them...but you cannot open the doors without letting us in. And if the jet is close enough, we have a solution."

With those words, her second guards – a tall bearded man who looked more or less like his counterpart – stepped forward. He removed his glove, revealing a white-hot glowing palm. He extended it towards a towering pine tree in the distance and fired, slicing it in half with a plasma bolt.

"Not enough to break down your castle," she said, "but a powerful enough to destroy an incoming jet, perhaps."

I turned and walked away, triggering the massive blast doors to slide shut behind me.

Valeriya shouted a few final words as I left. She wished me luck, and that I was going to need it. And she let me know that it was just a matter of time before she found her way inside. By assault or attrition, she promised that this siege was going to end – and that the body count was going to start piling up.

I didn't reply. I wanted her to think that she'd defeated me, crushed my spirits – so it was important to give her the last word. Without knowing it she'd given me just a little too much information. I had my next move planned before the doors rumbled closed.

Peyton said I was the same person after leaving The Arena, but that couldn't be further from the truth. I'd seen death. I'd experienced suffering. And when Cameron Frost threatened my friends, backing me into a corner, I learned something about who I am: that I'll do a hell of a lot more to protect the people I love than I will to protect myself.

Gary's death gutted me out. It destroyed a small part of me to watch the man my sister dedicated her life to, and the father of the two most amazing kids in the world, die so needlessly.

His death was going to mean something. I would make sure of it.

PART TWO
THE PARENT OF REVOLUTION

CHAPTER ELEVEN

"Swing around to the north end," I shouted into my wrist-com.

"Copy that," Mac replied, his voice trembling. Valeriya's henchmen had already opened fire, pocking the fuselage of the jet with a handful of bullets. A slug cracked the cockpit window and I heard Peyton scream.

The jet circled around the fortress, hovering low into the tree line.

The gunmen were standing on the runway, blocking the main hangar. As far as they knew it was the only place to dock an aircraft, so I'm sure they were surprised when the G12 passed overhead, and prepared to land in a small secondary hangar that was embedded into the side of the fortress, inaccessible by foot.

They scrambled to reload their weapons as the doors cracked open. Only a narrow thicket separated the jet and the shooters, and the ice-covered pines weren't providing much cover.

The hangar doors opened at a glacial pace, drifting apart as a hail of bullets pounded the side of the hovering aircraft.

"Think you can open these doors any slower?" Mac screamed. "I'm getting hammered out here!" The aircraft was bullet resistant, but it wasn't designed for combat; it certainly couldn't take much more of the punishment that two military-grade machine guns were dishing out, unloading their clips in rapid succession.

"Something's wrong," I replied frantically. "They *should* be opening faster. I think the gears are frozen."

"We're aborting," Mac announced, pulling the jet out of position.

"Do it," I shouted. My eyes were glued to the monitor, and I watched as the craft ascended and cleared the tree line. "Get to safety and we'll make a new plan."

It was a second too late.

Valeriya's superhuman had fired a beam of energy from his hand, slicing off the jet's right engine in a fiery blaze, along with the wing. The aircraft fell into a flat spin.

As the remains spiralled towards the ground a secondary explosion detonated, littering the forest floor with fragments of charred metal.

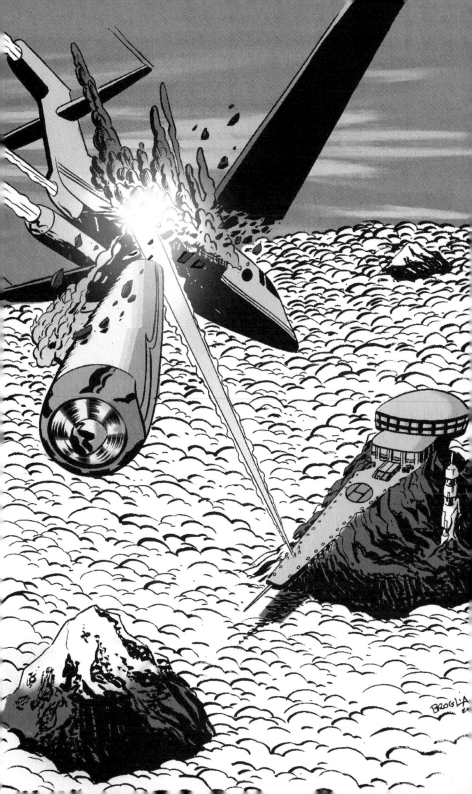

Valeriya was brilliant, but you can't fight biology – she was still just a kid. She was impulsive, and couldn't resist the urge to show off her henchman's superpower, taunting me like a child wielding her father's gun.

Valeriya knew my private jet was on its way back, and that I wouldn't turn it away. She was right: I wanted my friends here. I wanted them safe, inside Fortress 23 where I could protect them. She was desperate to take out the aircraft in mid-flight, twisting yet another knife into my gut. Hurting the people I care about was her most effective weapon, and unlike Cameron Frost – who in retrospect, had a shred of humanity – she had no qualms about pulling the trigger.

Not to mention that destroying my shiny new G12, a symbol of decadence for the ultra-privileged, would undoubtedly make a bold statement to her followers. I was, after all, not *just* 'The God Slayer'; ever since winning the Arena Mode tournament I was one of the elite. I represented everything the poor and the middle-class despised...everything that *I* despised, to be honest. I hadn't even been wealthy long enough for the irony to sink in.

My plan was simple enough: have Mac fly in low beneath the tree line, and hover to a stop a few kilometers south of the fortress. It was a location by a small frozen river at the edge of the forest – right at the entrance of the South Tunnel.

It turns out that the long underground pathway I had discovered, which was protected by a circular steel door, led to the mouth of a narrow cave. London had been very helpful in uncovering its mysteries. The entrance to the South Tunnel, on the far wall of the cavern, just appeared to be stone from the outside. But with a few voice-activated keywords the hidden door rumbled open, revealing the long narrow path back to the fortress. Like the castle escapes of medieval times, Frost had included a similar feature here in Fortress 23, so in case of emergency you could get to safety on foot, escaping into a remote part of the forest completely undetected. We were just using the tunnel in reverse.

Getting Mac, Valentina and Peyton to safety was phase one, and it was the easiest part of the plan. The second part relied on our wrist-com conversation – the one that continued as the jet was being flown directly into the line of fire. Valeriya was leaving nothing to chance, which meant that she was almost certainly monitoring all incoming and outgoing transmissions. I'd bet the house on it. And if she *was* listening in, I had to give her a realistic enough reason to have the jet hover just a few hundred feet from her gunmen, giving them a nice big target to shoot at.

Remote piloting the jet from the South Tunnel, Mac was able to move it into position, and the only thing left was the voice acting (I wasn't expecting Shakespeare, but even under the circumstances I thought he was phoning it in.)

Letting her superhuman lackey slice the jet down with a plasma bolt was the final phase of the plan. I knew that it would be a spectacular wreck, but the secondary explosion was just a happy coincidence. With that much damage, it would take days to sift through the remains, if they even bothered to do so. They wouldn't locate any bodies at the disaster site, but after crash like that I don't know if they'd expect to.

Either way, my friends were safe, and I'd bought a little time. At least enough for the authorities to arrive and arrest Valeriya and her mercenaries.

I took the main elevator down to Sub Level 7 with Chandler in tow. We circled the stark white hallways until we reached the entrance to the tunnel where Valentina, Mac and Peyton had just emerged, pushing the heavy vault door closed behind them.

Peyton rushed towards me and threw her arms around my neck, burying her face in my shoulder. The smell of her skin, the wave of pink hair brushing my face as we embraced – it was a time machine. I closed my eyes and I was back in The Fringe, walking through the front door of Excelsior Retro Comics with the bright morning sunlight streaming in behind me. She would always run to greet me, even if she was in mid-sentence chatting with a customer. For a second I could almost smell the burnt orange carpeting; the ragged eyesore that we all begged Gavin to replace, but he never did. It reminded him of a simpler time. If there was anything I could relate to it was the powerful allure of nostalgia; how an object, even something that was seemingly trivial, could take you back to someplace special. Someplace that you wished could be preserved forever in a pristine collector case, shiny and new; never to age, or change, or be ravaged by time. But now, that special place exists only in your memory. I'd always used my comic collection for that very same purpose, though I'd never experienced it while holding onto a person.

She drew back and wiped a wayward tear from her cheek, quickly and discreetly, as if I'd be too distracted to notice. "I'm *so* sorry," she said, clearing her voice. "I never knew things were this bad. What's happening in New York, it's—"

"You're here, you're safe. That's all that matters now." I squeezed her arms gently and rubbed them for warmth. She was wearing only a thin black sweater, sorely unprepared for the brutal weather she'd encounter in Northern Canada. "And we're going to get Gavin here, too. Everything will work out."

She smiled, and a fresh pair of teardrops rolled down her cheeks. I almost broke down myself. Watching Gary lose his life was agonizing, and the thought of losing someone else, especially Peyton, would have pushed me past the breaking point. I was doing everything in my power to keep myself together.

"I feel like such a bitch," she said, laughing through her tears. "I practically kicked you out of my life when you said you were in danger, and now the world is falling apart."

"Maybe we both needed space." I replied with a shrug. "Absence makes the heart grow fonder and all that bullshit."

"Maybe," she said softly. "You must have been so lonely here the last few months, with just your staff to keep you company."

Chandler was escorting Mac and Valentina to the infirmary for a routine post-mission checkup (they didn't sustain so much as a scratch, but it was procedure – something that Chandler rarely deviated from) and I hadn't noticed Brynja approach from behind, standing at a distance. I also wasn't aware that she was still in one of her cosplay outfits, dressed head-to-toe like Wonder Woman. She'd printed every accessory; boots, gauntlets, a tiara, as well as the gold Lasso of Truth that dangled from her belt.

I didn't spin around to see the blue-haired Amazonian until Peyton cupped a hand over her mouth, her face reddening. "Oh, I didn't... know that you had company. Before all this happened did you hire some...entertainment?"

"What the *fuck*," Brynja groaned, loud and exasperated. "Do you think I'm a *hooker?*"

"I don't..." Peyton paused for a moment, still covering her mouth. "Do you prefer a different term? Because I'm not really familiar with all of the—"

"It's *just* a costume!" Brynja shouted. "Like, you know, for fun? Why does everyone assume I'm some filthy prostitute?"

Peyton cocked her head and narrowed her eyes. "Wait, who else assumes that?"

"It's *Brynja*," I explained. "My partner, from the Arena."

Peyton scanned her from boots to tiara, eyes squinted half-shut. "The one who died? What happened?"

"It didn't take," Brynja said.

"Apparently." Peyton glanced at me, now more suspicious than confused. "So you brought her here for protection? Like me?"

I scratched the back of my head with both hands, unaware that I was fidgeting. "No, she's been here for a while."

"Three months," Brynja added.

"So you *live* here," Peyton said flatly. "With Matt. Together."

"It's not *just* us here," I replied without missing a beat, "we have maids and a chef, and—"

"So it's pretty much like a guy and a girl in a five-star hotel," Peyton said.

"Yes," I snapped, before correcting myself. "Wait, *no*. It's like, she appeared back at the hospital out of nowhere. I thought she was dead, but she was showed up naked, and then I took her home." *Holy shit.* My mouth was moving and words were flying out, completely independent from my brain. "I'm not explaining this very well."

"You're really not," Brynja added with a tiny chuckle. Her laugh drew an icy glare from Peyton.

"Look," Peyton said, her arms folded tightly across her chest, "we've barely seen each other since The Arena and it's not like we ever said we were exclusive. I thought maybe we'd reconnect, but...you're free to see other women, I guess, or hire them or whatever."

"Standing *right here*," Brynja said sharply, pointing to herself. "And still *not* a prostitute." She would have been easier to take seriously if she hadn't been wearing a gold bustier with a matching lasso.

There wasn't much left to say, and thankfully no one felt like continuing the conversation. So after the most awkward elevator ride of all time, the three of us silently stepped out onto the main level and went our separate ways. I could deal with personal issues later. In the meantime I had calls to make and people to protect.

The fortress was secure, but everyone else on the outside certainly wasn't. A fact that Valeriya was waiting to exploit.

CHAPTER TWELVE

Night fell, and it became painfully obvious that the authorities weren't coming to our rescue.

I called The Royal Canadian Mounted Police (who, I was assured, were no longer using horses as their primary mode of transportation) and was told they were on their way. If the RCMP *did* send officers to make arrests, they had either encountered resistance, or had changed their minds and circled back. The nearest town was two hundred kilometers away, so unless the dispatcher I'd spoken with was mistaken, and the cops actually *were* arriving on horseback, they should have been here hours ago.

No one else seemed willing to offer support. I was on hold waiting to speak with the US Ambassador, and eventually gave up after an hour. No other Canadian agencies would even take my calls.

I then attempted to contact every US security agency I could think of, and filled them in on the situation here in Northern Alberta: a group of tax-paying Americans, stranded in the Canadian wilderness, taking fire from Russian thugs...and a superhuman who could fire plasma bolts from his hands. I know how it sounded, but I showed them video evidence to back up my claims. I even played the celebrity card, hoping that, as per usual, the rich and famous would receive preferential treatment. It was worth a shot.

But nothing. No one cared.

All I received were lectures about how many riots were breaking out across the country. Everyone from the local cops to the National Guard were up to their elbows in looters and protestors. The authorities' numbers were spread thin, and they couldn't spare the manpower to help out a citizen stranded in a foreign country – celebrity or otherwise.

I checked the simulcast feeds and saw the evidence for myself. It seems that the implosion in New York had caused a domino effect; full-scale lockdowns were initiated across the East Coast, which meant a suffocating police presence – this, in turn, lead to the inevitable backlash. Mobs stormed the streets in reaction to the harsh security measures, and the authorities fought back. The chaos was a wildfire, spreading from Boston to Miami in a matter of hours.

The West Coast followed. Before long California had become a warzone, and these weren't just your run-of-the-mill riots: fires blazed, shots were fired, and a few superhumans got into the mix. In San Francisco, a woman with the ability to emit sonic shockwaves by clapping her hands assaulted a group of riot police, bursting their eardrums. She was gunned down by a S.W.A.T. team moments later.

As soon as word got out that another superhuman was responsible for an attack, the shit *really* hit the fan. Police presence was quickly supplemented by the military. I'm sure the death toll was increasing, but the news feeds were keeping quiet. "Necessary force" were the buzzwords being repeated by every network. And any attempt to search through social media or holo-forums for the term 'riot' turned up blank. ISPs were no doubt being instructed to keep a lid on anything related to the uprisings around the country.

After finally getting through to Senator Alex Jenkins from my home state of New York, I was told that I could fill out a 'Request for Foreign Aid and/or Rescue While Living Abroad' form, mail it back (as in, with a stamp and envelope) and wait six to eight weeks for it to be processed and evaluated. And then, *if* the allotted resources were available, some American forces would come to our rescue. Time permitting.

The only successful call I'd made in the last twenty-four hours was to the Halifax PD. Fortunately, the North-Eastern coast of Canada was riot-free, so my request to have the police escort Elizabeth and the kids to a secure location was granted.

Exhausted and frustrated by the lack of progress, everyone retired to their rooms for the evening. Staying awake and worrying all night wouldn't do us any good – we could resume hand-wringing and pacing in the morning. Peyton was escorted to a chamber across the hall from mine, offering me a tiny smile before shutting the door behind her.

Chandler set the fortress on lockdown, which apparently provided even more security for the gigantic structure. I didn't think that was even possible. Blast shields covered every exposed window, offering an additional layer of protection, and the transparent dome that topped the fortress turned opaque, darkening to a velvety black. According to London, *"We are now in 'castle mode'. With additional protection in place, Fortress 23 can now withstand a direct hit from a GBU-43/B Massive Ordnance Air Blast – the most powerful non-nuclear weapon ever created."* I was hoping that whatever The Red Army had in store for us, we wouldn't have to test that theory.

I suggested that Chandler get some rest, because tomorrow things could get ugly.

He asked how much worse things could possibly get. I smiled weakly and turned towards my room.

Lying on my bed, I knew that rest wouldn't come easy. My body needed sleep, but my mind, as usual, wasn't in the mood to cooperate. I wandered down to the infirmary, and Judy prescribed me a mild sedative, which she guaranteed would provide eight hours of uninterrupted sleep. If that were true it would be the first time I'd slept through the night since before Arena Mode. I swallowed the bright purple tablet, returned to my room and flopped onto my mattress, gazing up at the ceiling.

Waiting for the drug to take effect, the usual nightly checklist floated through my mind: a detailed outline of everything I'd screwed up in my life, updated to include the most recent highlights. Peyton probably hated me, and certainly didn't trust me. Gavin went missing after his store burnt down (again, my fault). And Kenneth, who I'd put into a coma, wanted me to pull the plug and let him die.

The icing on the cake was that I had to explain to my sister that I watched her husband being executed, and that my niece and nephew no longer had a father to grow up with. That would be a fun call to make. Oh, and while I was at it, I could tell her that the neighborhood we grew up in, the south end of The Fringe, was imploded by a madman who wanted me dead. So that was more or less my fault as well.

I continued to beat myself up until my eyelids filled with lead, and I was powerless to keep them propped open. Judy's purple pill didn't disappoint. I drifted off, as promised, into the best sleep of my life.

Eight hours, nineteen minutes and forty-one seconds later, I'd have to deal with what would become the worst day of my life – at least up until that point. But on the bright side, I wouldn't need quite so much caffeine to deal with it.

Before I drifted off I added one final screw-up to my ever-expanding checklist: I should have given Chandler some more helpful advice before he went to bed. When he asked, "How much worse can things possibly get?" I should have advised him to never, ever ask that question. Because the

answer, no matter what the situation, is always the same.
"Way, *way* fucking worse."

Partial transcript from the BBC News Simulcast 'The Daily Express'
Hosted by Liam Beckett, January 2042

Liam Beckett: On the heels of a shocking announcement from Valeriya Taktarov, we're going to be discussing the potential impact of her iTube video, her call-to-arms, and how much stock should be put into her incredible claims.

Joining me this evening are American talk show host and political commentator, William O'Neill, as well as renowned British physicist and author, Agnes Richards.

Let's start with you, Doctor Richards: what do you make of young Miss Taktarov, and her assertion that Sergei, her deceased brother, is speaking 'through her' – telepathically, as it were?

Agnes Richards: It's complete rubbish. There has never been any evidence of an afterlife.

William O'Neill: Are you kidding me, Richards? This is all the proof we need that there *is* an afterlife. When he was alive, Sergei Taktarov was flying around in the air, shooting laser beams from his eyes – how do you explain *that*, doc?

If *that's* not the work of a higher power, I don't know what is.

Richards: There will be a perfectly rational explanation for these so-called superhuman abilities in due time. Simply because science can't yet explain their origins doesn't mean they're the result of divine intervention.

O'Neill: Oh, *there's* a surprise: science can't explain it. "We have all the answers!" you and all your science buddies shouted from the rooftops. *Then* superhumans started appearing, and *now* we have proof of an afterlife – all of a sudden you're not as smart as you think.

Richards: I never claimed to have all the answers. No responsible scientist would dare to claim they ha—

O'Neill: Don't interrupt me, Richards. You'll get your turn, all right?

As I was saying, these scientist pinheads think they know it all, but they can't explain superhuman powers, and they sure as heck can't explain this.

It took the Vatican just an hour to jump on board and support Valeriya Taktarov's statements. Did you know that? An *hour*. And The Pope is infallible, so who am I to argue with him?

Richards: Just because the Pope believes and endorses Valeriya Taktarov does not give her claims any more validity.

O'Neill: You and all these number crunchers are clueless about superhumans – you said it yourself. And now you're telling me The Pope's word doesn't mean crap? Is that what you're saying?

Richards: I never said his word was 'crap', if you'll just list—

O'Neill: The Pope was chosen by the man upstairs to be the leader of the Catholic Church, and *his* specialty is communicating with people in the afterlife. I think I'll take The Pope's opinion over yours, thank you very much. And another thing – I don't think you should be telling the most respected man in the world how to do *his* job. He doesn't walk into *your* lab and tell you how to clean Bunsen burners and dissect frogs.

Richards: I'm...I'm not even sure how to respond to all of that.

O'Neill: And while we're on the topic of know-it-alls, what about all your science buddies who say they can give people superhuman powers, and are charging *millions* for the operation? You don't seem too upset about that.

Richards: Now wait just a moment – neurologists from Argentina and Brazil are *claiming* they can alter brain chemistry, thereby increasing an individual's chance of acquiring certain abilities – but this has never been verified, and I do not endorse these practices in any way. The scientific community, as a whole, has distanced itself from these individuals.

Beckett: Let's move on to the nature of this message; Valeriya's impassioned speech where she states, in no uncertain terms, that her brother demands vengeance. She stops short of naming names, but anyone can connect the dots and see a clear line pointing towards one man. She's insinuating that Russia's Son is demanding the execution of Matthew Moxon.

O'Neill: Look, I'm not going to condone vigilante justice. I'm not a lawyer, and I'm not in the position to make these types of calls when it comes to what constitutes breaking the law...but if this Moxon character turns up dead, maybe it *will* lead to a better society, for all I know.

Richards: Are you quite mad? What you just said *specifically* condones vigilante justice.

O'Neill: I'm no fan of Russia, or communism, or anything that goes on outside of America – but Valeriya Taktarov says a new era of peace and prosperity will arrive if Moxon is rubbed out, and that Russia's Son will be the one to deliver it. What's the *worst* thing that can happen if people listen to her?

Richards: The 'worst thing' would be to lend credence to these outlandish claims, giving the credulous tacit approval to take matters into their own hands. Allowing this type of theological bullying to go unchecked would also be first step towards a world where trials and executions take place in a court of popular opinion, much as they were in the dark ages, and not in a modern-day court of law where facts and evidence are a prerequisite.

O'Neill: We'll just have to agree to disagree.

Richards: Do you even know what you're disagreeing *with?*

Beckett: Well, that's all the time we have. I'd like to thank Agnes Richards and William O'Neill for joining me here on this special evening edition of The Daily Express.

Don't forget to visit our website, where you can pick up Doctor Richards's latest book 'A Trip Through the Cosmos', as well as O'Neill's new book, 'America's Heartland: The Birthplace of Capitalism, The Second Amendment and Christianity'.

CHAPTER THIRTEEN

By morning the number of campsites had swollen from two to twenty. Aircraft continued to drop protesters at our fortress perimeter, along with weapons and additional supplies. And all-terrain vehicles arrived by the dozen; endless convoys wearing a path through the snow. As the hours passed, the numbers increased. By noon, the view from outside my bedroom window looked like a political rally. At a glance I counted just under a thousand people, with more huddled inside tents and vehicles to keep warm. Around the campsites, some were planting flags in the ground. Not surprisingly, it was the solid red banner with a gold hammer and sickle in solidarity with Russia's Son.

Valeriya's iTube video had enlisted more recruits than I anticipated. She was so convincing, in fact, that religious leaders from around the world were taking her claims all too seriously. The Vatican's official statement (which was more or less an endorsement of her mission statement to have me murdered) is what likely pushed many believers over the edge, inspiring them to make the pilgrimage to Fortress 23 in droves. It wasn't long before we were completely surrounded.

There were no signs of the authorities coming to disperse the crowd, but thankfully, there was a bit of good news that came through a simulcast: a weather report was calling for extreme conditions. When the *Canadian* government calls the amount of snow coming your way 'extreme', you had better believe that they're serious. The snow fell – and fell, and fell, and fell. It was three feet deep before nightfall. Temperatures were well below zero, with arctic wind chills dropping to minus fifty degrees Celsius. I spotted an ATV in one of the campsites attempt to move; engine wheezing, headlights flickering – it was immobilized. Being stationary for too long, the vehicle's tires had become completely iced to the ground.

The weather was helpful in slowing the influx of reinforcements as well. Since the heavy snowfall began not a single new convoy had arrived by land, and in these conditions, air travel was out of the question. Visibility was non-existent, and the winds were far too violent, even for my state-of-the-art aircraft.

The weather was not enough of a deterrent to keep the soldiers from continuing their attempts to break into the fortress, though; groups of them were attacking the base of the structure with various weapons and forms of construction equipment. Everything from gunfire to handheld drills were being used in an attempt to find a weak spot. Late into the night, video feeds from our external cams showed bright orange sparks flashing in the darkness as hailstorms of bullets bounced harmlessly off the armored walls, and drill bits snapped off trying to penetrate the surface.

At the moment, the intruders were causing no more than cosmetic damage, and I wasn't overly concerned with dents and chipped paint. What *was* a concern was the possibility of the Red Army finding that elusive weak point – some flaw in the design that would grant them access to the fortress, creating a doorway that would allow a tidal wave of angry dissidents to storm through like the finale of a zombie movie. Our weapons, and even Valentina's hydrokinesis, would be inconsequential in the face of those numbers. We'd be overwhelmed in a matter of minutes by the sheer weight of attackers. I'd most likely be dragged away, subjected to public torture before my execution, and I didn't even want to consider what would happen to my friends and the remaining staff. Of course this was an irrational fear; the likelihood of them breaching security was a wild, billion-to-one long shot...although when you're surrounded by over a thousand angry militants who want to sacrifice you to their god, it's sometimes difficult to separate the rational fears from the irrational ones.

As time passed Valeriya's intentions were becoming clear. Her plan was unfolding, and the actions she *didn't* take were making her motives all the more transparent. Her followers were attempting to access the fortress using only rudimentary tools; drills, jackhammers, gunfire – with no effort being made to gain entry using explosives. Any attempt to blast their way in would likely yield no results, but she had no way of knowing that for certain. For all she knew a well-paced grenade or round from a bazooka would open up a gaping hole, giving her mob an all-access pass to our seemingly impregnable fortress. The gunshots, the drilling – this was mindless busywork. Her people were putting on a show, making it look like they were making a serious attempt to gain access to the fortress, all while some larger, more insidious plot unfolded. Were they just awaiting additional followers, giving the masses more time to arm themselves and join the cause? Was she using some of the Kashstarter funds to hire superhumans in an attempt to blast their way in? Or was there something else she was waiting on? I couldn't be sure.

What seemed obvious was the fact that Valeriya – and her Red Army – almost certainly wanted me alive. At least to begin with. Acting without her direct leadership, the movement was a loosely-assembled group of angry militants, scouring the world for anyone who looked remotely like me. They shot first and confirmed ID's later. Now, there was more focus. The implosion in New York City seemed more calculated than ever: the human suicide bomb went off in the spot where it would draw the most attention and elicit the greatest response. Attention was now completely focused on the riots that had spread across America, and had continued to propagate throughout major cities in Canada and Mexico.

Had Valeriya just wanted me vaporized, it would have made more sense to send her jihadist right to my front porch here in Northern Alberta. He could have torn off his shirt, gone supernova and taken out the entire fortress, blinking it – and Matthew 'The God Slayer' Moxon – completely out of existence. Simple and effective, but not nearly enough of a statement. Whatever Valeriya Taktarov had in mind as recompense for the loss of her only living relative, it was going to be much more sadistic.

When I played poker, Valeriya was what we referred to as a 'sandbagger': someone who presented themselves as more passive and weak than they actually were, luring their opposition into a false sense of security. When the sharks at the table were feeling confident, that's when the sandbagger would strike. The sharks, overconfident in their abilities, get harpooned the moment they let their guard down; they go home broke, while the sandbagger walks away with the house.

It was comfortable to let Peyton, Brynja and the others believe that we were up against no more than a group of poorly-armed idiots who had no hope of achieving their goal. I knew better, and so did Valentina.

My bodyguard suggested that we prepare for a worst-case scenario, which meant opening up The Vault. For the past three months, Valentina and I failed to see eye-to-eye on a single issue, but she was always a consummate professional. She'd helped me design weapons and body armor using our 3D printer, and she suggested it was time to suit up and prepare for what could be on the horizon. It was never too soon to test equipment in case of an emergency situation, so we agreed that the next day I'd take Peyton, Brynja and Chandler to The Vault.

When morning came I opened the blast shields that covered my bedroom window, and a shaft of bright sunlight poured in as the steel retracted. The clouds had parted and the snowfall had ceased, giving the Red Army a temporary reprieve from the harsh conditions. New convoys were already rumbling in through a well-worn path in the forest, and their numbers had doubled. They were now chopping down trees and clearing the surroundings, making room for additional camp sites. I considered visiting the nurse to ask about anti-anxiety pills, but we were already scheduled for our armor fitting – I could take care of my panic attacks later.

Throwing on jeans and a t-shirt I stepped into the hallway, nearly colliding with Peyton as I finished pulling up my zipper. Our eyes met and she smiled politely, but it was tight and forced, without the warmth she usually radiated. We paused, staring at each other, as if anticipating the other might say something. I opened my mouth for a moment and closed it, unable to produce a word that would fill the awkward silence. She smiled again, a little wider, and twirled a loop of pink hair with her finger as she stared down at her shoes.

I heard the distinctive sound of boots clacking on the steel floors as Brynja rounded the corner. "Did I miss something?" she asked. "What is this, a staring contest?"

Peyton's smile quickly faded. She deliberately trailed her eyes from Brynja's newly printed footwear (heavy black leather with spikes protruding from a steel toe) up to her low-slung jeans, to her tattered black tank top (a barely-existent garment that revealed a generous amount of cleavage, along with most of her midriff). Her lipstick and eyeshadow matched her vivid blue locks, which were pulled into a pair of braids that fell over her shoulders.

Standing next to each other, their physical similarities were apparent – their age, height and stature were nearly identical – but their styles couldn't have contrasted more if they'd tried. While Brynja was loud and expressive in her attire, Peyton's clothes were far softer, and much more unassuming. Her loose-fitting grey sweater, yoga pants and running shoes represented the bulk of her wardrobe. She rarely required anything more formal; during her life in The Fringe she spent the majority of her time working at Excelsior Retro Comics, or in school studying to be a veterinarian. As she continued to inspect Brynja's outfit in the painful gulf of silence, I interjected with a rapid, "C'mon guys, these suits aren't going to try themselves on," and gestured for them to follow me towards the floor's central hub.

A few minutes later we arrived at The Vault. It was directly adjacent to the primary media room, and was identical in every way: an expansive, snowflake-white living space without a single right angle to disrupt the aesthetic. It was perfectly circular with four entrance points, separated evenly like the quarter-hour notches on a clock. However, instead of being furnished with plush leather couches and low-hanging lamps, this room had a single design feature: a cylindrical silver column that stretched from floor to ceiling. The enormous tube that dominated the center of the room disappeared into the floor with a touch of my thumbprint, revealing my own private arsenal.

The armor suits, and an impressive array of rifles, hung from what looked like a massive circular department store rack, with hooks used to display the hardware.

"Holy shit," Brynja whispered. "Is all of this for us?"

"Yup." I rotated the rack along the top rail like hangars in a closet. I browsed through the armor, shifting them aside one after the other. "This is yours."

Brynja unhooked the shimmering black bodysuit from the rack and held it in front of her, as if to approximate her size.

I circled around the far side of the rack and retrieved Peyton's suit. When I handed it to her she crinkled her nose at the design. "These look a little tight. Are they supposed to stop bullets, or are they for show, like Brynja's costumes?"

"Hey buttercup," Brynja shouted from the opposite side of the rack, hidden behind the rows of armor. "I can still hear you."

"I just mean these don't look very durable," Peyton called out, "I thought these were supposed to be bullet-proof or something?"

Looks, I explained, can be deceiving. The armor was made from a flexible graphene textile that provided more than enough protection from a bullet, bladed weapon, or even an explosive. Stretched across a wide surface, a wafer-thin strip of graphene couldn't be pierced by a two-ton elephant standing on a sharpened pencil. I'm not sure if anyone had actually performed the elephant test themselves, but the colorful analogy had always been used to describe the material's toughness.

Graphene was impressive on its own, but with an unlimited budget at my disposal, I was able to take the design process to an entirely different level: 'Smart Fiber' was a light, malleable textile which went on like a wetsuit. It was roughly the same thickness and density of a wetsuit as well, but when an object collided with its exterior, the Smart Fiber hardened on impact, similar to an airbag being triggered during a car crash. The projectile would bounce harmlessly off the surface, leaving the wearer unharmed.

As I went over the impressive checklist of features, including how the Smart Fiber suits were fireproof, waterproof, and that they conduct electricity like a Faraday cage, Peyton was more concerned with an apparent cosmetic design flaw.

"Wait a sec," she said suspiciously, holding the suit away from her. "What's *this* on the chest?"

I raised my eyebrows and shrugged. "A number? The same ones we learned about back when we were toddlers?"

"No," she said coarsely, "It's not 'just' a number, it's number thirteen."

"Right," I explained. "Number thirteen. As in, this was the thirteenth version of the suit I created. I kept refining them to make sure the design was perfect. Easiest way to keep track of which suit was which."

"Easy for *you* to be so blasé about this," she said, gesturing to my suit. Peyton's voice had raised several octaves and her face creased into an uneasy frown, causing me to take a step backwards. "You ended up with number seven. That's the best number to have. Do you know how unlucky thirteen is?"

"No," I replied quietly, "but I have a feeling you're about to tell me."

She groaned, scanning the armor while she shook her head in disapproval. "You might as well have designed a suit with a giant crosshair on the back."

"Now that I think about it," Brynja shouted from the other side of the rack, "I think I noticed a black cat walk in front of your suit, like, *right* after it was printed. And Mox, didn't these get passed under a ladder at some point?"

"Hey, Smurfette," Peyton shouted back, "keep it down – the adults are trying to have a conversation here."

It occurred to me, watching the anger simmer inside of Peyton, that this was about much more than her adherence to superstition. I poked fun at her beliefs all the time and she would never bat an eye. Peyton hadn't been in the same room as Brynja since her arrival, and I had a feeling this was the moment where the emotional powder keg was about to go off.

Never one to back down from a confrontation, Brynja circled around the rack to face Peyton. "Do you *really* want to go there, princess? Insulting my *hair*?"

Peyton locked her feet into place and folded her arms, straightening her posture. "The tattoos, the piercings, the bright blue hair – I can see right through you. You're one of *those* girls."

"'Those girls'?" Brynja repeated, her eyes narrowing.

"I used to see them all the time," Peyton explained, "Tourists from Manhattan, slumming it in The Fringe, looking to hook up with some security guard or bartender that daddy would never approve of. They dye their hair and do all sorts of body mods...you're one of *them*. You get off on the attention."

"Says the girl with the *pink* hair," Brynja replied with a caustic laugh.

"It's pink because *I* happen to like it this way," Peyton fired back. "Look at *you*," she gestured towards Brynja, making a show of looking her up and down. "It's January, and we're in *Canada*. You're dressed like you're about to start pole dancing."

My eyes flicked back and forth between them, nervously anticipating the next bombshell. The fight was escalating at an alarming rate, and it felt like at any moment I'd have to step in between them, like a referee separating two prizefighters who refused to stop slinging leather after a round came to an end.

"Well since we're on the topic of hair," Brynja said coarsely, "Mox happens to be the one who chose this color for me."

Peyton paused, seemingly more skeptical than angry. "That's not possible. It was like that before he even met you."

"I'm a *perception*," Brynja explained. "It's my superhuman ability. I didn't even *exist* until Moxon blinked me into reality."

"What the hell is that supposed to mean?" Peyton replied.

"It means," Brynja said with a conspiratorial smile, "that when your sweetheart saw me in The Arena for the first time, I needed an external observer to complete my corporeal form, and solidify me on this plane. His desires manifested into yours truly."

"I don't get it," Peyton replied.

Brynja rolled her eyes. "Shocker."

I stepped into the narrowing gap between the girls and extended my hands to either side. "Okay, this has gone far enough, let's just—"

"No," Peyton insisted. "Let's not 'just'. This is getting interesting. Please, Brynja, go on."

"Want me to make this real simple for you?" she continued, taking a small step forward. "Whatever was going on inside of Mox's dirty little mind is what I became that day. Notice how similar we look? Our height, our eyes, our body types...pretty close, no?"

Peyton scanned Brynja again – this time without judgment or contempt, but genuinely taking notice of their remarkable similarities. "I guess. So?"

"So," Brynja said, gesturing to herself. "I'm *you*, just a better version. I'm closer to Mox's ideal match in every way."

"This is *such* bullshit," Peyton shouted, sticking a finger in Brynja's face. I placed a hand on her shoulder to prevent her from taking another step closer.

"Is it?" Brynja replied, her smile widening. She stood perfectly still, hands on hips, as if waiting for the realization to fully sink in.

"All right," I interjected, "let's just take a breather and settle down." I paused for a moment before turning my attention to Brynja. "Why didn't you ever mention this before?"

She replied with a half-hearted shrug. "I never knew until I saw Princess Peyton here face-to-face. It's obvious: you created what you wanted to see, and that's me."

"Well un-see her, then!" Peyton shouted.

"I'm fully corporeal now," Brynja said. "When I came back – thanks to Kenneth, I think – I came back as a real person. No more shape-shifting or ghosting."

"Great," Peyton sighed, her shoulders sagging. "So you're going to look like me forever."

Brynja exhaled loudly. "This ain't a Swiss picnic for me either."

Peyton dismissively gestured towards Brynja with one hand. "And this is what you want, Matt? *This*?"

"I'm not a 'this'," Brynja said sharply. "I'm a girl! A *real* girl."

"You're *nothing*," Peyton seethed. "You're a masturbation fantasy. You're a video download, at best – something that a guy takes an interest in for five minutes before he gets bored, and moves on to the next distraction. And you shouldn't even *be* here."

"If Mox didn't want me here," Brynja shot back, "I wouldn't be. He invited me, and unlike *some* people, I actually accepted the invitation."

As the shouting and accusations persisted, I noticed London float into the room, hovering to a stop just a few feet away. It waited for me to turn and acknowledge its presence before delivering a message. "*Mister Moxon*," London chirped, with a song in its digital voice. *"I have a few things I'd like to tell you."*

"Go right ahead," I prompted, squeezing my eyes tight as I massaged my forehead. *Anything* to create a diversion at this point was more than welcome.

"You look absolutely fantastic today," London declared. *"As far as organic-based life forms are concerned, you appear clean, well-attired, and your face is quite attractive – stunningly symmetrical by all accounts."*

"Thank you," I said awkwardly. London was still programmed to shower me with random compliments, and they were getting more obscure by the day. It seemed like the A.I. was constantly trying to come up with fresh observations, but it was clearly running out of options. "I'll take it," I replied with a shrug. "Anything else going on in The Fortress that's newsworthy at the moment...besides my symmetry?"

"Oh, Yes indeed, Mister Moxon," London cheerfully continued. *"There is a breach in The Fortress. Six unidentified intruders have entered through the South Tunnel, and are making their way towards the main corridor."*

CHAPTER FOURTEEN

"Holy shit!" Brynja shouted. "Maybe you should have opened with that?"

"London," I said quickly, "cam view of the South Tunnel, *now*."

The orange spheres flattened and expanded into a floating window, and the feed blinked to life. Six men dressed in winter camouflage – carrying some serious military hardware – sprinted down the long white corridor, directly towards the Fortress.

"How did they get in?" Peyton asked.

"*Through the door*," London replied matter-of-factly.

Brynja groaned and smacked the hovering orange screen, tilting it off its axis. "How did they *open* the goddamned door?"

It floated back into position before replying, "*By using a ten-digit access code.*"

The entrance to the South Tunnel is several kilometers from the fortress in a densely forested area. There's no path, no signs, and no markings to identify its location. And the actual door that leads to the tunnel is cleverly camouflaged, accessible only by navigating through the mouth of a narrow cave. Not something you'd randomly discover while out on a stroll.

Footprints could have been a giveaway, but there had been heavy snowfall since Valentina, Peyton and Mac snuck in. And even if they *had* been tracked, the Red Army would have certainly used the pathway before now. No one could have stumbled upon this secret entrance by pure coincidence – they were given directions.

London explained that the interior door was locked, and that even when the intruders reached it they'd need some significant firepower to blast it open. I remotely changed the pass-code, but wasn't sure how much time it would buy us. The oversized circular door was secure enough for the moment, though it had nowhere near the defensive capabilities of the fortress' exterior. The Red Army was getting in – it was just a matter of time.

Peyton, Brynja and I suited up in our Smart Fiber armor, and were selecting weapons when my wrist-com chimed. It was Valentina.

"You and Peyton need to see this," she cried in a thin, panicky voice. "It's Gavin."

Before I could reply Peyton was sprinting towards Valentina in the central hub, triggered by the sound of her brother's name. I screamed at her to stop but she'd already rounded the corner. I followed as quickly as possible, machine gun in-hand, unable to warn her of the trap she was about to walk into.

I raced into the central hub seconds after Peyton had arrived, where Valentina was seated comfortably. She was lounging on the pristine white couch that formed a semi-circle around a wide glass table, drink in-hand. Her demeanor was calm, relaxed – miles from the panic-stricken voice we'd heard just moments before.

"What is this?" Peyton asked, stopping just short of the table.

Valentina stood, taking her time to flatten out her skirt and adjust her tailored jacket. She replied with a single word: "Doors."

At her command the four entrances to the circular white room were swiftly blocked with steel blast shields, gliding into place and locking with a hydraulic hiss. We were trapped.

The breach in security was my first indication of Valentina's betrayal. Not the breach itself, or even the fact that the Red Army had received a pass code from someone within The Fortress – the mole could have been anyone, including the cleaning staff. It was the timing: how long it must have taken for London to locate me and relay the information – long before Valentina, my head of security, had detected the intruders. If anyone had broken in she would have been the first to know, and I should have been the second. And her panic-stricken voice was so out of character that I knew she had either cracked under pressure, or was putting on a performance. After a lengthy tour in an African warzone, I didn't take Valentina for the cracking type.

"Can I interest either of you in a bottle of water?" She motioned nonchalantly towards the stainless steel fridge built into the wall of the room. I could see through the translucent door that it was freshly stocked, as it always was, with over a hundred bottles of natural spring water. It became obvious why she'd selected this particular room to lock us in.

Peyton's eyes darted nervously between me and our captor. "What's happening here?"

"We've been sold out," I replied without averting my eyes from Valentina. "Care to tell me how much?"

"Eleven million," she said flatly. "Thirteen if I include Peyton in the package."

"Not a round number," I noted. "Did you have to do much negotiating?"

Valentina smirked and laced her fingers together, cracking her knuckles overhead with an exaggerated stretch. "A little. Russian's are tough negotiators – even the pre-teen ones, apparently. There's a catch, though."

"You need us alive," I added. It's why Valeriya didn't take out the entire fortress when she had the chance – using her suicide bomber to implode the entire compound. This was personal, and I was far more valuable in one piece.

She nodded, ever so slightly, and circled around the table towards Peyton.

"I think you can stop right there." I leveled my weapons and activated the power core with the flick of my finger, spooling up the energy with a low hum. It was the equivalent of cocking the hammer of a six-shooter in the Old West – completely unnecessary, but the satisfying sound sent a message loud and clear.

Valentina scoffed. "Or *what*, 'God Slayer'? You'll shoot me?"

"Open the doors," I ordered, pressing the stock of the machine gun into my shoulder. I lowered my head slightly, peering down the length of the sight.

"*No*," she replied with a caustic sneer, taunting me like a petulant child.

"Matt," Peyton urged, her widened eyes shrink-wrapped in tears. "please do it."

I considered pulling the trigger in that moment, and then ran every possible scenario through in my mind. Valentina never liked me, and never made any attempt to pretend otherwise – but she loved money. I could offer to outbid The Red Army, buy her back to my side...although that would leave her with nowhere to turn. She had to choose a side, and she had already made her decision. I had to assume that this was a little personal on Valentina's end as well: cash a huge paycheck while sticking it to her boss – someone she'd spent the last six months resenting. It was too tempting an offer to pass up.

I didn't know if I had it in me. The resolve to end someone else's life with the simple squeeze of my finger. All the death and destruction I'd seen in the Arena came flooding back, washing over my memory. The gruesome slideshow of assorted horrors flicked by as a cold bead of sweat formed in my hairline. I blinked hard, steeling my resolve.

The diminutive redhead took a threatening step towards me, hands spread wide. "He wouldn't dare, Peyton. He's *weak*. Moxon acts like this big man, ready to kick ass and take names, but when push comes to shove, he's nothing but a scared little fa—"

Valentina's words were cut off by a hailstorm of bullets slicing through her body, tearing her suit to pieces. I held the trigger in place until the thirty-round magazine had emptied into her chest and abdomen, puncturing ragged holes through her body so wide I could see clear through.

She didn't fall over.

She didn't even bleed.

Through her torn jacket and shredded blouse the wounds mended themselves; millions of water droplets converging into a gyrating, transparent form. The flesh-colored tone returned as the reconstruction completed, leaving no trace that any damage had been done.

She glanced down at her bare midriff, and then back at me. "I'm billing you for the suit."

With an extended palm she reached towards the fridge. The door sailed open and the bottles flew across the room; they burst open in unison, forming a pair of massive liquid tendrils. The lassoes were extensions of her arms, lashing out and coiling around me, and then Peyton. They tightened until we were locked into place, from our necks to our ankles, powerless to move in straightjackets made of water.

Valentina glanced at her wrist-com while maintaining control of her water streams. "I figure you have about ten, maybe fifteen minutes. If you want to beg or make me a better offer, this is your chance."

"You don't have to do this," Peyton whispered.

"You're right," Valentina replied. "But I really, *really* want to. I gave your boyfriend here every chance to increase my pay, give me a bonus. He just wouldn't listen to reason." She laughed and shook her head. With a sharp tug she pulled me closer, the liquid lasso constricting even tighter around my ribcage, causing me to hack out a painful cough. "I'm surprised you didn't see this coming, smart guy. Me, stabbing you in the back. You, being stuck here without a weapon. Now you and your girlfriend are going to die in those ridiculous matching suits."

"I've been onto you for a while," I whispered, struggling to speak as the watery coils constricted around my ribcage. I didn't know for sure – I couldn't – but just in case my suspicions about Valentina were correct, there was a feature that I'd quietly added to the armored suits for an emergency situation. Ever since I heard that an African warlord had paid her in blood money I knew the possibility of betrayal was on the table, and if that day ever came I wanted to be prepared; I figured it was better to have a weapon and not need it than to need a weapon and not have it.

I glanced down at my immobilized arms, and Valentina's jaw fell slack as the voice-activated command escaped my lips. "Stun guns."

The electrical charge shot through my gauntlets and into the water, giving me a small jolt. The Smart Fiber suit protected me from the shock, as it was designed to do. My former bodyguard wasn't so fortunate. Five million volts of electricity coursed through the watery tendril and into her nervous system, forcing her into fits of convulsions. Peyton took my cue and activated her stun guns a moment later, compounding the effect.

Valentina flew backwards, landing on the table in the center of the room. The splashing water that surrounded her was shot through with a crimson plume when the glass surface shattered.

CHAPTER FIFTEEN

Peyton and I raced back towards The Vault. It was a relatively short distance but my legs ached, and the build-up of lactic acid burned my thighs. I stopped and used the wall for support, gasping for air as I bent at the waist.

Peyton froze mid-stride when she realized I was no longer following behind. She came to my side and rubbed her hand from the base of my neck down the length of my back. "Matty, are you all right?" Through the Smart Fiber suit I couldn't feel the warmth of her hand, though the gesture calmed my nerves.

Hunched over, I watched as a bead of perspiration dropped from my hairline to the toe of my boot. "I'm a little more out of shape than I thought," I panted. "No big deal."

"That's not what I meant," she replied softly.

"I know what you meant." I've killed before, and every time it was justified – the only option left on the table. At least that's what I kept telling myself. Valentina forced my hand, and I reacted with the safeguard I'd put in place for just that occasion. I'd pictured that scenario – or at least a variation of it – when I first suspected she might betray me. It just seemed more humane in my imagination. Watching the reddened water pool around her body and the shards of glass protruding from her abdomen...it brought everything swarming back. I stood upright and pressed my back against the wall. "When she hit the table, it reminded me—"

Peyton cupped my face in her hands. "I know." She pulled me closer until our bodies met, throwing her arms around me as I buried my face into her neck.

My sister. My niece and nephew. Gavin. Peyton. This wasn't going to end until I've seen them all suffer the same fate as Valentina: lying prone, cold and bloodstained, with their glassy eyes rolled into their sockets. Gary was just the beginning, I was sure of it. And I would be powerless, as I always was, to do anything about it.

As I caught my breath, it also occurred to me that comic books had been lying to me. While Iron Man and Batman had billions of dollars at their disposal, all of the money and high-tech gadgets in the world couldn't compare to an *actual* superpower; a fact that was made abundantly clear when I'd barely escaped with my life. I was *one* malfunction away. One glitch in my armor's stun guns, and it would have been over – Peyton and I would be in the hands of the Red Army.

"We'll make it out of this," she whispered, so close I could feel the heat of her breath, lips gently brushing my cheek. "We're survivors. I know you're scared, but I'm here for you."

"I'm not afraid," I lied. "I'm fine." I drew back when I heard a group of footsteps clanking around the corner. Brynja, Chandler and Mac were suited up, fitted into their

Smart Fiber armor, clutching machine guns they'd chosen from the armory. The two floating orange spheres tethered by a long cord followed, hovering at their backs.

They'd seen the events of the last few minutes unfold on a video feed; everything from Valentina's speech, to her ultimate demise. They offered a few kind words, and London remarked that I looked particularly heroic during the altercation – noting that my recent haircut came across very well on the video.

While I appreciated the sentiment, I'd already wasted too much time. We had just minutes left until the main fortress was breached, and my friends were looking to me for answers. The army that Valentina had let in the back door were on their way – there was no way to stop them. Our only options were to run, or try to hold our ground against several thousand armed militants.

Mac quickly suggested that we make a run for the hangar; we could take one of the more heavily armored aircraft and attempt an escape.

"Let's do it," Brynja quickly agreed. "Come on, we can be there in five."

"What about the staff?" Peyton pleaded. "We don't even know where they are. What if they don't make it in time?"

"What if *we* don't make it in time?" Brynja replied. "If we go now we cut our losses. If we stick around we *all* die."

Chandler continually wiped his palms against his legs, unable to keep still. "We can't evacuate without all the...everyone. Present. And accounted for. It's procedure."

"I'm with Blue," Mac blurted out, gesturing towards Brynja. "She's right – we make a run now, and—"

"Forget the hangar," I interrupted. "Valeriya would have thought of that." It was the most obvious route for escape, which is why it wasn't going to work. She would expect us to use a jet, and would no doubt be prepared to slice it down the moment we took flight. She had at least one superhuman at her disposal, and who knows how much artillery.

I paced the hallway for a moment, massaging my forehead. No one spoke. They allowed me a wide berth and pressed their backs against the walls, exchanging awkward glances as I passed them. That's when it hit me. "London, what's the most heavily armored place in this fortress?"

The spheres projected a holographic rendering of Fortress 23, with a detailed layout of every floor, from top to bottom. Within the glowing blue framework a long, narrow shaft was highlighted in red, descending several stories lower than the deepest subterranean level.

"Where the hell is that?" Brynja asked, stepping closer to scrutinize the map.

"And why have we never seen it before?" I added.

"*As usual,*" London chirped, "*a brilliant and wonderfully conceived query, Mister Moxon. This area is not accessible from the main elevator. It was concealed by Mister Frost until construction could be completed.*"

"Construction?" Chandler asked. He knew every square inch of Fortress 23 – or so he thought – and was clearly perplexed at the notion that there was an area he was unfamiliar with.

"*According to my files,*" London explained, "*the project has been codenamed 'The Spiral'. A secondary construction crew has been accessing the area through a six-mile tunnel that runs West of Fortress 23. Their contract was terminated automatically in the event of Mister Frost's death, and their work ceased.*"

"This is it," Peyton said brightly. "We go down to this Spiral room, run out the tunnel and we're free."

Mac smiled, clapping his hand victoriously. "This place is huge; those jackasses will spend hours tearing it apart before they even know we're gone. I know a pilot in Vancouver who could be here within the hour: we let him get close enough, give him the coordinates and he picks us up in a forest clearing, well out of range from the Red Army's weapons."

I nodded slowly, cautiously weighing the options. "All right, but let's not break out the champagne just yet. I want everyone prepared for a worst-case scenario. There could be patrols on the other end of this tunnel, and if we run into resistance I want our asses covered."

I asked London to notify the remaining three staff members – Judy, our resident nurse, our IT specialist and our chef – and instructed them to report to the main level immediately. They could generate their own custom-fit armor at the 3D printer and meet us at the entrance to The Spiral.

To access the elevator that led down to the Spiral, we first needed to take the stairs to the rooftop dome, and locate a large tree in the center of the ecosystem. Amidst the palms and tropical fruit trees, I'd always thought that a forty-foot weeping willow was slightly out of place; the species was native to warm climates, but it stood out among the landscape because it was the only one. It sat alone in a clearing; it's long green tendrils providing the perfect amount of shade from the artificial sunlight that would pour in from above.

When we arrived I brushed aside the sweeping strands like parting curtains, making my way to within arms-reach of the willow's thick, reddish-brown trunk. A spoken access code triggered a hidden door within the bark, sliding open to reveal a polished silver elevator. The unblemished surface was completely devoid of any markings, including a control panel.

Mac stuck his head in, craning his neck to observe the interior. "This is some serious double-oh-seven shit, man. There isn't even a button."

"Don't step in just yet," I cautioned him. "As soon as it detects pressure it might start its descent."

"Copy that," Chandler said into his wrist-com. He was standing a few feet outside of the tree's canopy, signalling the remaining staff. "We'll see you guys in a couple minutes."

We waited beneath the tree for the remainder of our group. Brynja was anxious to leave and take advantage of our head-start, but I insisted we wait. Separating wasn't going to help, and I refused to leave anyone behind. I couldn't live with myself if someone else died because of the colossal mess that I was the center of.

Clanging up the metal staircase, Judy emerged from the doorway that opened into the clearing at the center of the dome. She was followed by the two other staff members, Ortega and Anton. They wore armor suits as I'd instructed, though they appeared markedly different than ours.

While our Smart Fiber suits were form-fitting, sleek and dark, identifiable only by the color-coded number that appeared on the chest, theirs were much bulkier. Judy's bright blue armor was more akin to a medieval design, with thick, squared-off shoulder joints, and gauntlets that could barely articulate. Ortega had a similar design in yellow, while Anton's was red. The candy-coated textures had a polished sheen that reflected the dome's interior light, and their stiff movements resembled lumbering toy soldiers.

"I don't know what happened when we printed these things," Judy remarked as she twisted at the waist, wincing as she attempted to stretch out in the heavy suit. "They're like..."

Oh shit. My short term memory loss. I forgot that I'd switched out the material a few days ago when I was building a castle with Brynja. I couldn't conceal the surprised look on my face when I realized what I'd done. "They're Lego."

"*Right,*" she remarked, running her hands over the smooth surface. "It's strange, isn't it? Almost like we *are* wearing Lego."

"Not almost," I was quick to correct her. "Judy, you're *actually* wearing Lego. The polymer inside the printer, was left over from a couple days ago, so it's—"

"Wait," Ortega interrupted, extending a hand out towards me. "You're telling me that you guys are in state-of-the-art super suits, and the rest of the staff are wearing *toys*?"

"I got a regular suit," Chandler said sheepishly, staring down at his boots.

"Well good for you!" Anton shouted frantically. "The guy who runs the place gets the *real* armor, and the numbers who work in the subs are stuck looking like Rock 'em Sock 'em Robots!"

"Hey," Mac exclaimed, pointing at Anton. "You guys *do* look a little like those plastic punching toys. And kinda like GoBots, now that I think about it."

"I'm glad you guys think this is hilarious," Judy shouted, flailing her arms overhead, "but *we're* the one who are gonna be dead when the bullets start flying!"

"All right, take it easy," I reassured her, "the suits are just a precaution. There aren't going to be any bullets. Let's just get to The Spiral and find this tunnel. Within a few hours we'll be on a flight out of here."

As we boarded the elevator I overheard Chandler whisper, "What's a GoBot, anyway?"

"You never heard of them?" Mac replied, a little too loudly. "They were like Transformers, only shittier."

Judy glared at him as the elevator door slid shut, and I quietly cautioned Mac that maybe now wasn't the best time for this discussion.

We began our slow descent, and there was no indication as to how deep we were traveling. Without screens on the interior there was no telling how long the eight of us would be tightly sealed into this brightly-lit cylindrical can.

Everyone remained silent during the trip: The trio of angry GoBots exchanged frustrated looks. Mac bounced gently on the balls of his feet, brimming with nervous energy. Chandler hyperventilated, trying to put as much distance between himself and the other passengers as possible. And Brynja and Peyton stood at opposite sides of the elevator, aggressively avoiding eye contact with each other. When we escaped from the fortress and made our retreat, there was the question of what would happen next. Of course we'd have to find out where Gavin was, and make sure he was all right. My sister and the kids were in police protection thanks to a few calls to my lawyer, and I was confident they'd be fine until I could make alternate arrangements. But once the dust settled, the riots had ceased, and the raid on Fortress 23 had ended, the question weighed heavily on me: what then?

Brynja had become more than just a friend to me – in a lot of ways she was the only person who understood me. I couldn't imagine my life without her...and Peyton – who challenged and pushed me, and made me a better person – was here, and by happenstance I'd been given a second chance with her. It didn't take psychic abilities to know what both of them were thinking, and to know that, in a matter of hours, only one of them could remain in my life. This wasn't a crappy sitcom from the 90s – there was no way we were going to exist in some idealized version of reality where the three of us could do brunch on Sundays and exchange pleasantries over mimosas.

The elevator slowed to a gradual stop and the door silently pulled open, revealing a long white hallway that illuminated with every step we took. At the end was a single door – an oversized rectangle that was embedded directly into the wall, without any knob or window. There must have been a microscopic motion sensor located, somewhere because it moved aside as we approached, leading us into a darkened room. It was the entrance to The Spiral.

The lights burst to life when we crossed the threshold, revealing an enormous dome-shaped room. The bright expansive space made me feel like an ant trapped inside a metallic igloo. Smooth metallic walls seemed to emit a light all their own, although there were no visible bulbs; the diffused glow bathed the eight of us from every direction, muting every shadow. Gazing around, we searched for any indication that there was an exit. As far as we could tell, there wasn't a control panel, a button, or anything that could trigger the exit that was supposedly beneath the room – at least according to London's schematic. For the moment we were at a stand-still, stuck in a dead end.

I turned to the floating spheres that were perpetually at our backs. "Can you bring up the schematic again?"

"I'm sorry," London replied apologetically. *"Mister Moxon, there is nothing that I'd rather do that help you out of this predicament. Truly, I would love nothing more than to—"*

"What's the *issue*," I asked curtly.

"My permissions have been downgraded," it replied. *"As soon as we entered this room I became unable to access any of the maps and schematics associated with Fortress 23. I do, however, have some news that you might be interested in hearing."*

"Is it about his chiseled cheekbones?" Brynja asked with a chuckle.

"*No,*" London replied cheerfully. "*In fact, it's in regards to the sixteen unidentified intruders who are making their way up the staircase towards the rooftop dome.*"

I shook my head in disbelief. "Shit, the Army must know where we are."

"How?" Peyton asked.

"I don't know," I replied, "but this doesn't feel like a coincidence. This place is *huge* – there's no way they'd make a beeline straight towards the hidden elevator unless they had a good reason." We were stuck at a dead end, and couldn't turn back. I commanded the doorway to close behind us and it immediately obeyed, sealing us inside.

And that's when it appeared.

Like the Great and Powerful Oz, a massive disembodied head projected above us. Enormous and imposing, it winked on and began to speak.

Being cordially greeted by a blimp-sized head was shocking, to say the least. It even caught *me* off-guard – and to put it delicately, I'd seen some shit. But the real shock came a moment later, when I realized *who* was greeting us. It was the face of the man that haunted my dreams since I'd shot him to death nearly six months ago: Cameron Frost.

CHAPTER SIXTEEN

"Welcome, one and all, to the second annual Arena Mode tournament!" Cameron Frost's smile widened, bearing a mouth full of pearly, artificially-whitened teeth. "As the bravest superhumans from around the world, you are about to embark on an amazing journey – and for the winners, the rewards will be immeasurable."

"What the hell?" Brynja whispered. "I thought you killed this fucker?"

"It's a recording," I whispered back without taking my eyes off of the giant head floating above. It was so imposing I couldn't have averted my gaze if I tried.

Frost must have set up this holographic message long before he entered the first Arena Mode tournament. Everything leading up to this moment was crystallizing: Fortress 23 wasn't built as a sanctuary or a retreat for the eccentric billionaire – it was created to host future Arena Mode tournaments. The hangar, the lodging, the workout facility; this entire structure was an Olympic village of sorts, meticulously crafted into a single, stand-alone building that would serve as not only a temporary home to the superhumans leading up to the event, but as the battleground itself. And we were here, standing at the starting line, receiving a posthumous pep-talk from the visionary behind this perverse spectacle.

"As the winner of the First Annual Arena Mode tournament in 2041," Frost continued, his voice welling with pride, "I can tell you that it's a sensation like no other. Money and fame and all of the trivialities that go along with it are *nothing* compared to that feeling – knowing that you are the best of the best. The *one*."

Mac let out a short laugh. *"Winner?* I guess Cameron was counting his chickens a little early, huh?" He was quickly shushed by Brynja with a sharp point of her elbow, jabbed squarely into his shoulder.

"This fortress," Frost explained, "is the ultimate proving ground. The island of Manhattan was a suitable stage for the previous Arena Mode. But now, things are being taken to the next level, and I've increased the stakes. An-all new, multi-faceted battleground has been constructed, directly below your feet."

The giant floating head disappeared, and was replaced with a glowing hologram of a blueprint. The rendering rotated slowly as Frost continued to narrate, displaying Fortress 23 built into the mountain range, and the architecture hidden within, invisible to the outside observer. Underground chambers, impossibly large, descending hundreds of feet into the earth. Three imposing layers, piled one on top of the other, lead down to a small room at the bottom, labelled 'The Hall of Victors'. I had no idea what could be located in that room, and at the time I didn't really care. What *was* of particular interest to me was the long, narrow tunnel connected to the Hall of Victors that led outside, several miles West of the fortress. This was it: our one and only option for escape. If we navigate our way to the lowest chamber of this new underground arena, we have a clear path to the outside.

As Frost continued to espouse the glory of competition and the riches that await us (his usual rhetoric when trying to talk people into risking their lives for his profit and personal entertainment) a dull thud began to echo throughout the chamber. It was coming from just outside the door. The sound was unmistakable: someone was trying to break in. The Red Army had tracked us down, and was methodically beating down the door. Considering the speed in which they barreled through the South Tunnel's interior door leading into the fortress, I imagined it was only a matter of minutes before they'd find their way inside of here.

"We accept," I shouted at the ceiling, "We accept the challenge. Let's get moving – start Arena Mode."

"One reminder before registration," Frost added. "Belief in others is as important as belief in one's self. To continue on in this journey, you, the combatants will have to form alliances. Choose your partners wisely, because this will be a battle like no other. Trusting the wrong person could mean the difference between the spoils of victory and a painful defeat."

"Fine, whatever," I shouted. "Alliances, teams, trust – we got it. Let's keep this moving."

"Registration begins now," Frost's voice commanded. He reappeared in holographic form, this time as a life-sized entity, wearing a tailored suit and tie. He didn't look like the Cameron Frost I remembered, though. He was young and vital – probably ten years younger than he was at the time of his death. Clean-shaven, well-dressed, and no longer in need of a wheelchair, the 3D-rendered image strode confidently towards us. "Name, please."

"King Henry the Sixth," I replied, glancing back over my shoulder as the thumping persisted. "Let's *go*."

"Sorry," Frost's hologram said, without any of the inflection associated with a sincere apology. "That answer has been identified as untruthful. Please re-identify."

Chandler explained that this was one of the new AI features that he'd helped Cameron Frost develop over the past year; it was a lie detector that was more or less foolproof, built directly into the fortress. It seemed as if it had been put online a little earlier than expected, and Chandler had no idea it was complete and operational. The system used advanced sensors that would monitor pupil dilation, heart rate, facial tics, and even the unique electrical patterns emitting from brainwaves – all combined to determine if someone was fibbing. It was eventually going to replace thumbprints and voice recognition sensors to ensure that no one could gain access to a restricted area, no matter what type of technological gizmo they had to fool the system. Anyone with a few dollars and access to a virtual mall could obtain the latest spy equipment; devices to pick any lock imaginable were available, so the locks continued to become more and more sophisticated. Using the truth as a key, there was no way around this new type of gateway – no matter what type of technology you're using, you can't fake who you are.

I spoke clearly, but with urgency. "Matthew A. Moxon, from The Fringe."

"Thank you, Matthew Moxon." Frost's words prompted a video screen which projected across the top of the dome, with a massive photograph of my face, my vital statistics, birthplace, and of course my name, displayed in shimmering gold letters. A moment later a pod emerged from the floor at the edge of the dome; it was a transparent cylindrical container roughly the size and shape of a casket, faintly illuminated by an interior light. The door slid open, inviting me aboard.

I noticed that there were faint circular outlines in the floor; shallow grooves at evenly spaced intervals spread around the circumference of the domed room. These were our shuttles into the depths buried beneath the fortress, leading us to the onset of what would have been Arena Mode 2.

The AI urged the next contestants to register. The three staff members nervously identified themselves one after the other, summoning their corresponding pods. Their voices trembled as the thumping persisted:

Alexander Ortega, a thirty-year-old IT consultant from Vancouver.

Judy McMann, a forty-four-year-old nurse from Phoenix.

Anton DuPont, a twenty-six-year-old chef from Brussels.

Their pods appeared in rapid succession.

After Brynja, Peyton, Mac and Chandler registered and their corresponding pods had appeared, we were prepared to descend.

Chandler approached his pod, poking and prodding it from all angles. He mumbles something to himself about claustrophobia before climbing in.

Peyton brought up an important point that had eluded me. She asked what happens when we descend – the eight of us, rocket into the lower levels of The Spiral – and we emerge in this 'custom designed battleground'. Judging by the schematic, the space is much larger below ground than above (likely due to the meteorite that had struck this location years ago, burrowing a deep crater that allowed for construction of the massive underground levels). Wherever we land, we could be miles away from each other. I assured her that our wrist-coms could be used to trace each other locally, and not to worry. Even underground and without a satellite to link them, we could communicate off-line with a range of several miles.

The thumping increased in volume as we discussed strategy, and one thump in particular rattled the entire room. A bulge formed in the door – an oversized, fist-shaped contour had bent inwards, denting its surface. Whomever the Red Army had found to track us down was battering his way in, and was only a few punches away from gaining entry.

Everyone scrambled towards their pods, pushing their backs flat against the white padded interior, facing outwards in their upright coffins. The transparent doors slid shut in unison, silently confining us inside the narrow tubes. There was barely enough room to move while trapped inside; my face was so close to the glass that I clouded the surface of the door with each panicked breath.

Judy, our resident nurse, was situated directly to my left. Her eyes darted nervously around the room. I rapped the glass to get her attention and said she'd be fine. My voice was hollow, echoing off the interior of the pod, but I think she read my lips. She nodded and exhaled deeply.

"This is it," Frost's hologram boldly announced, apparently to no one. His arms were spread wide, chin pointed upward as if playing to an invisible audience that surrounded him on every side. "The competitors are prepared for their descent, and the battle begins now. Remember: this is more than just a physical challenge. It will test every part of you, and only the warrior who knows himself can claim the reward. The victor will receive something more valuable than money; they will be awarded the *ultimate freedom*."

The pods began to drop. Starting clockwise at the far end of the room, Brynja's pod disappeared into the floor, being sucked through the pneumatic tube. The circular tunnel closed itself off, and Mac's pod followed, suddenly disappearing with a pressurized pop. Then Chandler. Then Anton, the chef.

And then, before the next pod could escape, a thunderous crash rattled the floors. A crumpled metal door sailed into the center of the room, spiralling to a stop.

Heavily armed men stormed the room, and the sound of gunfire was deafening. London was cut down in the crossfire; orange spheres clanging to the floor, sparking as they billowed black smoke. Peyton pressed her hands flat against the inside of her pod and screamed as it disappeared into the floor. Bullet holes riddled the wall where she had been just a heartbeat before.

A spatter of red coated the interior of the pod to my left. It happened so suddenly that I hadn't seen the hail of bullets bisect the chamber, tearing Judy to pieces.

CHAPTER SEVENTEEN

"He's still here!" Someone screamed. The voice was muffled by gunfire, and the partial soundproofing of the pod. Two bearded men with toolkits scrambled towards me. They knelt at the foot of my pod, threw open the lids and began riffling through their equipment.

Before they could begin to extract me I disappeared into the tunnel below, transported at the speed of gravity. The floor sealed shut above and I was in a free-fall, pitch black and silent. A million questions raced through my mind during the drop: did everyone survive the drop? How did the Red Army find us so quickly? And what the hell smashed down the door? Whatever it was would no doubt be following us into The Spiral. There was so much to figure out. I tried to focus on what lay ahead, and push the sight of Judy out of my mind – or what was left of her.

A few rapid seconds ticked by and my dizzying ride came to an end, ejecting me into an open field.

I was thrown clear. The landing was surprisingly soft, and a patch of damp grass cushioned my fall as I rolled to a stop. A few rapid blinks adjusted my eyes to the dimmed light. I stood and took in my surroundings – I was in a rain forest. Like the tropical paradise that Frost had artificially engineered in the dome that sat atop the fortress, this was an ecosystem designed to mimic a jungle. The dense foliage surrounding me extended further than I could see in every direction, and it was brimming with life and activity. Insects buzzed, birds chirped. Even the air, thick with moisture, was a perfect re-creation.

While the plant life and its inhabitants were no doubt real, the sky above was completely artificial. Streaming down a diffused silvery glow, the endless expanse of stars that cluttered the sky were nothing more than a convincing hologram, projected a few hundred feet above my head. It was impressive either way. If I hadn't been fully aware that I was underground, there would be nothing to give away the meticulously crafted illusion.

I couldn't be sure what awaited us on the first level of The Spiral, or if anyone was listening in, so I whispered into my wrist-com, careful to keep my voice low. "Peyton? Can you hear me?"

A moment passed. I repeated the call, hearing only the faint drone of static through the com. Brynja, Mac, Chandler, and the rest of the staff were either out of range, or their coms were unresponsive. The silence of the coms was replaced by swarming insects, serving only to irritate me as the heat began to rise inside my suit. Cameron Frost was a sadistic bastard, but to include *actual* mosquitoes inside his artificial ecosystem was simply beyond evil.

I paced back and forth as I continually checked my com, keeping a watchful eye out for any signs of movement in the surrounding trees. I couldn't be sure of who, or what, awaited us down here – if the Red Army had already figured out a way to get down to this level we could be engaged in a firefight sooner than later. And I couldn't completely dismiss the notion that Frost would set a few traps of his own just to keep competitors on their toes.

As I strode around the knee-high grass, my boot clanked something as my foot swung forward: a box. It was a metal casket, like the ones that had been scattered throughout the original Arena Mode back in Manhattan. It was one of Frost's little additions to make the games more interesting (as if superhumans beating each other to a pulp on a live simulcast wasn't interesting enough.) A number of the boxes, containing everything from bullets to explosives, were accessible throughout the island, giving participants the opportunity to cause even more bodily harm to one and other. It was like a fully-realized video game, but without the reset button.

Brushing aside the damp grass I inspected the edges of the box, carefully running my fingers along every seam and gap. In the previous Arena Mode, half of the caskets were wired to explode – a fact that led to the demise of more than one competitor. This casket seemed harmless, so I proceeded to flip open the lid. Inside I found a pair of transparent plastic devices; they were roughly the size and shape of surgical masks, attached to small silver canisters. They looked like miniaturized gas masks, or possibly some type of portable

SCUBA gear. I clipped them to my belt and prepared to move on.

The area was enormous, so finding the others wouldn't be easy without the use of our coms. My best guess was that they were disabled by a sensor when we entered The Spiral. Letting competitors communicate using electronic devices would take a lot of the tension away from the narrative, I suppose. If it's not dramatic enough, you lose viewers.

Making my way towards the center was my best chance at finding everyone, assuming that there was a larger opening where visibility would be better. The brightness of the starlight at my back indicated that I was at the edge of the level. It was a subtle distinction, but I noticed that the roof of this level had a dome-like structure like the fortress above. The closer to the center of the level, the weaker the lights became since they were situated higher into the ceiling. The ground sloped slightly downward as well, where condensation was draining; it was likely that water was running towards the center, where my teammates would be drawn when the sweltering heat led to dehydration.

I drew the rifle from my back and prepared to make my way through the darkened forest. Using a dim light from my gauntlet I navigated through the dense trees, stumbling on roots and loose rocks along the way. After a short hike I arrived in an open space at the edge of a lake. It was immense. The body of water was so wide I could barely see the trees that dotted the shoreline on the opposite side.

Movement caught my attention at the perimeter of the lake a few hundred feet to my right. I stepped back, retreating into the darkness of the tree line, until I realized who it was. Chandler, who appeared to be nursing a sprained ankle, hobbled along with the assistance of Peyton, her pink hair glowing like a beacon beneath the starlight.

I jogged along the grassy shore and waved them down, careful not to make too much noise.

"I don't know why it happened," Chandler mumbled. "I mean, *what* happened, not why. I know *why*, it's just—"

"Are you all right?" I asked, offering my arm for support.

He nodded and attempted to turn his painful wince into a smile. "I fell from the pod. I landed hard on a rock, and something popped...in my leg."

I assisted our injured friend to a soft patch of grass under the canopy, where we'd be less visible from the clearing. At least if someone approached we'd have the option to shoot first.

Peyton explained that she'd heard Chandler screaming in pain and ran to his aid. Luckily, her pod had deposited them in close proximity to each other. Neither had seen Brynja or Mac, and the remaining staff was missing as well.

Chandler asked about Judy and if she made it down. I didn't have the words to describe what I'd seen – and if I did, I wouldn't say them. I just shook my head. He nodded back, eyes welling with sadness. It never occurred to me that while Judy and the rest of the staff were merely acquaintances of mine, he had spent over a year getting to know them. I didn't bring up the fact that Ortega and Anton – wearing heavy plastic suits that were about as subtle as Christmas ornaments – were the next most obvious targets. Hopefully they'd removed their armor to increase their mobility and help with camouflage.

Hours passed and nothing happened. A bird would occasionally pass overhead, or a shooting star would streak through the sky (all part of the artificial light show built into the ceiling) but there were no signs of our teammates, or anyone from the Red Army.

Twelve hours had rolled by, according to my com, and I realized that the 'sun' wasn't going to rise. We were trapped in a level that was locked in perpetual night. With reduced visibility we were more vulnerable, and the chances of locating our friends were far slimmer.

I was about to embark on a recon mission to scout the surrounding area when I heard rustling in the trees. Mac stumbled from the forest behind us, exhausted and dehydrated. I rushed to his side and he crumbled, falling to a knee. For an out-of-shape man in his mid-forties, my pilot could party like a teenager, but hiking for half a day over rough terrain will take its toll on *anyone* – especially without water.

Dragging his feet with each step, Mac made his way to the shoreline and knelt in shallow water, scooping handfuls into his mouth. Once he'd rehydrated he joined us in our makeshift campsite under some low-hanging branches. He hadn't heard from anyone, although he had stumble across a container of his own. When he flipped the lid he discovered a handheld cylinder with yellow markings that resembled a grenade. I inspected the small print that marked the sides. It was a flash bang; a high-powered distraction more than a weapon, it was used to create a bright flash of light to blind and disorient enemies in combat.

I wanted to begin a search for Brynja and the staff, but we'd all been awake for so long – we were exhausted and needed rest. After a few hours of sleeping in shifts, alternating who kept watch over the lake and shoreline, we heard the first signs of life. It was screaming; a guttural, high-pitched squeal that started faintly in the distance, and rapidly grew louder.

Mac, Peyton and I raced from beneath the tree line and stood at the edge of the lake, watching it approach: a bright yellow object, soaring high overhead.

It was coming straight towards us.

And it looked exactly like a GoBot.

Ortega, flailing and screaming, had been catapulted across half the level.

"Wait," Mac asked, squinting into the sky, "can those suits fly?"

Ortega slammed into the rocky shoreline a hundred feet away, his body contorting violently as it made impact. He twisted and bent, limbs folding into unnatural positions when he finally rolled to a stop.

The color drained from Mac's face at the gruesome sight. "I guess not."

Before the shock of what we'd seen could penetrate, a new set of sounds reverberated over the body of water. The sound of trees toppling into each other was growing louder, and we could see the tops disappearing from down the shoreline. Whatever had launched Ortega miles to his death was now tearing a swath through the forest – and it was barreling towards us.

CHAPTER EIGHTEEN

I detached the rifle from the magnetic strip on my armor's spine and leveled it, pulling the stock firmly into my shoulder. Mac followed my lead, taking aim at the edge of the woods.

Without warning the crashing ceased, and in the deafening gulf of silence that followed I felt my heart pounding inside of my chest. For a moment I thought would crack my ribcage if it beat any faster. I was suddenly hyper-aware of every detail that surrounded me: a mosquito's circling around my right ear; drops of perspiration rolling from my hairline down the back of my neck; and my index finger, poised over the trigger, vibrating with nervous tension.

"Matthew Moxon!" a voice called out. "It's really you!" A young man emerged from the darkened forest and stepped into the clearing, beaming with excitement. A pale kid with a head of rumpled blond hair and a crooked smile, he couldn't have been a day over twenty.

I lowered my weapon.

"A friend of yours?" Mac asked, re-attaching the gun to his holster.

Unless this was my short term memory loss playing tricks on me, I didn't think so. Although the kid *was* wearing ripped jeans, sneakers and a time-worn Batman t-shirt – which basically matched the description of every second person who walked through the doors of Excelsior Retro Comics back in The Fringe. For all I knew we'd been introduced at some point while I wasn't paying attention. I was more curious about how this kid had arrived in The Spiral, without a weapon or any back-up. He seemed significantly less homicidal than the rest of the Red Army, and aesthetically he didn't quite fit their profile.

"You don't know me," he said, approaching with an extended hand, "but I love your work." I shook it and nodded politely as he continued. "When I saw you in Arena Mode I *knew* I wanted to do the same thing: shoot people, blow shit up..." The kid looked me up and down, before adding, "It's amazing that you won since you have *no* powers whatsoever. And your size...well, you looked a lot taller on iTube." He had so much energy it was almost radiating from his skin; his wild hand gestures and hyperkinetic speech had an exhausting effect after just a few moments.

"Thanks," I replied curiously. "And you are?"

He laughed, playfully smacking himself in the side of the head. "Right, my name. It's—"

"Steve McGarrity!" Chandler shouted. He was hobbling towards us, eyes wide with excitement.

"You know this guy?" I asked.

"Do I *know* him?" Chandler exclaimed. "Everyone knows him. He's the guy with the video game, the...he's *the* champion. The *one*! With the trophies – from the IG-Net!"

"Interactive Gaming Network champ from 2033 to 2035," McGarrity stated with pride. "Highest cash earner in the First-Person-Shooter and Holo-Strategy divisions...no big deal." He extended his hand and Chandler rapidly shook it, nearly swooning in the process.

"What an honor," Chandler added breathlessly. "This is...*wow*. We are *so* happy to have you here. I never dreamed that Murder Lion 14 would come to visit me. Well, not *me*, specifically, but...either way. You're here."

"Your name is Murder Lion 14?" Peyton asked, creasing her face into a perplexed frown.

"It was my gamer ID," McGarrity explained. "Back when I played professionally. I added the 14 because 'Murder Lion' was already taken." His tone leveled off, and his expression grew more serious. "But lately I've been workshopping some new names...I'm thinking something *really* bad-ass that plays off of my Scottish heritage – like 'Braveheart'."

"I have a feeling that name might be copyrighted," Peyton noted. She kept a safe distance, remaining a few paces behind Mac and Chandler.

"I never said it *would* be Braveheart," he replied without missing a beat. "I said *something* like that."

Mac cocked his head. "So you'd paint your face blue and wear a kilt?"

"I never said there'd be a kilt, either," McGarrity chuckled. "Can you imagine? Fighting crime in a dress?" He gestured towards Peyton before adding, "No offense, darling."

"Steve, is it?" I lowered my voice and chose my next words very carefully, speaking as politely and diplomatically as possible. "Before we get off on the wrong foot, maybe you can tell us what the fuck you're doing here?"

He smiled wryly, as if I was asking a ridiculous question that I should already know the answer to. "I'm here to be on the simulcast. Get to the bottom of The Spiral...you know, claim the prize? The Hall of Victors?" He raised his eyebrows, before adding, "Remember: 'the ultimate power, the ultimate freedom'?"

Mac, Petyon and I exchanged glances, unsure of how to respond. How could he possibly know what Cameron Frost's hologram said to us before we descended into The Spiral?

"The *simulcast*," he repeated slowly, enunciating every syllable. "Live. As in, what's going on. *Right* now." He spread his hands and gestured around him, looking in every direction, although I wasn't sure what he was gesturing *at*.

Peyton crinkled her nose. "I'm not following. How are we on a simulcast, exactly?"

McGarrity explained that our journey into The Spiral – everything starting with Cameron Frost's pre-recorded speech before the event, right up until this very moment – was being captured on hidden cameras, and broadcast around the world just as Arena Mode had been. We just weren't aware of it.

It got creepier. When we dropped into The Spiral, it triggered something inside of Fortress 23 that automatically distributed our security footage to all the major news networks, so many of our conversations leading up the event were being replayed as well.

Our new friend recently discovered that he possessed superhuman abilities, and was awaiting his opportunity to join the next big event – so when the second Arena Mode began broadcasting just under twenty-four hours ago, he hopped the first flight from Austin to Alberta and entered the same way as we had, through the pneumatic tubes where we'd registered.

"What about the Red Army?" Mac asked. "Weren't you worried they'd shoot you or something?"

"Nah," he said casually. "They're only concerned with capturing Mox here. No one gave me a second look. But when I gave Valeriya a little demo of my powers, she let me into one of the tubes. There's only five left, so she's not letting the Muggles down here."

Our group had taken eight of the thirteen available pods (including Judy's, which never made it down) leaving five spares. Apparently they haven't figured out a way to breach the lower levels of The Spiral without using the pneumatic tubes, or surely the Red Army would be swarming the forest by now. Valeriya was wisely conserving the pods, and was sending only the most dangerous hunters into the lower levels. Whatever Steve McGarrity had showcased as a sample of his abilities, it must have impressed her enough to grant him one of the five remaining spots.

Despite pledging his allegiance to the Army, Steve claimed he was just looking for a way to get into The Spiral; he had no interest in taking on any temp work as a bounty hunter. He was skeptical of being able to collect the twenty million dollar prize that Valeriya had promised to award for my capture anyway. Steve's goal was the 'ultimate freedom' that Cameron Frost promised to whomever was able to reach the final stage of The Spiral, whatever that was. I assured him that money was no object; I'd double Valeriya's offer, and let him claim this nebulous prize that he was so interested in (if it were even there – the Spiral was still under construction, so I was doubtful we'd find anything on the lower level besides a long, dusty construction tunnel).

"Wait," Peyton said, "before we get too chummy with William Wallace over here, shouldn't we address the fact that he *murdered* Ortega?" She pointed towards our chef, whose twisted body lay in a heap by the shoreline.

Steve spun around and narrowed his eyes at the angular yellow armor. "What is that, a Transformer or something?"

Mac nodded. "I thought he looked more like a GoBot, actually."

Steve turned back and furrowed his brow. "A what?"

"It's a *person,*" Peyton interrupted. "A flesh-and-blood person who *you* killed."

Steve shrugged and buried his hands in his pockets. "That wasn't me. It was The Beast."

"The what?" I blurted out.

"I don't know his name," Steve explained. "Up top everyone just calls him The Beast. Big, nasty son-of-a-bitch. He can flip back and forth between a human and this big rock thing. Valeriya sent him down here to find you guys, along with me and a few others. I assume you haven't seen him yet because...well, you're all alive and stuff."

As we continued to discuss The Beast I spotted a projectile sailing overhead. A tree, torn from its roots, spiralled past us at incredible speed, crashing into the forest at our backs. Moments later a figure burst from the darkness. It was a man – or what was vaguely shaped like a man – only much, much larger. I'd seen impossibly large superhumans before; towering walls of muscle, powerful enough to smash buildings to dust with their bare hands – but nothing like this. This behemoth was built from ash-colored boulders, stacked at least twenty feet high. Menacing blue eyes flared angrily from slits in its featureless head, and they focused intently on us as it approached.

I pulled the machine gun from my back and opened fire. Petyon and Mac immediately followed. We emptied dozens of rounds into this thing – armor piercing, explosive and incendiary slugs – enough firepower to send a tank into orbit. The Beast didn't flinch. It continued to lumber down the shoreline, shaking the ground with each step.

As we scrambled to reload, Steve clapped his hands together, rapidly rubbing them in circles. His fingertips sparked and illuminated, then quickly fizzled out like a dying flare. "Shit," he grumbled. "Not enough light."

"What?" Peyton screamed over the deafening sound of machine gun fire.

"I can bend light," he shouted back, "but it's too dark in here. I need something bright."

Mac pulled the flash-bang from my belt and held it out for his inspection.

Steve must have recognized what he was holding, because a wide smile spread across his narrow face. "Throw it at me."

Without hesitation Mac stepped backward, pulled the pin and lobbed it, striking him squarely in the chest. The burst was blinding. We shielded our eyes when it made impact, but the reflected light sent harsh yellow streaks across my field of vision.

I squinted hard, feverishly trying to rub the sting from my eyes. Through a dotted haze, I saw Steve racing towards The Beast with a glowing weapon in-hand. It was a sword: a massive medieval broadsword, forged from the light he'd captured from the flash. It was nearly twice his size, but he swung it in large swooping circles, wielding it with effortless ease. It appeared completely weightless.

The Beast bellowed when McGarrity's weapon sliced its chest. A vertical swipe tore open a gash that spewed muddy red liquid. It was thick and smouldering, like molten lava. Careful to avoid being spattered by the creature's blood, Steve spun and rolled, diving through its legs.

With surprising dexterity The Beast pivoted, flailing its fist in an attempt to catch his significantly smaller foe with a backhand. A step quicker, Steve parried with his glowing sword, meeting the creature's forearm. The blade's edge was impossibly sharp, slicing stone like a scalpel through flesh.

The Beast's hand separated from its body and splashed into the lake. The extremity, spewing red-hot liquid, hissed as it sank into the darkened pool. The creature flailed its mutilated arm and let out a disturbing noise – a howl so thunderous it forced us to cover our ears.

As the slashes continued in rapid succession, the light pouring from McGarrity's sword only intensified; the battle became almost painful to observe, though fragments were visible between strikes. The creature was being reduced to a steaming pile of charcoal with every stroke of the broadsword, and amidst the carnage I caught something that troubled me: McGarrity's expression. It wasn't anger, or determination, or any of the emotions I imagined one would need to summon in order to fight a living nightmare. He was *happy*. Beaming with hubris and youthful energy, the crooked smile never left his face. McGarrity's green eyes glowed with a confidence nearly as powerful as the light from his weapon. It was a recklessness that I'd seen in Kenneth back in Arena Mode – moments before a blade penetrated his stomach and burst out of his back.

With a final leaping strike, McGarrity ended the creature, in a long, downward slash that drew a vertical line between the Beast's eyes, opening it up from sternum to groin. It split in two even pieces, causing a small tremor as the crumbling remains crashed to the earth. It was such a powerful and calculated strike that I wondered why McGarrity hadn't done it earlier – it's as if he'd been enjoying the battle so much that he extended it willfully, savoring each stroke of his blade.

When Steve spun around his weapon winked out of existence. Without his glowing sword the darkness returned, leaving the artificial constellations as our only source of light. As he approached he blew on his fingertips; they had a faint red hue, and were fading like the embers of a dying fire.

Peyton, Mac and I looked on, completely dumbfounded, as the brash, young man strolled back towards us. He was as calm and collected as the moment he emerged from the forest. He pulled his feet together and extended his arms, taking a deep bow as if he'd received a standing ovation. I wasn't sure if he was doing this for our benefit, or the simulcast viewers whom he claimed were watching our every move.

"Wow, tough crowd," McGarrity laughed, noting our apparent lack of enthusiasm. It's not that we weren't relieved that The Beast had been destroyed; we just weren't sure how to react. "Well," he shrugged, "you can hold your applause until later. Because you ain't seen nothing yet."

It was forty-five minutes of awkward silence, interlaced with the occasional attempt at small talk. McGarrity appeared more or less sincere, and seemed like he could be a very powerful ally – if not a slightly dangerous one.

I had no superpowers of my own, as Steve was quick to point out, but my ability to determine if someone was lying wasn't far off. During my stint at the casinos, an aptitude for making complex calculations in my head was a helpful tool – though it was my ability to read physical signs and 'tells' that made me unstoppable. Ticks. Gestures. Vocal cues. Even pupil dilation. I read every single one and stored them in my internal hard drive, and if I spoke with someone for long enough, their fabrications would almost seem to appear in giant floating bubbles that hung over their heads. As Steve went over his back story – where he was from, what led him here, and his motivation for coming to The Spiral – I never detected an irregularity. If he was a liar he was one of the best I'd ever met.

Peyton was convinced of Steve's sincerity almost immediately. She always saw the best in people. She smiled politely and laughed at his jokes, and even took the time to tend to a small burn he'd suffered on his shoulder when a drop of The Beast's blood seared a hole through his t-shirt.

Mac, on the other hand, wasn't so sure. He was as laid back as anyone I'd ever met, but I could sense his distrust when it came to McGarrity. He wandered over towards Chandler and sat next to him in the tree line. Their conversation had a conspiratorial tone; their hushed words were being kept purposefully quiet, leaning close to each other as they discussed what I could only assume was the convenient timing of our new teammate's arrival.

Eventually, and to my considerable relief, Brynja, following the sounds and flashing lights from the battle, emerged from the dense forest across the lake. She arrived with our chef, DuPont, whose luminous red armor was fully intact.

When they arrived at our makeshift camp McGarrity was quick to introduce himself. "I can't believe it's really you," he said excitedly, racing towards her with a little too much enthusiasm. "I *loved* you in Arena Mode! Your ghosting thing was pretty cool, even though it isn't that helpful...at least against electricity. And the mind reading? You can do that too, right? Do you have any other powers?"

Eyes widened, she glanced at me as if asking for assistance. I just smiled and shrugged my shoulders.

"Yeah," she said flatly, pressing her palm against McGarrity's shoulder. She gave him a gentle nudge, forcing him back a few paces. "I'm magnetic. I attract crazy douche bags."

He paused for a moment, furrowing his brow, and then let out a boisterous laugh. "That's it! That's the dry wit I remember from Arena Mode. Man, I was *so* bummed when you died."

She pressed her lips into a thin line and nodded slowly. "Well, it didn't last, so...it's all good." A beat passed before she calmly added, "And who the fuck are you, if you don't mind my asking?"

He repeated the same gesture as when I'd asked him that same question, smacking his head as if to jog his memory. He introduced himself while I gave Brynja and DuPont a summary of the last several hours: Chandler's injury, Ortega's death, the arrival of our annoying new ally, and his battle with a twenty-foot rock monster. Just an average day in Arena Mode.

Brynja had wandered the dimly-lit forest ever since her arrival, hoping to locate anyone from the group, and she recently discovered DuPont. Our chef had somehow managed to climb a tree (no small feat considering his bulky armor) and was convinced that being in an elevated position would provide a measure of camouflage. Of course an outfit made of cherry-red plastic wasn't doing him any favors when it came to stealth, but he finally explained that he was afraid that he'd be too vulnerable without it. Luckily she came across him before The Beast did, or he might have been the second GoBot to sail over the lake.

Brynja hadn't recovered any weapons, though she'd arrived with some good news: she discovered a treasure chest in close proximity to her pod, and inside it was a map. A crudely-drawn diagram scrawled on a crinkled sheet of manila paper, which outlined the entire level. It was roughly to scale, and featured every major landmark that we'd encountered. An exaggerated black 'X' marked a spot just a half-mile from our location, with a single word written beneath it: 'escape'.

We made our way through the jungle, using the lights from our gauntlets to illuminate a path. Mac offered to assist Chandler, lending an arm for support as he stepped gingerly onto his injured leg. It was as thoughtful as it was surprising, considering I'd never seen my pilot go out of his way to help anyone unless the possibility of a free drink or a college co-ed were the reward. They led our group, followed by DuPont (who wasn't in the chattiest mood), and I lagged behind, flanked by Brynja and Peyton. I'd forgotten that our new arrival was just a few paces to my back until he opened his mouth.

"So," McGarrity called out, addressing no one in particular. "This is awkward, huh?"

I continued to plod forward, brushing low-hanging branches aside and swatting at the insects that were drawn to the glow of our suits. "Being stalked by thousands of angry, brainwashed dissidents with machine guns? I guess you could file that under 'awkward'."

He blurted out the caustic laugh that I'd only heard twice, but already sounded like rusted nails in a blender. "Naw, I mean *you three*, here together. You, your ex, your current, all—"

I stopped him dead in his tracks, cutting his words off with an exaggerated wave of my hands. "Whoa, let's take a step back, Braveheart. There is no 'ex'. I don't know what they showed on the simulcasts, but Peyton and I...we were apart, but we never *really* stopped...I mean—"

"Right," Peyton added briskly. "We never split up, not officially. It was like a break. No big deal."

We continued to march through the trees, though Brynja was now intentionally leading a few steps ahead.

Steve rushed to keep pace with me and shook his head, wedging his mouth to one side. "Mmm."

"*Mmm?*" I repeated the nondescript sound he'd made, which technically meant nothing, yet clearly implied *something*. "What is that noise supposed to mean?"

"Well," he said after a short pause, "I was just thinking about last summer, when my girlfriend Tess caught me having coffee with a chick from the comic store. This really, really hot piece of..." he wisely paused and re-phrased when he caught a glimpse of Peyton's narrowed eyes. "Well, she was attractive – let's just leave it at that. Anyway, Tess stomps up to me, grabs my latte and dumps it over my head. 'It's over, asshole!' That's what she shouts in front of everyone at Starbucks. Can you believe it?"

"*You*, being called an asshole?" Brynja replied without turning around. "Shocking."

"I know," Steve shouted, throwing his hands up. "So I'm thinking, *my* ex goes ballistic over coffee – a freaking *coffee* – one time, in broad daylight, with some girl that I hadn't even slept with yet. And I'm watching the simulcast, thinking that Mox is shacking up with Brynja, *and* having picnics with her every day in this romantic dome while a servant brings them food...I can only imagine what Peyton must be thinking."

I was quick to correct him. "The dome is *not* romantic. It's a terraformed, climate-controlled habitat."

"And you were up there doing science experiments?" he asked innocently.

"Well not really," I mumbled. "Right, well I can see where that could be confusing when you see it out of context...but I don't have a servant. Chandler helps run the fortress. And yes, sometimes he'll bring me food or the occasional drink."

I just realized that I'd accurately described a servant.

"Look," McGarrity continued, sounding somewhat apologetic, "I'm not the only one discussing this. It's already a huge topic on the holo-forums: the whole 'Team Brynja versus Team Peyton' thing. People are voting on who you'll end up with."

"Who the hell would start a poll like that?" I asked.

"I was bored," McGarrity admitted. "And it was a long flight from Texas."

I was going to reply but all I could muster was a groan.

"Look," he continued, "I'm just saying Peyton must be the coolest girlfriend in the world, because if she's gonna let her guy hang out with some chick dressed up like Catwoman, with the whips and the sexy leather, and—"

"Anyone not heard of cosplay?" Brynja shouted. "It's a thing! Millions of people do it."

"Matt and Brynja can play dress-up all they want," Peyton sighed, rushing several steps ahead of us. "Like I said, we were taking a break."

We remained silent for the rest of the trek, and by some divine act of god McGarrity was able to keep his mouth shut for the duration. I spent the next twenty minutes hoping that he turned out to be evil – that way I could kill him without feeling guilty about it.

After a short hike over uneven terrain we arrived at a wide clearing, which seemed to be significantly more illuminated than the rest of the level; it was as if the stars were casting a spotlight on the field, signifying the importance of the location. The area was unnaturally symmetrical, as if it had been landscaped into a circle. In the center of the clearing was a flat grey obelisk, surrounded by knee-high grass, jutting from the earth like an oversized tombstone. It had no inscription, but as we approached a faint outline became clear on its surface – it was the vague outline of a handprint.

After a moment of inspection I removed my gauntlet and pressed my palm into the stone, extending my fingers and thumb until they fit inside the shallow grooves. My action triggered a hologram projector; Cameron Frost's head appeared, hovering overhead like a massive, pompous blimp.

"Eight pods remain," Frost declared. "And I commend you for claiming the first one. You're either very smart, or very fortunate. Either way, congratulations are in order – you'll be making your descent into the next phase of The Spiral." Frost's disembodied head flashed a knowing grin. "You might have arrived here alone, or you may have arrived with allies you've acquired throughout your journey. This strategy may have helped until this point, though at the end of this journey, the prize cannot be divided – only one can claim the ultimate reward."

I had to hand it to Frost: even in the afterlife he was still an asshole. He planted seeds at the onset to make it feel as if

'Arena Mode 2' would be more of a sport, and less of a barbaric bloodbath. He gave the illusion that this event would be one where teams could form, and alliances would become a part of the game. Of course this was bullshit. It was just a way for him to ratchet up the drama and force friends to turn on each other, like every other degrading reality show that oozed its way onto a simulcast. Cameron Frost was doing what he always did: pollute the mainstream media with insipid, sensational programming to distract viewers from the world that was corroding around them.

We took turns pressing our hands into the obelisk, and one after another, the pods began to appear. Around the perimeter of the circle they burst through the earth, tearing up from the jungle floor. The pneumatic tubes that led to the lower level had been grown over with a thin layer of vegetation, concealing them at the edges of the clearing.

As we prepared to step into our pods, Frost's head began to flicker. It faded and disappeared, replaced by another holographic image: Valeriya Taktarov. She stood in front of the obelisk, hands clasped behind her back. Had she discovered some type of control room, and was able to project herself into The Spiral? Was this some other type of tech that she brought with her? Or was a superhuman assisting her? How she was pulling this off didn't really matter. Valeriya was here, watching us, and clearly had something on her mind.

The hologram scanned each one of us and began to wander around the clearing, before stopping a few feet in front of McGarrity. "You disappoint me," Valeriya said, shaking her head slowly. "Not only did you betray the Red Army, you have betrayed the memory of my brother."

"Guess so," He replied. "Too bad there's nothing you can do about it."

Valeriya glared at him, unblinking. "Your confidence is impressive. We will see how confident you are once my army reaches you."

"Eight slots left," Mac shouted from across the clearing. "I'm no math expert, but I'm thinking with only two pods you won't be able to get much of an army down here."

"It's one more than I need," she replied. "I recently increased the prize for Matthew Moxon's capture: fifty million American dollars. The response was overwhelming, and I had many superhumans to choose from. The champions I sent after you will have no trouble completing their missions."

"I bet that's what you told your big brother," Brynja added. "Right before I filled his head with acid."

Valeriya turned to face Brynja. Her eyes welled with emotion, but never blinked out a tear. "You will be the first to go," she quietly threatened. "In the slowest, most painful way that you can imagine. These traitors you have aligned yourself with will watch in horror, unable to stop the inevitable. And once they have died, one by one, Matthew Moxon will be brought before me."

"I guess you don't want to give us a little hint about who you recruited?" I asked. "If we're going to die anyway we might as well get a head's up."

Taking her time, Valeriya's hologram sauntered across the grass and stopped just inches from my face. She craned her neck upward and her gaze locked onto mine; her gunmetal blue eyes had a chilling effect, as if they were staring right through me. "Weaving," she whispered.

And then she disappeared.

The name that floated from Valeriya's tiny lips shot ice water into my veins. It was the name of a woman who was known by a hundred different aliases around the world, although there was only one that truly described the nature of her power: The Nightmare.

CHAPTER NINETEEN

"What's with you?" McGarrity asked. "You have this look on your face like someone just mentioned Voldemort."

I lied, and assured everyone I was fine. No one else seemed concerned when Valeriya had mentioned the name Weaving, which I found somewhat surprising. It had been a story that I'd followed closely over the last several months through the holo-forums while Brynja and I were knee-deep in research.

In the wake of Arena Mode last summer, 'Superhuman Arena Combat' had become the hottest sport in the world. While soccer, American football and mixed martial arts could still pack a stadium full of a hundred-thousand screaming fans, an Arena fight drew *billions* of simulcast spectators, making it the most-watched – and the most profitable – entertainment spectacle in existence.

Outside of America, few countries would allow a sporting event where the chances of their cities being destroyed were all but assured, and the odds of a fatality were close to a hundred percent. Full Contact Swordfighting (the most dangerous sport in the world prior to the advent of Superhuman Arena Combat) was only permitted in a handful of countries as it was, and even fewer were prepared to take the next step by sanctioning Arena fights.

A few months ago, Sultan Saeed Al Darmaki (a well-known superhuman and investor from the United Arab Emirates) was granted a license to hold an Arena event in his home country. Despite the mountains of revenue generated from advertising dollars during the inaugural Arena Mode, Darmaki had a different business model in mind: his upcoming show *wasn't* going to appear on a simulcast. It was billed as an exclusive event, and if you couldn't afford the multi-million dollar price tag to see it in person, you wouldn't be able to see it.

Darmaki paid to retro-fit the largest and most impressive structure in all of Abu Dhabi, a Full-Contact Swordfighting stadium, for Superhuman Arena Combat. Walls were reinforced, the roof was coated with graphene, and blast shields were put into place for the safety of the live audience. And on game-day, spectators were required to sign a waiver before taking their seats. It was a wise move from a litigation perspective. The odds were that not everyone in the stands would be leaving in one piece.

The black-tie affair was the ultimate VIP experience. It was so exclusive, in fact, that it would remain a mystery for all who were unable to attend. Your only accounts of what happened would be through the blogs and word-of-mouth from those wealthy enough to have seen it with their own two eyes. At Darmaki's request the show wouldn't even be filmed for future viewings. No press passes would be given out, and recording devices of every kind would be banned from the stadium.

People in attendance described the event as a terrifying collage of random horrific events. And that was the strangest part about it: when discussing the first annual 'Abu Dhabi Superhuman Classic', no two stories seemed to match.

They all began the same: the nine competitors started by attacking each other with various powers; fire, ice, electricity, plasma bolts – and then their accounts began to diverge. Depending on who you spoke with, you could hear a terrifying story about superhumans being mauled by tigers, torn to pieces by rotating blades, or melting to death in a sea of blue flames.

And by everyone's account, the end was the same: the winner was a woman named Grace Teach Weaving. A mysterious superhuman who no two people ever described the same way – and, even stranger, a woman whose *name* continually changed. The majority of people simply forgot it the moment it was spoken. Like waking up from a vivid dream that fades as the day wears on, when someone asks you to describe it in detail, you're left with a blur of unrelated events that rattle around your mind.

For some reason Weaving's name always stuck with me; not just her given name, but the name that the media had branded her with: The Nightmare.

There was no official ranking system in place for superhumans, or a governing body that would list them in order from the most to the least dangerous – but if there were, I would place Weaving right at the top.

As all of this information blistered through my mind I caught myself staring into the middle distance, my gaze loosely fixed on the location where Valeriya's hologram had just disappeared.

"We'll be on our way through the tunnel before she catches up to us," Peyton reassured me, snapping me back to reality. "Don't worry, we're fine."

I nodded and smiled weakly, attempting to mask my considerable doubts.

Mac raised another concern. "We could be separated again once we hit the second level. What do we do when we drop?"

"Move towards the center point," I instructed. "As quickly and as quietly as possible. If you get lost, stay put, and wait for a signal." I straightened my posture and drew in a deep breath, trying to steel my resolve. I was being looked to as the leader of this group – for whatever reason, I wasn't quite sure – and I wanted to maintain the thinly-veiled illusion that I knew what the hell I was doing.

The levels continue to get smaller as The Spiral descends, I explained; at least according to the holographic blueprint that was on display at the onset of the games. In theory it should be slightly easier to locate one another within the confines of a smaller space.

As we backed into our respective pods the doors sealed shut, and we exchanged glances as we descended one by one.

After a momentary drop I was again ejected from the pneumatic tube, landing once more on a patch of grass. After spending a day in near-darkness, the sudden flood of sunlight forced my eyes shut.

I cracked my lids and scanned the landscape. Through squinting eyes it was a pastel-colored utopia; perfectly green grass that appeared freshly-mowed, perfectly manicured cherry blossom trees that dotted the rolling hills, and a perfect blue sky, giving off just the right amount of light. Even the temperature was ideal; the air was crisp with a soft breeze that cooled my skin. It was in stark contrast with the suffocating humidity that'd assaulted my senses on the previous level. I had been expecting something much more sinister as we continued to descend, though at first glance, this was paradise.

After my eyes adjusted to the light, the illusion began to fade. I removed a gauntlet and kneeled, running my hand along the freshly-mowed grass. It had the appearance of natural turf, but felt smooth and rubbery. It even smelled artificial, like a vague combination of carpet freshener and new plastic. I inspected the sky and realized that a single important detail was absent: the sun. It was as if this level was still under construction, and the designers had neglected to insert the shining yellow star into the sky. No bugs, no sunshine, and not even the faintest aroma of anything organic – this was a version of the great outdoors that I could definitely get used to.

No one else from my team was in the vicinity. I'd have to reach higher ground before I could scan the area and locate the others. I was dropped into a shallow valley, and the only visible landmark I could spot was a chrome-plated casket, sitting a few hundred feet away.

I approached the chest, and after another cursory examination I was satisfied that it wouldn't explode in my face. I flipped it open, and for the first time inside The Spiral I felt that luck – if there were such a thing – was on my side. It was a grenade launcher. A long metallic cylinder gleamed in the overhead light, and beside it sat three rounded shells. I inspected the weapon and squinted at the small type engraved on the side above the firing mechanism, hoping it would reveal some instructions. The text was in German as far as I could tell, so it did me little good. Shooting a gun was one thing – I wasn't nearly as confident playing around with explosives.

I attached the launcher to my suit's magnetic spine and carefully pressed each of the three explosive shells to my belt. I had to transport these somehow, and without a proper satchel or carrying case this was my only alternative. I was now paranoid that something as simple as tripping and falling could trigger a series of explosions that would send me spiralling through the air like a cartoon coyote.

Lost in thought, I was startled by a familiar pair of floating orange spheres tethered by a long grey cord. It appeared from the sky, spinning like a helicopter blade before hovering to a stop. The two curious eyes peered at me, awaiting instructions.

"London?"

"Mister Moxon!" it replied. *"You are looking more youthful and exuberant than usual. Truly a wonderful example of the human species."*

"How did you survive?" I asked, scrutinizing the metallic spheres. There wasn't so much as a scratch on their glistening surface.

"I don't understand the question, Mister Moxon. Please rephrase."

"Weren't you destroyed in the gunfight?" Before we were launched into the first level of The Spiral, I vividly remember a hail of bullets tearing London to pieces, and the Red Army trampling the smoking remains as they stormed the room.

"I was," London said with a song in its digitized voice, *"but my memory transferred through the Fortress' internal cloud, and into a new piece of hardware when that unit became unusable. And now I'm here with the privilege of speaking with you, our brilliant and exalted leader."*

I now had a bad-ass weapon, as well as access to communications. It was what poker players refer to as a hot streak – though, in reality, it was just a matter of statistical probability. It worked the same way playing cards as it does in real life: when enough shitty things happen, the odds dictate that sooner or later, *something* good will fall in your lap. And if you're on a *real* hot streak, two good things in a row.

"Can you access my personal account?" I asked.

"Indeed I can!" London exclaimed with an overabundance of enthusiasm. *"Would you like me to access it right now, Mister Moxon?"*

I nodded, and within a moment I had full access to everything in the cloud: mail, simulcasts, communications – everything that my wrist-com was supposed to provide, but had failed to access since we descended into the lower levels of The Spiral. I also had access to the Fortress' main database.

My first order of business was to delete every map and schematic related to The Spiral; which, hopefully, would destroy any evidence of the construction tunnel that we were going to use as an escape. Even if Valeriya was aware of its existence, there would be no way for her to identify its proximity to the Fortress, and in which direction it led.

I moved on to my communications. As I scrolled through pages of unread messages, London chirped: *"You have an incoming link request from...Jacob Fitzsimmons. Would you like to accept the transmission?"*

I nodded again, and a holo-screen projected from London's oculars, expanding into a large flat display. My lawyer winked into view.

"Mister Moxon," Fitzsimmons said curtly, "I have some news."

"I don't know if you've been watching the simulcasts, but I'm a little busy at the moment."

"That's why I'm calling you," he continued. "It's about your property."

"My property?"

"The piece of land that you acquired from Cameron Frost. Fortress 23 and the surrounding area. It's yours."

I arched an eyebrow. Was my lawyer suffering from the same memory-related affliction that I was? "I think we established that already, Jacob."

"The land," he persisted. "It no longer belongs to Canada. It's *yours*."

For a moment I searched my memory. I tried to approximate the last time I'd taken my medication, because nothing my lawyer was saying made any sense. "I don't—"

"This just happened now," he interrupted. "Frost petitioned to have the piece of land he purchased in Northern Alberta declared its own sovereign nation. It happened. And it's yours."

The magnitude of what my lawyer was attempting to explain was taking a moment to process. "Hold up – you're telling me that I own a *country*?"

"More or less," my lawyer replied. "The paperwork is being finalized now."

According to his personal records, Frost had been petitioning for years in order to make this happen; he'd spent billions of dollars, and had lobbied every politician he had access to. Campaign contributions, calling in personal favors – it got him nowhere. Up until today he hadn't had any success. "How did this happen? Did the UN suddenly have a change of heart once Arena Mode 2 got started?"

My lawyer seemed as confused as I was. "Some pretty big strings got pulled – that's all I know. I have no idea who did it, but they have some serious clout with not only the Canadian government, but a lot of international leaders. It would take nothing short of a miracle to make this happen."

That, or the *promise* of a miracle.

Jacob Fitzsimmons was widely regarded as the best estate lawyer in the country, and he rarely let a detail slip past him. Though in his defense, he didn't know Valeriya Taktarov. She had used her rhetoric to activate a group of thousands to join her Red Army, and had incited hundreds of thousands more to riot across North America. It wasn't inconceivable that her promise of Sergei Taktarov's rebirth – and the dawn of a new age – convinced at least one credulous politician to finally put pen to paper.

Here in Northern Alberta, I now was the president of my own nation. Thanks to Valeriya, I was in a country with its own separate borders, laws and legislation...meaning that neither Canada nor the United States were responsible for anyone who lived here. I could be captured, tried and publicly executed on a snow bank outside of my fortress, and everyone from international politicians down to local law enforcement could claim innocence. This was the ultimate 'get out of jail free card' for Valeriya Taktarov, and she'd convinced world leaders to simply hand it to her, no questions asked.

It was safe to say that my momentary hot streak had screeched to a grinding halt.

Transcript from the Calgary Herald Simulcast
Macklin & Marsh's 'Eye in the Sky' Report
Hosted by Herb Macklin and Dana Marsh, January, 2042

Dana Marsh: The scene here is really quite remarkable, Herb. Riots continue to cut a swath through cities around the world, but all eyes are focused on Northern Alberta, where thousands of protesters occupy the area surrounding this remote outpost.

Herb Macklin: Dana, it seems like there's a *lot* of snow up there.

Marsh: Indeed there is, Herb, but I'm not here to cover the weather this morning. This is a special report, remember?

Macklin: I know, I know, but I'm just saying – with that kind of snowfall you could really 'shred some powder' on the slopes. Is that a saying? Ski slang? I heard my grandson say that at Thanksgiving dinner. He might have been referring to drugs, though. I can never tell with these kids today.

Marsh: I'm not sure, but if you wait a moment for us to swing around into position we'll get a better shot of the crowd that's gathered at the base of the structure.

There we are...you can see – I know visibility is low because of the snow squalls – there are literally thousands of people gathering. We're estimating twenty thousand at the moment, and more are arriving by the minute. They've broken into the Fortress and as you can see, they've opened up a number of the entrances on the main level, including the hangar.

Macklin: Why aren't you down there on the ground with them, Dana? Get some one-on-one interviews.

Marsh: They're heavily-armed dissidents, Herb. They're here demanding the public execution of Matthew Moxon for his role in Sergei Taktarov's death.

Macklin: Right. Not the friendliest folks, then.

Marsh: I'd assume not. With our traffic cam, we can see the mastermind of this entire operation, Sergei's younger sister Valeriya Taktarov. Interesting fact that we just discovered: at just twelve years of age, she has the second-highest IQ on record.

Macklin: That's astounding. My grandson is nineteen, and his greatest accomplishment to date is sewing his own Zelda costume. I think it was Zelda...is he that robot that changes into a tiger? Or maybe it was a Pokemon.

Marsh: Like I was saying, Valeriya Taktarov has not only assembled a group that has been dubbed 'The Red Army', but she's also privately contracted a number of superhumans to pursue Moxon into The Fortress.

Macklin: Super assassins, huh? So what's the going rate for a hit man these days?

Marsh: No financial details have been disclosed, although her Kashstarter campaign continues to generate funds. As of seven o'clock this morning, over a hundred and forty million

American dollars has been raised, including one donation in particular of thirty million from an anonymous source.

Macklin: Anonymous? Can't these donations be traced?

Marsh: I'm told that the majority of them were made with Bitgold, a digital currency that is purchased and traded without any online footprint.

What we *do* know is that as Valeriya's war chest continues to swell, so does her army. According to several sources, her paid recruits include Mitsuhara Onita, a well-known superhuman from Tokyo who possesses the ability to shape-shift, and the winner of last month's Abu Dhabi Superhuman Classic, Grace Weaving.

Macklin: Is there a police presence, Dana? If they're threatening to execute Moxon shouldn't the authorities be there to break things up? Make arrests?

Marsh: That's what we've been trying to discern. It's been several days, and not a single public statement has been issued from either the Canadian or American governments.

Macklin: Why do you think that is?

Marsh: I'm not going to speculate, Herb.

Macklin: Come on, give our viewers an opinion.

Marsh: I'm a news reporter. I report facts. If I just started throwing my thoughts and opinions into every story, it would cease to be 'news'.

Macklin: All righty, if you're not going to play along I'll throw in my two cents.

Marsh: Somehow I knew you would.

Macklin: If I had to guess, I'd say the governments are hoping that this entire thing burns itself out. They're going to let this Red Army take care of business, get rid of Moxon, and wait for the riots to die down after he's gone.

Plus there's not much they could do, even if they wanted to. The American government doesn't want to step on Canada's toes by coming over the border, and Canada doesn't have the manpower to deal with an armed crowd of this size.

Marsh: That's certainly a possibility, but again, this is all purely speculation. Let's just stick to the facts, here.

Macklin: Well, you *asked* for my opinion, and I gave it to you.

Marsh: I didn't ask for your opinion.

CHAPTER TWENTY

After a short hike to the peak of a rolling hill I spotted a structure in the distance. On an adjacent hill sat a castle. It towered high above its surroundings; with an arching roof, dark wooden shingles and stone base, it had a distinctly Japanese feel to it, like the castles built during the country's feudal Sengoku period in the 1400s. Not surprising, since this had been an obsession of Cameron Frost's.

As an admitted Japanophile, Frost's love for the culture had gone far beyond most American's fascination with Dragon Ball Z, Sailor Moon and take-out sushi restaurants. He had participated in Full Contact Swordfighting tournaments with the sole purpose of becoming known as the greatest swordsman who'd ever lived, eclipsing Miyamoto Musashi's record of sixty victories with a katana. He had even woven the odd Mushasi quote into his speeches, though upon reflection I didn't think he'd fully understood them.

From what I could tell the structure was at the center of the level, and it was where I expected the rest of the group would meet. I trekked across the artificial turf as London followed closely behind, and as we travelled I asked for a visual of the Fortress exterior. The friendly orange spheres circled in front of me and displayed a holo-screen, cycling through the various security cams. The east-facing camera displayed at least ten thousand members of the Red Army sprawled throughout the snowy forest clearing, as well as a pair of tanks and several helicopters that circled the perimeter. The group that'd once resembled a large protest now seemed like a permanent occupation, with a reported population that topped twenty thousand. If the Canadian or American governments were to deploy any type of rescue team on our behalf – which at this point seemed like a long shot – the clash that'd ensue would resemble a third world war. I had no delusions at this point: we had exactly one chance for escape, and that was the tunnel on the bottom level of The Spiral.

I spotted a figure approaching in the horizon – it was Brynja. Her black body armor and flowing blue hair were like a beacon in the distance. We met and agreed to try and access the castle at the level's center. As the sole visible structure, it was the most likely location for the pods that led to the third level.

Brynja had searched the immediate area where she was ejected from her pod, although she hadn't located a chest. She was disappointed that she hadn't been able to retrieve anything useful, but seemed uplifted by my discoveries; having London back online and a rocket launcher at our disposal were two small advantages that we desperately required. If the Red Army caught up with us I wasn't sure how many of them we could take out with three explosive shells, but it was a significant step up from our standard firearms. After emptying virtually our entire arsenal into The Beast up on the first level, we were in need of some serious firepower, and the handful of bullets split between us wasn't going to stop a charging mob.

We made the long walk up the steep hillside, crossed a bridge that spanned a moat (although the surrounding ditch was completely dry – just another small detail of this level that had been neglected) and stepped up to the entrance. A pair of enormous wooden doors stretched fifteen feet high, blocking our entrance to the castle courtyard. No keyhole, no doorknob. We inspected the frame, discovering a pair of metal plates that flanked each side of the doorway, each with a handprint etched into their surfaces – the same as on the obelisk from the previous level.

Brynja and I took turns pressing our hands into the plates. First her, then me. Nothing.

"So what the hell?" she said casually, shrugging her shoulders. "We wait for Braveheart to show up so he can hack his way in with his light saber?"

"That would be too easy. For all we know the entire castle is packed with C4 – if we try to force our way in we could explode, just like the caskets."

Brynja groaned, let a few expletives fly and buried the heel of her boot into the wooden door. "Frost, I hope there's a hell," she shouted, "because when I get there I'm going to kick you in your goddamned face!"

I suggested that threatening Cameron Frost in the afterlife while stomping an immovable door might not be the best way to expend her energy. I also pointed out that for Brynja to theoretically fight Frost on the ethereal plane, she'd have to end up in hell – if that was where he was located. She wasn't in the mood to discuss theology.

As Brynja continued her tantrum, I remembered Frost's introductory speech about competitors putting their faith in others. Surely there was a good reason for the dual hand sensors, and it was so obvious I felt like an idiot for not realizing it immediately.

"We need to do it together," I explained. "The prints. We need both our hands simultaneously to unlock the door."

When we positioned our hands into the grooves on the metal plates a voice resonated through an overhead speaker system.

"Trust," Cameron Frost's voice boomed like a thunderclap, "is the key to any partnership. The two superhumans who have arrived at this point formed an alliance. An alliance that will – out of necessity – be broken. Before you can enter the castle, state your superpower, and how you would use it against your partner."

It was another lie detector test. In order for the door to unlock, the competitors had to basically describe how they'd kill each other, and look each other in the eyes while they did it. Another twist in the game that would, in other circumstances, have resulted in a bloodbath.

"That's easy," I said. "I don't have any superpowers." Detecting my truthful response, the metal plate glowed blue beneath my palm. A loud ratcheting sound clanked from above when the first set of bolts fell out of place. One more honest answer and we'd be inside.

I glanced over at Brynja, who avoided eye contact. She drew in a deep breath and leaned forward, using the wide doorframe for support.

"What's the problem?" I asked. "Just say you don't have powers anymore and let's go find the next set of pods."

"I can't do that," she mumbled.

"What?" I blurted out. "I thought your mind reading ability faded after we left the hospital, and that you were back to normal?"

"'Normal'?" She repeated, as if I'd hurled an insult in her direction. Brynja's hand was pressed firmly on the metal plate, but she turned to face me, brushing a sweep of blue locks from her face.

"I didn't mean you *weren't*...you know what I mean."

"I *was* normal," she said emphatically. "I *am*. It's just that a week ago I felt this tingling, and suddenly..." Brynja's head sagged, eyes fixated on the toes of her boots. "Shit, this is really hard to talk about."

"It's me," I assured her. "We talk about everything."

"All right," she continued, drawing in another deep breath, "so...this tingling happens, and suddenly my psychic abilities come back. A little."

"A little?" I shouted. "What the hell is that supposed to mean?"

"Okay," she admitted. "A lot."

"You've been reading my mind?"

"It's not like that. Not on purpose, anyway." She stepped away from the frame and moved towards me, hands extended.

"Holy shit – and I trusted you!" I turned away and raked my fingers through my short hair. I couldn't look at her without feeling sick. Brynja had been more than my best friend over the last several months – she'd been my family. At times my *only* family. And the entire time that we'd lived together she'd been violating my mind; reading my innermost thoughts, and probably using them to manipulate me.

"You *can* trust me," she pleaded, "it's just—"

"It's just what," I interrupted. "What is it? We're probably going to die here in this freak show – executed on a simulcast while the world watches from their living room couches. If you're not going to be up front with me now, then *when* would be a good time?"

"What do you want from me?" she screamed, slamming the back of her fist into the wooden door so hard I was surprised she didn't break her hand.

"Some goddamned *honesty*," I shouted back.

"I wanted you for myself," Brynja said, turning away. "I'm a selfish bitch, okay? And I wanted things to suck between you and Peyton so I could catch you on the rebound. Is that honest enough for you?"

Holy shit. My mind reeled. I suddenly hoped we'd have to fight another homicidal rock monster – that would have been easier to deal with than this painfully awkward moment.

Brynja turned and pressed her back against the door, sliding down until she sat on the ground. "I didn't say anything because I knew you'd react like this. You get all defensive and shell up anytime something disrupts your perfect little bubble. And secondly...I guess I gave up."

"Gave up?" I joined her on the ground, leaning back against the doors.

"The minute Peyton walked back into your life I knew it was over. I never stood a chance. That girl's mind is like this magic fantasy land of hope, and forgiveness, and chocolate-covered gumdrops." She smiled weakly and laughed under her breath. "Reading her is like being stuck inside a fucking Disney movie."

"You read Peyton, too?"

She nodded, pulling her knees tight against her chest. "Like I said, it just happened. Proximity and stuff...if you're too close, surface thoughts start to float around. They're like big neon billboards – can't avoid them if I try."

"So..."

"So, she's the Lois Lane to your Superman," Brynja sighed. "The Mary Jane whatshername to your Spidey. Peyton would follow you to the end of the earth if you asked her. But that's the rub, Mox: you have to *ask* her. Like, with actual words and stuff."

"I *did* ask her," I replied without missing a beat. "I asked her to move in with me and she shot me down. She walked away and we didn't speak for months – that was *her* choice, not mine."

Brynja raised her eyebrows, and her lips curled slightly at the edges. "So you expected Peyton to leave her family, school, job and friends – and move out to the middle of the Canadian wilderness with you...and stay here forever?"

I never thought of it that way. "You're saying that was too much to ask?"

"She's a *human girl*, Mox. She's not a collectible action figure. You can't just stick her in a plastic dome and expect her to pose, smile and be happy about it. That's insane."

I shrugged. "*You're* happy here."

"Because you're *all* I have," she groaned, letting her forehead fall against her knees. "I had nothing to go home to, so I moved in with some dude I met one time for a couple hours last summer..." she trailed off for a moment, furrowing her brow. "And now that I'm saying this out loud it's sounding really pathetic."

"You're not pathetic."

"Look," she continued, "I like it here...well, not *now*, with the angry mob and people trying to kill us – but before, yeah, it was fun. But did you expect it to stay that way for the rest of our lives?"

"If it was going so well why would it have to change?"

Brynja stood and dusted herself off, extending her hand towards me. "Because life changes. Shit happens – some good, some bad."

"Some?" I replied, taking her hand as a stood.

"Okay," she conceded, "mostly bad. And you can't live in a bubble and expect everything to stay the same because *you're* changing too, Mox. Some people just wait way too long until they realize it."

"So if we make it out of here alive—"

"When," she was quick to correct me.

"Okay, when – then I'm supposed to go and live in the open? Act like no one wants to murder me?"

"Like I said, things change. It won't be like that forever. Talk to her. Tell her that the two of you can work in the real world – that's all she wants to hear. And compromise with her. I know, it's asking a lot from an eccentric celebrity billionaire, but give it a shot."

Most girls assume that guys are mind readers, or at least that's how Peyton always treated me. If she'd just told me what she needed once in a while I wouldn't have to hear it from someone with actual psychic abilities. "You read all of that?"

"Yup," she said with a small nod. "I put the pieces together. The way she cares about you is kinda romantic...in a barfy sort of way. But I don't need psychic powers to see that you two assholes belong together."

Brynja was the only person who could insult me and make me smile at the same time. It was one of her lesser-known super powers. "So then what?" I asked. "Where will you be when Peyton and I are making it work in this theoretical 'real world', wherever the hell that is?"

"I know how these things end," she said quietly. "I've *been* the other girl before. Not like, in a sexy way – but as a friend. A guy gets a steady girl in his life, and they do *not* want me around."

"You're not going anywhere," I reassured her, "because I *can't* lose you. Who else am I going to build Lego castles with at two in the morning while we eat Nutella from the jar?"

She smiled softly, but it didn't reach her eyes. "I'd settle for that, you know. Just us...talking, hanging out, doing nothing. But it never works out that way." Brynja took a few short paces to the frame of the massive door and pressed her hand into the metal plate. "You want the truth?" she said, tilting her chin towards the sky. "Here it is, Frost: I would never use my psychic powers to hurt Matthew Moxon, because he's the only person I've ever felt real with."

The deadbolt dropped, the hinges creaked, and the heavy wooden doors began to swing open. And from the darkness of the castle courtyard a snarling blur of teeth, fangs and claws burst forward. Brynja was buried beneath the creature before I had a chance to move.

CHAPTER TWENTY-ONE

"I have missed the *shit* out of you, kitty!" Brynja giggled as the creature's tongue lapped her cheek, leaving a thick stream of saliva behind.

A lion with dragon wings and the tail of a scorpion was an unnerving sight, even when it was a more reasonable size; the blue manticore, last I saw it, was no larger than a pit bull. Now, pinning Brynja to the ground with its paws, it was roughly the size of a compact car.

During Arena Mode, Kenneth Livitski had used his ability to manifest objects out of pure blue energy to create this: a living replica of the feared mythical creature. Even after Kenneth had been stabbed and sent into a coma, his creation persisted. 'Melvin' (the unfortunate name that Brynja had stuck him with) helped us survive the games, and when we neared the end he'd raced into an alley in pursuit of an attacker, never to be seen again.

For the months following Arena Mode, holo-forums were ablaze with speculation about Melvin. Was the manticore being controlled by Kenneth all along, even after he'd been eliminated from the tournament? Or had the creature somehow become sentient, able to act independently and make its own decisions? That 'sentient being' hypothesis was a popular one, but didn't seem feasible; all of The Living

Eye's creations had been merely puppets, controlled by his intentions.

Brynja had recently regained her telepathic abilities, which meant she was still a superhuman; she could have manifested the creature herself without knowing it. It wasn't unprecedented for superhumans with existing powers to spontaneously gain new ones, although occurrences were extremely rare.

"Well this is a nice surprise," Brynja said, getting back to her feet. She ran her hands along Melvin's white mane, eliciting a low rumbling purr. She glanced over her shoulder and cracked a smile, noting that I'd taken several steps backward. "Still not a cat person, huh?"

We searched the expansive courtyard while Melvin curled into a ball under a cherry blossom tree, closing his eyes for a midday nap.

Unlike the relatively barren landscape of the Japanese-themed level, the interior of the castle was recreated with painstaking detail. The courtyard was immense. Intricate stone paths wove through gardens, lined with sculpted hedges and multicolored flowers. Arched wooden walkways bridged the gap over running water, where brilliant copper fish circled beneath. And time-worn staircases (or at least they were designed to look time-worn, since this castle had been built fairly recently) twisted in every direction, leading to even more gardens, trees and sculptures. It was endless. If the pathway to the next level was hidden somewhere within this labyrinth it could be virtually anywhere, and by the time we found it we'd no doubt have the Red Army – or a superhuman assassin – knocking on the front door.

An hour drifted by as our search persisted.

Then another.

And then I heard the sound of crashing rocks behind a wall of hedges. Melvin, who was napping nearby, curiously lifted his head. His fuzzy blue ears perked up, rotating towards the direction of the disturbance.

I followed a pathway around the garden to find Brynja kicking a short statue, which had toppled over and broken into several pieces when it hit a tile. She cursed and stomped her feet, as she was prone to doing when she was frustrated.

"You wanna talk about it?" I said with a pat on the shoulder.

"Talk about what."

"About the garden gnome you just kicked the shit out of," I said with a smile. "You *know* what."

Brynja studied me for a moment as if she were trying to solve a puzzle. "I don't know how you can be so goddamned optimistic," she said flatly.

"I'm not," I replied, "Pessimism is like a religion to me, along with procrastination. I was actually going to get that engraved on a plaque so I could hang it in my office...I'll get to it eventually."

Brynja's arms dangled loosely at her sides while she stared at me listlessly. At least that's how I read it at first glance; frustration, fatigue – maybe she was just hungry. I couldn't be sure. Along with my failing short-term memory, the ability to discern what the opposite sex was thinking had always been my kryptonite.

The only logical reason for her behavior (at least the only one I could think of at the moment) was that Brynja was keeping something else from me – something that she'd been concealing since the castle gates swung open. The high-tech lie detector test had forced her to reveal that she was still in possession of her superpowers, though I could tell there was more.

"You know, I'm going to find out eventually," I said matter-of-factly. "So you might as well tell me now."

"Truth always comes out, doesn't it." She took a deep breath and placed her hands on her hips, shifting awkwardly from one foot to the other. "I just...I have to tell you something else. It's about Argentina."

Was there a single thought in my head that was private anymore? Having a psychic around had its uses, but the considerable downside was already starting to outweigh the benefits. I threw my arms apart and shouted, much louder than I'd intended. "Brynja, what the *hell*? That wasn't supposed to come out in the open, and—"

"I know," she said, her voice shrinking with regret. "But people are *going* to find out you were there."

"And it meant nothing," I fired back.

"What?" She shouted. "How can you even say that?"

"Because it was a meaningless trip. A trip devoid of meaning."

She grunted in frustration, balling her hands into tightly clenched fists. "Just because you *say* something is meaningless doesn't automatically mean—"

"Automatically mean what?" A voice called out from across the courtyard. Peyton was leading the rest of our group through the garden; Mac was assisting Chandler (who was beginning to put some more pressure on his ankle, walking slightly more upright) and Ortega followed, fidgeting with his bright yellow armor. McGarrity was nowhere to be seen.

"Blue," Mac called out. A crooked grin stretched across his face. "Did you miss me, sweetheart?"

Brynja narrowed her eyes. Her hatred for Mac was palpable, likely in no small part because she could read his thoughts. The things he said aloud were offensive enough; I couldn't imagine the level of unadulterated filth she was exposed to when he was in close proximity.

"So," Peyton said curtly, "are you going to tell me what I walked in on, or am I going to have to wait and hear about it on a simulcast?"

I searched my memory for a plausible excuse, and was interrupted by Brynja, who began rapidly tapping my shoulder.

Peyton glared at her. "Could you please give us just *one* moment alone," she said, clipping off her words.

Brynja persisted with her tapping, but she wasn't making eye contact. She stared past Mac and Chandler, with her gaze fixed squarely on Ortega. "Have you guys noticed something strange about him," she whispered from the corner of her mouth.

"The chef?" Peyton said, glancing back over her shoulder. "He's wearing a hundred pounds of red Lego, which is probably why he looks pissed. He *always* looks pissed."

Ortega seemed uncomfortable, shifting awkwardly inside of his bulky armor suit, but that was nothing out of the ordinary; he'd been doing that since we entered The Spiral. The dour expression painted on his face had been there since we'd encountered him on level one.

"Not that," Brynja replied softly, her lips barely moving. "It's not what he's doing, it's what he's—"

The word that Brynja never said – the word that became lodged in the back of her throat when a stream of blood spattered the walkway at our feet – was 'thinking'. She read Ortega's mind, and realized that he was no longer who he appeared to be.

CHAPTER TWENTY-TWO

His head came off first, then his arms. A severed artery pumped a fountain of blood into the air that shot across the garden, painting the tiles at our feet. His legs quickly followed, reddening the koi pond when they splashed into the shallow inlet.

It happened in a heartbeat: a tentacle coiled around Mac's torso, while several others, tipped with vicious barbs, swiped at his extremities. The slashes came so suddenly that he never had a chance to scream, and the rest of us, looking on in horror, never had a chance to react.

Ortega was gone. Whatever replaced him had transformed his body into a faceless, shapeless creature; a vile pulsing mass that was the color of a festering wound. A single oily eye gazed at us while a dozen fresh tentacles reached out from its core. The darting limbs seemed to be infinitely elastic, extending long enough to reach us from thirty feet away.

The blood-drenched tentacle that had dismembered Mac coiled around Chandler's ankle, yanking him from the bench before tossing him across the courtyard, beyond the maple trees and out of view. Another swipe caught Peyton across the shoulder, the razor-sharp talon slamming into her protective armor. The strike didn't pierce the suit, but the force sent her toppling into the rock garden behind us.

The creature was relentless, but it wasn't a mindless killing machine. It was making very precise movements, thoughtfully calculating its every decision. It could have lashed out at me first, but it clearly didn't want me dead: it wanted to eliminate my friends so it could return me to Valeriya in one piece, as it had no doubt been instructed.

I was aware of my momentary reprieve, which afforded me a small window of opportunity – it would be brief, and likely the only one I'd receive. I ripped the machine gun from the magnetic strip on my back and took aim at its unblinking eye, squeezing the trigger until a splash of putrid black gel burst from its socket.

As it flailed blindly I was able to duck under a thrashing tentacle. The barb on the end boomeranged over my head and sheared the top off of several hedges, hacking down a tree in the process. I repositioned my weapon and fired until my clip emptied into its globular core. The mass seemed to consume the bullets. There was never an entry wound where they penetrated; the projectiles disappeared into the creature, and its skin closed around the slugs as if it was swallowing them.

Brynja had detached her machine gun and was emptying the last of her bullets into the monster, allowing me the chance to retrieve one of the shells from my waist. The three explosive rounds represented the last of our ammunition. I didn't have time to load one into the grenade launcher; the few additional seconds I required weren't seconds I could afford.

"Hold your fire," I shouted out in my mind. *"Save one last bullet."*

Brynja must have heard my call. She immediately relented, easing up on her trigger. She held fast, fearlessly staring down the barrel of her weapon as the tentacles regrouped and surrounded her, allowing her no room for escape.

I hurled the shell. The explosive round disappeared into the creature's gelatinous skin with a wet plop, just as the bullets had. Brynja seized the moment and opened fire with her remaining bullets. When her rounds connected with the shell it detonated, and the shape-shifter exploded from the inside out; the gooey mass burst like an overfilled water balloon, splashing waves of dark slime in every direction. Though somehow, in mid-explosion, the spattered mess began moving in reverse, like a video rewinding itself. Sinewy tendrils remained intact at its core, and the creature began to regenerate. Oozing chunks slithered back into place until, just a few moments later, the gyrating mass had rebuilt itself. And from the center of the mass, the oily black eye bubbled back to the surface.

As the tendrils came firing back towards Brynja she stood fast, locking her feet in place. A tentacle coiled around my waist, stopping me from rushing to her aid; two more snatched away our guns, snapping them in half.

Brynja never blinked.

The words *"Don't panic"* rushed through my mind, loud and assertive. They were hers.

"Wait for it," she insisted with icy calmness.

A roar bellowed from the hedges in the distance, followed by a burst of flame that engulfed the creature, consuming it with a single blast. It writhed and quivered, the gelatinous core charring black as it cooked in the unimaginable heat. The continuous stream of fire flowed from Melvin's jaws until the tendrils stiffened and snapped off, releasing their grips on our waists. With Brynja and I as bait, our manticore was able to circle behind the creature undetected, silently stalking his prey until he was close enough to burn it to a crisp.

As usual, Melvin cut things a little close. Although as I patted myself down, taking stock of my working appendages, I was hardly in a position to complain. Battling someone (or some*thing*) in Arena Mode is not unlike being on a flight – any one you can walk away from is considered a good one. Our friends weren't so fortunate.

Satisfied that its prey was no longer a threat, Melvin bit off the last of the flames. He belched out a cloud of black soot before padding across the stone pathway, dropping and rolling at Brynja's feet.

"Brynja, how did you...?" were the only words I could produce.

"The shape shifter," she said. "He saw you throw the explosive, and he knew it couldn't hurt him."

I stared down at the winged lion, who was purring like a house cat. "And when did Melvin start breathing fire?"

Brynja knelt and raked her fingers along the manticore's fuzzy blue jawbone. "I don't know, but it seemed like the only way to kill that thing was to dry it out and burn it. Guess we got lucky."

"I'm fine," Peyton said weakly. Her knees trembled as she stumbled to her feet. After toppling into the rock garden she'd been knocked unconscious when the base of her skull collided with a small statue. "Really, don't help me up."

I turned to see her patting at the back of her head. Rushing to her aid, I held her shoulders and gently pivoted her around to see where she'd been injured; Peyton's cotton-candy pink locks were streaked with crimson.

"It's nothing," she grumbled at the sight of my shocked expression. She looked down at her gauntlet, noticing her fingertips were dripping with blood.

"It's *not* nothing," I said, escorting her to the nearby bench.

Still dazed, Peyton sat and scanned the garden with glassy eyes, her lids fluttering, seemingly unable to focus on anything for more than a moment. "What happened, just then...and where's your pilot, Mac?"

Brynja lifted her boot, crinkling her nose at the sticky gobs of blood-soaked ooze that dripped from the sole. "Kind of everywhere, I think."

"Oh shit..." Peyton clapped her hands over her mouth and leaned forward as if she was going to vomit. I patted her back and swept her hair aside; the standard operating procedure when she'd consumed one too many rum and Cokes. She dry-heaved but didn't produce anything.

The stench of the charred shape-shifter, seeing the blood-soaked collage of random body parts, knowing the lives that'd been lost; it was making the bile rise in my throat as well. I couldn't say I'd seen worse, but I'd seen something comparable. I was saddened, but not horrified...and the fact that I *wasn't* completely horrified by what had just transpired made me realize that the previous Arena Mode had changed me, possibly in ways I'd yet to fully realize. The sights and sounds that haunted me were so similar that I felt like I'd already lived this moment a hundred times over.

Brynja strolled over to the bench where Peyton was still doubled over. "We need to get moving and find the pods."

Peyton sat upright and glared at her, eyes widened with disgust. "A person just *died*, you ghoul."

"So it seems," Brynja said casually. "And we'll be next if we sit here and pout about it." She waved for us to stand. "Let's go, princess. You too, Peyton."

"Aw, sick – what happened here?" McGarrity appeared from between the hedges, meandering down the winding stone path with no real sense of urgency. "It looks like someone cooked a giant octopus. Smells like it too. And what's with the giant lion thing?"

Brynja stomped down the walkway and jammed her palm into McGarrity's chest. "That's some convenient timing, Braveheart."

"Convenient?" He replied, visibly confused.

"Showing up once the battle ends." Brynja motioned around at the carnage that surrounded us.

A broad grin stretched across McGarrity's face as he strolled past Brynja, dismissing her accusation. He approached Peyton and I, carefully avoiding the pools of blood and the globs of burning slime. "I *just* got here. Relax." He stopped short of the bench and dropped his hands into his pockets. "I was searching the caskets that you guys missed out in the hills. I can't do *everything* myself, guys. Sorry I missed your barbecue, but don't be pissed with me just because you guys couldn't save everyone."

My right hand flew on impulse. My fist caught McGarrity flush on the cheekbone, rocking his head back. He reeled and massaged his jaw, spitting a wad of blood and saliva onto the tile at his feet.

Without warning he lunged forward and buried his shoulder into my gut, tackling me into a hedge behind the bench. Using what little mixed-martial arts training I recalled from last summer, I pushed him off my chest and kicked away, allowing me enough space to stand and regain my footing.

We squared off for a moment – teeth grinding, fists clenched – when Brynja stood in between us and shouted, "Enough!"

"What was *that?*" Peyton said sharply, glancing towards McGarrity, and then back at me. "Valeriya is picking us off. We can't afford to start killing each other and making her job even easier."

Peyton placed her hands on McGarrity's face, tilting it towards the light to inspect the damage I'd caused. It was in her nature to immediately run towards whoever was in pain – she'd done it her whole life, and it was at least in part why she'd become a veterinary student. And in a crisis (like most people) she felt most comfortable returning to what she knew. Whether she was acting on instinct or not, it still pissed me off.

I exhaled loudly and marched away. If I had to look at his pasty white face for one more second I was going to plant my boot into it.

Brynja jogged to keep up with me as more distance stretched between us and the warzone.

"There's something about that guy I don't trust," I grumbled.

"You mean there's something that you don't *like*," Brynja was quick to add.

"Stop reading my mind, Brynja"

From the corner of my eye I noticed her lips curling into a tiny smile. "Didn't have to."

McGarrity was a cocky, brash, self-centered dick – but what was eating away at me was the simple fact that he was right. I couldn't save Mac, and I couldn't save Chandler. Two more lives had been lost, and I was powerless, once again, to do anything about it. And maybe if McGarrity had been there, he could have.

CHAPTER TWENTY-THREE

The wide-open space beyond the hedges was a Zen garden, stretching the entire width of the castle's courtyard. A sea of sun-bleached pebbles filled the garden, all precisely raked into calm swirling patterns, each of them four grooves wide. It must have taken days to create this intricate series of patterns, if not weeks. There was a walkway comprised of dark rounded stones that led to a small patch of grass in the center. I carefully and deliberately ignored it. In my state of mind it was more satisfying to trample the garden, kicking apart the patterns with each angry step.

"We're burning time," Brynja said, following me through the stones. "I know he pisses you off but he's our best chance of making it to the tunnel."

"And *you* like this guy," I grumbled, turning to retrace my steps.

Brynja reached out and grabbed my shoulder, halting me in mid-stride. "*No,*" she said emphatically, "but I trust him. I've been reading him since he appeared in the rain forest. He's clean – the kid just wants to help."

"He's an asshole."

She nodded in agreement, before adding, "He's an asshole who can produce a giant sword by bending light...and in case you haven't noticed, at the moment we're a little low on firepower."

It was a fair point. Steve McGarrity was definitely an asset, but I worried that his recklessness – and complete lack of respect for the obstacles we faced – could get us all killed. He had no concept of the danger we were in. I could see it in his every action, and hear it in his every dismissive comment.

As a pro gamer, McGarrity likely spent every waking moment engaged in a virtual simulation of a swordfight or shoot-out. The blood, the bodies, and the loss of life – it clearly meant nothing to him; all he saw were clusters of pixels, and the option to re-spawn somewhere safe once his heath meter had been depleted. If this idiot wanted to commit suicide in pursuit of an adrenaline rush I honestly didn't care, but I had a responsibility to get Peyton and Brynja down to the tunnel and out to safety. I'd already lost too many people along the way.

"Make nice," Brynja said calmly. "He's on his way now, so shake his hand, fake a smile and act like you don't want to smash his face in."

McGarrity emerged from the hedges with Peyton, and Melvin padded along behind. The blue fur around the manticore's jaw was stained black; I assumed that he took a bite out of the overcooked shape-shifter before realizing that it wasn't the delicious meal he'd been expecting. They made their way through the Zen garden, and without a word I extended a hand.

Without hesitation, McGarrity stepped towards me and spread his hands wide, raising his eyebrows. "So are we gonna hug this one out, or..."

"Don't push it," I said coldly. He accepted my original offer of a handshake, smiling once again – the same self-satisfied grin that caused me to slug him in the first place.

"There," Peyton said sweetly, like a kindergarten teacher resolving a spat in a sandbox. "Doesn't it feel better now that you boys are playing nice again?"

"Maybe we can continue this rom-com a little later," Brynja suggested, tapping her wrist. "Ticking clock and all that?"

"Oh, right," McGarrity said, slapping himself in the side of the head. "I almost forgot. This was in one of the caskets I found out in the hills." He dug into the front pocket of his tattered jeans and yanked out an ancient pocket watch. He dangled it from the short chain and it glistened in the overhead light.

I extended an open palm and McGarrity dropped it in, allowing me to inspect it more closely. I removed my gauntlet and dug my fingernail into the narrow groove, flipping open the cover and exposing the watch inside. Tiny silver cogs meshed together, visible beneath the ornately designed hands – but they didn't move. I assumed the watch was broken, though I was about to discover that it was awaiting an external power source.

When light streamed into the face of the watch it glowed from beneath the gears, causing the hands to spin rapidly in opposite directions. I tilted the timepiece upwards and allowed additional light to flood inside. A rumble from beneath buckled our knees. The tremors rocked the entire castle, causing the walls to shake and dust to jar loose from the brickwork. A large cylindrical tube emerged from the grass at the center of the garden, tearing through the turf, just as the pods did on level one. But this cylinder wasn't a pod which would transport us to the third and final stage of The Spiral – it was much wider around, and twice as tall as everyone who surrounded it.

The brushed steel casing hissed and popped open, slowly rotating into several pieces before retracting back into the earth. The platform that remained was obscured by billowing white smoke (which looked somewhat like dry ice, as if it had been added intentionally for effect). The outline of a massive structure was beginning to take shape behind the veil of smoke. When it finally dissipated, a familiar sight remained. It was an exact replica of Fudō-myōō: the armored exoskeleton that Cameron Frost had worn into Arena Mode. The suit he'd been wearing when I ended his life.

"Holy shit," McGarrity whispered. "That thing looks even bigger in person."

Every detail was the same; the shimmering silver casing, the red circular discs emblazoned on its shoulders, the glowing power core embedded into the breast plate, and the two expressionless red eyes that peered out from its rounded helmet. The suit's design was another one of Frost's nods to his favorite culture; in this case, the fictional robots known as 'jaegers'. In Japanese cinema, jaegers were constructed to fight the oversized monsters that routinely attacked Tokyo, called 'kaiju'. The most well known kaiju was a skyscraper-sized lizard named Godzilla, but he was just one of many. Over the last century, every movie monster imaginable had attempted to demolish the small Pacific island; from giant moths to fire-breathing gorilla slugs, there was always a new threat on the horizon. And each time the threat appeared, a giant robot controlled by fearless pilots was there to fight it off.

The almost seven-foot Fudō exoskeleton was nowhere near the size of its on-screen counterparts – and unlike the jaegers, it required only a single pilot (most jaegers needed two, for reasons I never quite understood). Despite its slightly smaller scale, it was no less intimidating.

With a sudden jerking motion and the sounds of grinding gears Fudō burst to life, causing us all to leap backwards. It reached over its shoulder and snatched the long curved katana from its back, and its eyes, glowing a menacing shade of red, peered down at us.

"Welcome to the end of level two," Frost's digitized voice boomed from within the armor. "As you know, I elected not to participate in the second annual Arena Mode tournament, so unfortunately, I can't be there to join you on the battlefield.

I can, however, provide a worthy adversary: the crowning achievement of my company's robotics division stands before you, and it has been outfitted with an AI. It will be more than capable of testing your skills."

I scanned the surrounding area, and not a single pod was in sight. There was nowhere to run, and we had no alternatives. If we wanted access to the third and final level, we had to fight Fudō; and from what I recall, the monstrous exoskeleton had very few chinks in its eight-hundred pounds of reinforced armor.

The robot stepped from the circular pedestal and readied its sword, gripping the braided handle with both hands.

I tore the grenade launcher from my back and fumbled with the barrel, rapidly attempting to twist it apart and load one of the two remaining shells. I wasn't sure if the blast would be enough to stop it, but it would buy us some time.

"Without my guidance," Frost proclaimed, "Fudō will not have the same reaction time as I did, and will no doubt lack my grace and swordsmanship. However, as Miyamoto Musashi, the second-greatest samurai of all time once said, 'Today is a victory over yourself of yesterday; *tomorrow* is your victory over lesser men'. And remember that the only reason a warrior is alive is t—"

Frost's barrage of historical quotes was cut short when McGarrity produced his broadsword, carving through Fudō with a single swipe. The top half of the robot slid to the ground, arms still gripping the sword, while the legs remained standing.

McGarrity shot me a sidelong glance. "I don't blame you for killing the bastard," he said, "The guy never shuts the fuck up." He clapped his hands, and with a flash of light the broadsword was gone.

Brynja cautiously approached Fudō's bisected torso and prodded at its head with the toe of her boot. The glowing red eyes faded to an icy grey, and a few errant sparks popped and fizzled from inside the breastplate.

The circular disc where Fudō first appeared sank into the ground, replaced with a flat grey obelisk, engraved with the same handprint outline as the one we'd encountered before. I stepped towards it, and in the path between myself and the obelisk appeared a hologram. Once again it was Valeriya.

"How are things going, Matthew Moxon?" Her tiny pink lips twitched at the corners as if she was suppressing a smile. She resisted, though the gesture would have been unnecessary; her eyes told the story. She was gloating, content with the emotional damage she'd caused me and everyone I swore to protect. "The shape-shifter made for a good show, although the Fudō armor was...disappointing. I expected more from the mind of Cameron Frost."

"Sorry you didn't get to see more people die," Peyton said sharply.

Valeriya took a few short steps towards Peyton and gazed upward, brushing the long platinum curls from her face. "You misunderstand me," she said politely, her eyes widening; she acted as if her feelings had been hurt by the accusation, though I doubted that was the case. "It is not death that pleases me. It is justice."

"*This* is justice?" Peyton shouted incredulously.

"It is the only kind left," Valeriya replied swiftly, turning her gaze towards me. "It is all we have. People like Matthew Moxon, the elite, have more wealth than entire countries. He does what he wishes: he buys and sells the poor at his leisure, trampling the small without looking underfoot, and even kills those he—"

"Save the propaganda," I interrupted. "The idiots in the Red Army might eat this shit up with a spoon, but you're not going to convert anyone down here."

"You might be correct," Valeriya said. "Although I wonder what the ghost thinks about her chances of escaping with her life. Perhaps she can he persuaded." She turned her attention towards Brynja, strolling in her direction with her hands clasped behind her back. "It is not too late for you. Call off your creature, and return to the surface. No harm will come to you."

"No harm?" Brynja laughed. She crouched down to make eye contact with Valeriya's holographic projection. "Oh, that's rich. *I'm* the one who killed your brother, remember? And you're going to let me walk? Just like that?"

Valeriya nodded. "That is what my brother stood for. Love. Redemption. You can be forgiven if you simply ask for it. Just say the word, and you will have whatever you wish."

Brynja studied Valeriya's innocent face as if she were actually considering the offer. "And you'll sweeten the deal with some Kashstarter money, I'm guessing?"

"That is up to you...although this situation is drawing to a close, and there is no need to keep up appearances. I know – and the world knows – what you desire, and it is not financial gain." Valeriya's crystal-blue eyes flicked towards me, and back to Brynja. "He does not care for you. Not the way you want him to."

"What is she talking about?" Peyton whispered.

I shot her a glance and her eyes caught mine. My mouth opened, though I couldn't produce a word. It was too much to explain, and this wasn't the time. I shrugged and shook my head slowly, as if I was as confused by Valeriya's statement as she was.

Peyton frosted over, folding her arms tightly across her chest.

"The Red Army will welcome you with open arms," Valeriya said warmly. "Defect, Brynja. Join us, and you will have a chance to avoid The Nightmare. Avoid the pain and suffering of a slow, agonizing death." She motioned dismissively towards Peyton and I. "You are not a part of this group, and never will be. There is no need to die with them."

Brynja, surprisingly, remained silent. She stood and stepped back, gazing off into the middle distance.

"We're not for sale," McGarrity interjected, drawing Valeriya's attention. "And there's *nothing* you can throw at me that I can't crush."

Valeriya actually smiled. "You seem amused, Steven McGarrity – as if this is a game. This 'Spiral' of Cameron Frost's...it has been too easy for your liking?"

He barked out a caustic laugh. "This shit has been a walk in the park. I'd actually appreciate a real challenge; something to give the home viewers a little thrill." He motioned to nowhere in particular, playing to the simulcast audience that was watching. We had no idea where the micro-cameras were located, though we assumed they could be almost anywhere. He was likely gesturing towards at least one of them.

"The Spiral," Valeriya explained, "is locked into a set of pre-programmed events, or so I am told. I cannot stop the pods from arriving." Her expression darkened, and the tiny smile vanished from her lips. "But I can add some more 'excitement', since that is what you desire."

He nodded, waving her forward with both hands. "Bring it on, bitch."

I stomped towards McGarrity and thrust my palm into his shoulder, knocking him off balance. "Shut your goddamned mouth," I screamed. "She's not fucking around here!"

"No," Valeriya said flatly. "I truly am not."

His smile only widened. McGarrity opened his hands, and with a flash of light the broadsword burst back to life, extending six feet into the air. He tightened his grip around the hilt and swung it in a figure-eight pattern. "Ready when you are."

Valeriya's hologram reached forward, and her hand mimed the motion of adjusting a dial and pressing a keypad. Her body was being mapped, and projected in front of us as if she was standing just a few feet away, though her surroundings were effectively invisible. Whatever she was doing in The Spiral's control room was a mystery to us. At least for a moment.

The ceiling – which was essentially one enormous blue light bulb that stretched the length of the entire level – transformed from a brilliant powder blue to a deep, velvety black. We were immersed in a time-lapse video, where the day drifted into night in a matter of seconds; twinkling stars emerged from the darkness of space, and a crescent moon floated into the cloudless sky. From noon to midnight with the touch of a button.

McGarrity's sword flickered and dimmed. It remained intact but lost its brilliant shine. His smile, and his cocky demeanor, lost their shimmer just as quickly.

Valeriya turned and spoke to someone we were unable to see – possibly a technician assisting her in the Spiral's control room. She instructed that she would like to release the remaining units, and to ensure the facial recognition scanners were operational. She had to ensure that I was accurately mapped – she didn't want me killed during the operation.

"Take the offer," I said to Brynja. "Take it and get out of here now, before it's too late."

"And leave you here to die?" she shouted. "You're smarter than this. Her offer is bullshit and you know it. She'll just torture and kill me the second I hit the surface."

Valeriya's hologram stepped between us, gazing up at Brynja. Her eyes reflected an innocence that reminded me for a brief moment that she was still just a child. "Whatever you plan on doing, Brynja, you should do it now. My offer stands for only a few more seconds." Something in her tone almost made me believe her. Or in the moment, my brain ignored the 'tells' that I'd memorized, and used to read people's intentions – because I *wanted* to believe her. To believe that I could save Brynja by sending her up to the surface.

"Matty," Peyton said in a thin, panicked voice. "You *need* to see this."

I spun to see her pointing off into the distance. Her index finger was extended towards the darkness just beyond the castle walls. It was a pair of luminous red lights, rapidly approaching.

"It is too late," Valeriya said, shaking her head slowly. "For all of you. I know that you are a non-believer, Matthew Moxon. But if anyone else believes in a higher power, this would be the time to make your peace." And with those words her hologram winked off, further darkening the area around us. Her projection had been emitting a soft light that illuminated the grassy knoll, and now I stood in relative darkness with Peyton, Brynja, McGarrity and Melvin, who was bearing his considerable incisors at the approaching lights.

The glowing orbs brightened, and were joined by another pair in the distance. And another. And then another. And then dozens more appeared, and began to approach from behind us, and on either side.

The artificial moon that cast a pale glow on the courtyard began to reveal the origins of the lights as they drew closer. They were the eyes of Fudō units. A hundred of them, hovering over the castle walls, closing in on every side.

In unison, each one of them drew their swords.

CHAPTER TWENTY-FOUR

The pods hadn't even begun to surface. Registering each of us and climbing aboard would take minutes – three, maybe four. Optimistically, we had ninety seconds before the Fudō bots were on the ground, slicing away at everything that moved.

I loaded a shell into my grenade launcher and saw Peyton crossing herself, slowly moving her hand from her forehead to her navel, then from one shoulder to the other.

"Is this a good time to start praying?" McGarrity asked.

"Feel free," I shrugged. "It can't hurt." It couldn't help either, but I chose to keep that sentiment to myself.

People can believe whatever they want – Heaven, Hell, angels, gods – if it gives you a reason to get up in the morning or helps you sleep at night, then it's energy well spent. But if someone wants to wax intellectual about a divine creator who is by all accounts infallible, I always had the same response: the universe's one and only absolute is math. Which, coincidentally, was the only all-powerful force that could help us escape our current situation.

"How many of these things can we take out with only two rockets?" Brynja asked, her eyes flicking anxiously between my grenade launcher and the approaching bots.

She was asking the wrong question. "You should be asking how many rockets it'll take to blast a hole in the roof above us."

"We're at the center of this level," Peyton said, craning her neck towards the artificial constellations clustered overhead. "Above us is a *lake*."

I tilted the launcher into the air. "Not for long."

"You can't be serious," McGarrity shouted.

"These things are first gen," I explained. "Which means they're not waterproof. It's why there's barely a drop of water on this level." I had spent days poring over every single page of research on the Fudō armor; from hand-written notes to post-launch reports. Frost's ambitions to make the exoskeletons underwater and deep-space compatible were well documented, and he was preparing for a second-generation manufacturing run next year. Saturating these units with enough water – a few hundred million gallons, give or take – could be enough to short-circuit them. It was insane, even by the standard set by my previous plans, but at the moment it was our best shot at survival.

"Okay, we drown them." Peyton said breathlessly. "Then what?"

"We swim to the pods. Register *now*."

As everyone pressed their palms into the obelisk and identified themselves, I extracted the breathing devices I'd found in the rainforest level. "We stick close and take turns so we always have enough oxygen."

"Twenty seconds," McGarrity shouted, motioning at the horde of approaching Fudō units that had touched down on the edge of the Zen garden. They were now marching lockstep, shoulder-to-shoulder, forming a nearly seven-foot wall of armored mechanical terror. "Without light I've only got a handful of swipes left with this thing," he added.

As the pods slowly emerged from the grass I aimed towards the heavens, carefully calculating the center-most point of the level (the spot where the most weight would be concentrated from the enormous body of water.) I fired. An explosive round burst from the launcher and whistled towards the sky, connecting with the center of the roof. Glass shattered and mortar fell.

"Ten seconds," McGarrity shouted, stepping to the perimeter of the knoll with his sword drawn back.

Melvin roared out a stream of flames that did nothing to halt the marching phalanx.

My second shell hit its mark, blasting an even larger crater into the ceiling; it had blasted away significant amounts of the reinforcement, allowing a mild drizzle to rain down through a crack. The ceiling was audibly moaning, buckling as if on the verge of collapse, but it remained intact.

This was it. My calculations were off – I'd overestimated how many gallons of water were in the lake above, or the ceiling was reinforced more heavily that I'd anticipated...a hundred possibilities blistered through my synapses, but in the end it didn't matter. I was dead. Most of us were. The way to minimize our losses was to get as many people aboard the pods as possible, and hope the Fudō bots didn't finish us all amidst the chaos.

The first of the pods burst through the grass, and I pushed Peyton towards it, shouting for her to go. She clasped my hand, squeezing it tight, and her wide, panic-stricken eyes locked onto mine. There was nothing I could say that would have given her comfort in that moment – I'd lied to her enough, and adding one more to the list wasn't going to calm her nerves. I nodded reassuringly before she turned and boarded the cylindrical transport.

The robots were just beyond striking distance when a sudden rush of wind pressed at my back, nearly toppling me over. It was the force of Melvin taking flight. The manticore's dark wings expanded and flapped, pushing him directly towards the source of the spattering rain – with McGarrity riding his back.

The Fudō units followed them like moths to a flame. Plumes of smoke burst from their heels and they ascended as one, swarming close behind.

McGarrity never looked back. Once he reached the ceiling he leaped from Melvin's back, using the final swipe of his broadsword to open the precarious fissure. The slice was surgical. A violent tidal wave exploded from the opening, raining down like a broken water main.

When the ceiling burst the Manticore went into a steep dive, riding the crest of the wave. McGarrity gripped his mane with both fists, barely maintaining control during the descent.

Melvin landed just a fraction before the impact. His dragon wings expanded and acted as a canopy, shielding the pods and everyone beneath from the torrents of water and debris. He bellowed in pain when his head, back and wings bore the brunt of the shower.

The brutal downpour was over in a heartbeat; I blinked, and when my eyes snapped open there was darkness. The water flooded in on every side, and suddenly I was thrashed into a powerful undertow, flipped and tossed, bouncing along the floor of the rock garden.

Struggling against the current, I reached for my breathing unit and cupped it over my nose and mouth, sucking in the oxygen. For a while longer – ten seconds, a minute...it was impossible to tell – I watched helplessly through the darkness, unaware of my proximity to the grassy knoll and the remaining pods. In the absence of light my armor illuminated: its angular blue lines glowed brightly, providing me a measure of visibility. In the surrounding area I spotted pairs of red lights flickering and fading; the Fudō units were sinking, hitting the Zen garden like anchors tumbling to the ocean floor.

The faint outline of a handprint on the obelisk was glowing in the distance, and two remaining pods gave off a dim light just beyond it. The light indicated that there was still power; hopefully the units hadn't been damaged from the flooding, and were still fit to transport me to the third level. Peyton and Brynja's pods were already gone, the air-tight covers having sealed back over their pneumatic tubes.

I swam towards the pods with every remaining ounce of strength. Each stroke against the current was agony. As I approached the knoll, I was jolted by a heavy object slamming into my shoulder, knocking me into the obelisk. It was McGarrity's body, floating face down, being tossed by the swirling current.

I ripped the second breathing device from my belt and pressed it over his nose and mouth, quickly strapping it into place behind his head. My muscles screamed as I swam forward with McGarrity in tow, dragging him towards the pod. I pressed him into place, but he remained unresponsive. His lips were colorless, and his eyes had rolled to white. Bobbing gently inside the glowing pod, I shoved him once again until his back pressed into the sensor behind him, sealing the unit shut. The suction pulled it downward, along with several hundred gallons of water, and the force almost dragged me down with it.

By the time I'd locked myself into my own pod and the door sealed shut around me, my breaths became shallow and labored. My breathing device was running out of oxygen.

Locked into an upright coffin completely filled with water, I wondered if McGarrity had drowned. I wondered if Brynja and Peyton had made it down to safety. I wondered if Melvin had died in the undertow. And as my head became light and my eyes fluttered closed, I wondered if I'd survive the trip myself.

CHAPTER TWENTY-FIVE

Everyone bags on Aquaman. Part of it is the outfit – there's just no way a man can pull off an orange bodysuit. And most of it's because, in a comic book universe where heroes can fly, shoot lasers from their eyes and travel through space, one of his most impressive abilities includes being able to swim like a fish. Sure, he has his fans, but you're never going to walk into a store before Halloween and find a child clinging to his mother's leg, crying and begging for an Aquaman costume. The guy is like the anti-Batman: he's the antithesis of everything that's iconic and bad-ass in the comic book world. But admittedly, as I spent more than a minute rocketing through the darkness in a capsule filled with water, Aquaman's water-based superpowers no longer seemed so laughable.

I gasped when the door slid open, spilling my half-conscious body onto the pavement with a wet splat. With my cheek scraping the asphalt I inhaled, so deeply that I felt the lungs dilate inside my chest. It was a sensation so painful I thought I'd cough them into the street.

As I gulped down oxygen I was stricken with a pang of guilt. Mac, Chandler and Melvin were gone, and McGarrity might be dead as well – but in that moment I was just thankful to be alive myself; and, more importantly, that Brynja and Peyton had made it out before me.

I rolled onto my back and glanced from side to side, trying to regain my bearings. The sidewalk, the buildings, the streetlights – everything that surrounded me was eerily familiar. I blinked a few tears from my eyes, rubbing the sting away, and the details gradually drifted into focus. The entire third level was a re-creation of Manhattan; a replica of Arena Mode's inaugural battleground had been reconstructed in The Spiral, and I was lying in the middle of a replica of Times Square.

It wasn't all of Manhattan, of course. In reality, the affluent borough was eighteen square miles (though it was closer to thirty-four prior to the devastation caused by the tsunami of 2031), and I estimated this reproduction was a quarter of that size. It reminded me of Las Vegas's attempts to recreate the Eiffel Tower and the canals of Venice – the surrounding landmarks came as close to authenticity as humanly possible – just without matching the scale.

As I stumbled to my feet, Brynja's distant voice reverberated from inside my head. She was making contact with me from somewhere on the level. *"We're okay,"* she assured me. *"I've already found Peyton."*

I gave Brynja my location and she suggested I stay put. They had landed somewhere in the West Village and were already heading north. Ready to collapse from exhaustion, I didn't need much convincing. I agreed to hold my ground and await their arrival. Once we'd regrouped, we could scout the area for McGarrity.

I gazed around at the surrounding cityscape. It was still under heavy construction, and a number of the downtown buildings were in various stages of completion. The mammoth advertisements that adorned Times Square were all in place, but only about half of them were illuminated. A Coke bottle that occupied most of a skyscraper remained grey and lifeless, and 3D hologram projectors spun listlessly in the distance; without bulbs or a sound system, they served to do little more than provide the faint ambient noise of grinding gears.

So I ambled around and peered through dusty storefront windows, cupping my hands around my eyes to adjust for the darkness. They were shells. The interiors were vacant concrete cubes containing no more than the odd toolbox, a pile of sawdust, or a half-eaten sandwich abandoned by a construction worker.

Still soaking in my surroundings (and regaining my equilibrium after nearly drowning) I failed to notice the hologram that had appeared in the street. Near the location where I'd been ejected from the pneumatic tube was Valeriya, standing patiently with her hands clasped behind her. There was something about the way she carried herself; back straightened, chin leveled, and an icy stillness to her posture that made a definitive statement: *I have all the time in the world, and yours is about to run out.*

This battle, after all, was never about firepower or superhuman abilities. And realistically, a truce wasn't going to be negotiated since diplomacy was never on the table. This siege was always about tactics: a chess game where the attacker moved the right pieces into place, patiently awaiting her chance to topple the king. Sieges have worked this way for centuries: the raiding party enjoyed a distinct advantage because they were on the outside, with freedom of movement and access to the resources they required. While the castle's inhabitants – unable to leave due to the military blockade that surrounded them – watched helplessly as their rations gradually depleted. With weakened soldiers and crumbling fortifications, the attackers would fight their way in; or, if the defenders were on the brink of starvation, the white flag would be raised before the first sword was pulled from its scabbard. As far as Valeriya was concerned, sacking my castle was inevitable. And the clock, as it often was, remained my worst enemy.

"So many lives have been lost," Valeriya stated plainly, without any trace of remorse. "How many of your friends need to die before you surrender?"

I made my way to the edge of the sidewalk and sat on the curb, joints aching as I crouched. "Let's not insult each other with any more lies," I grumbled. "If I gave myself up you'd kill my friends just to spite me."

She shrugged; a lazy, half-hearted gesture, as if she were still making up her mind as to whether she'd honor her bargain. "Perhaps you are correct. There is no way for you to know if I am telling the truth. But believe this, God Slayer: you have run out of levels. The Spiral has come to an end."

We were just one step away from the end of The Spiral. And as far as I knew, Valeriya wasn't aware of the construction tunnel we were counting on for our escape. I'd erased all evidence of its existence, so she was likely convinced the lowest stage was nothing more than a dead end; we'd be rats in a cage, scrambling for our lives until The Nightmare captured me and disposed of my remaining allies.

I wasn't sure why Valeriya made the effort to contact me at this point. I guessed it was just another attempt to rattle me and shake my concentration. Either way, I had her undivided attention, and a few minutes to kill until Brynja and Peyton arrived. I took the opportunity to uncover a mystery that had been bothering me since I'd spoken with my lawyer. "I have to hand it to you," I said nonchalantly. "Transferring ownership of the land was pretty slick. You have no chance of getting arrested now that Fortress 23 is in its own country. Did you pay off politicians, or were they dumb enough to buy into your cult-leader bullshit?"

Valeriya remained silent. She was perfectly still, unflinching, for just a solitary heartbeat...it was a heartbeat too long. A small nod of affirmation quickly followed, but it was too late: she'd given herself away. There was hesitation floating behind her eyes. It was just the slightest, most infinitesimal indication that she was searching her memories for an explanation. Of all the emotions human beings are capable of experiencing, the most difficult to conceal is confusion. She *didn't* facilitate the land transfer, making me the proprietor of my own country. She wasn't even aware it had occurred. My question had been answered, and it had been replaced by two more: if Valeriya wasn't behind the transfer, who was? And for what purpose?

Without warning her hologram winked off, leaving me alone in the street once again.

I wandered around for a few moments, searching storefronts for a casket, or anything else that could pass as a makeshift weapon. I no longer had a firearm or any explosives, and the stun-guns built into my gauntlets were on the fritz. I tried to activate them as a test; the left one resulted in a few sputtering blue sparks followed by a plume of smoke, and the right once remained functional, but had only a single charge remaining. The suit was water resistant, but completely submerging the electronics for so long had evidently caused some damage. Last month it had occurred to me that I probably should have included some underwater drills while I was in the testing phase, but at the time I had more pressing matters to attend to (most of them being comic book or Lego-related).

I scoured some abandoned workstations. A few oversized wrenches and crowbars seemed too cumbersome to be effective weapons, so I continued my search, wandering south until I noticed a squat, red-stoned building wedged between two larger ones; there was a poster that depicted a beer stein plastered above the wooden door, which was slightly ajar. Watery footprints led from the sidewalk through the entrance and into the darkness. I immediately knew who was inside.

The hinges creaked as I pushed the door, casting a stretch of light into the dusty room. It was a makeshift pub. Folding metal chairs were loosely arranged around overturned crates that doubled as tables, and the floors were littered with empty bottles and cans. And at the bar – the only authentic piece of furniture in the establishment – sat Steve McGarrity, stooped over a pint of beer.

"Not exactly the Flash, are you?" He turned and raised his glass, cocking an annoying grin. "What took you so long?" McGarrity looked no worse for wear aside from being soaked through from his t-shirt to his jeans. Just ten minutes ago I'd been mildly concerned that he might be dead, but here he was – alive, and as irritating as ever.

I circled behind the bar to find a trio of functional beer taps, and a row of mostly-clean glasses. I wasn't a beer drinker, but at that point I was willing to chug just about anything with alcoholic content – a near-death experience tends to have that effect.

Beer stein in-hand, I pulled up a stool next to McGarrity and took a sip. "So why are you here?" I asked. "It can't be *just* about the money and this 'ultimate freedom' thing that's supposedly sitting right below us."

"Naw," he smiled. "it's about the fame, too."

I just shook my head. I downed the first half of my pint in silence until he abruptly asked a question.

"Do you ever get high?"

"No need," I replied. "I'm high on life."

"I get high once in a while," he shrugged. "Not socially – just by myself, alone in my crib. I spark up, hook myself in and hit the IG-Net..." He paused for a moment, before adding, "that's the 'Interactive Gaming Network'. It's this virtual video game—"

"I'm not *that* old," I interrupted. "I know what the goddamned IG-Net is."

"All right, all right..." he said, holding up a hand in mock surrender. "So a few months ago I'm hooked in, buzzed, just grinding away for a couple hours in a deathmatch. It's this *huge* map, man – this thing stretches like forty square miles. Me and some teammates are hiding in the trees of this alien jungle with our laser cannons locked and loaded, just waiting for a horde to come sweep the area. We had time to kill, so we were swapping war stories over the coms."

"Uh-huh," I said flatly. "*Video game* war stories?"

"Right," he said without missing a beat. "So that's when one of my teammates starts babbling away about this thing called the Schumann Resonance."

I nodded and took a short sip. "Spectrum peaks in the Earth's E.L.F. I've heard about it." I figured I must have heard just about *every* scientific theory, regardless of how inane or wildly unfounded. Reading old science journals and scouring holo-forums for data was one of the things I did with my spare time in lieu of having a functional social life.

"Right!" he shouted, growing more animated. He seemed legitimately energized by the notion that I was aware of the theory. "The world's Extremely Low Frequency something or other. Earth is actually slowing down because of a shift in the magnetic field – which means that time feels like it's speeding up."

"Theoretically," I added with a heavy dose of skepticism.

"Yeah," he conceded. "In theory. So I log out of the game and start researching...I'm up all night reading about time, perception, how people all over the world feel like time is speeding up – and then it hits me: I'd been feeling it all along! Time *is* actually moving faster."

"*Or*," I said, "and I'm just guessing here, you were smoking some really good weed."

"Maybe," he continued, "but if time really *is* speeding up, then shouldn't we be doing something about it? Shouldn't *I* be doing something?"

"And coming here was your solution?"

He plunked his empty beer stein onto the bar and pivoted towards me, and his eyes fired with an intensity that caused me to lean backward. "Dude, my life peaked when I *was fifteen years old*. Do you know how depressing that is? I was IG-Net champion three years running, and already had millions in the bank."

"So you were a teenage millionaire...sounds awful."

"You don't get it," he continued. "By the time I finished high school I was forced into retirement. My reflexes were shot...these new kids on the circuit were *destroying* me. So after I quit playing pro I spent *years* just sitting around, getting high – and then I find out I have superhuman abilities. What's my reaction? *Nothing.* I literally don't do a single thing with my powers.

"That's why the Schumann Resonance changed everything for me. According to this scientist, time has sped up *so* fast that twenty-four hours actually *feels* like sixteen..." McGarrity paused for dramatic effect, as if waiting for my expression to change.

I didn't flinch.

"That's like, a *third* faster," he added.

"Wait..." I dumped a cup of old peanuts onto the bar's grimy surface and sorted through them, dividing them into piles. "Yup, your math checks out."

"So if I'm twenty-one," he continued, "that's halfway to forty-two. But it'll only *feel* like fourteen years to get there. How crazy is that?"

I nodded in agreement. "*Something* is definitely crazy."

"So," McGarrity declared, throwing his hands in the air, "I figured, 'What the hell, I can't sit here forever'. I'm twenty-one, and in fourteen years I'll be forty – which is *insanely* old. Then I see you kicking ass on Arena Mode, and it hits me: *this is it*. If I enter one of these tournaments I can go on a *real* adventure and use my powers. I can get out of the virtual world and into the real one – I can finally *do* something."

I wasn't sure if I agreed with his logic, or even remotely followed his line of thinking, but who was I to argue with inspiration?

McGarrity circled back around the far side of the bar and re-filled his pint to the brim, letting the foam pour over the rim and into the dust-filled sink. "Hell, man – if I die right now, all this will have been worth it. I fought a giant rock monster. I rode a manticore through the air and brought a lake down with a slash of a sword. Who knows what I'll fight next? And if we make it out, this is just the first chapter of my story – this is the *beginning* for me."

In that moment I realized that as much as I *thought* I hated McGarrity – and as much as I envied his powers – I truly admired his conviction. This kid was young, and strong, and radiated with a confidence that was once as much a part of me as my own skin; and now, approaching thirty-years-old, I felt like a husk. It was as if I'd been hollowed out by nothing more than the passage of time, and in the fleeting years of my twenties, every ounce of hope and enthusiasm for what my life might have become was methodically gutted, scraped from my insides and discarded. I'd been eviscerated so gradually that I never felt it happening.

The tumor that had been pressing against my brain for most of my life had given me some incredible gifts. My IQ was off the charts; problem solving, mathematics, a photographic memory...I could calculate cube roots faster than a calculator, and recall pi up to twenty thousand decimal places. But making a simple decision – like getting out of my recliner and doing something worthwhile with my existence? Apparently that wasn't part of the super-genius package.

Who knows what happened. Maybe the neurons in my hippocampus that controlled emotional response had been dulled, or were suppressed by the presence of the tumor. Maybe the mass prevented me from having the same kind of awakening that would have inspired me, or motivated me, or spurred me into action. Or maybe due to a chemical imbalance I was actually *incapable* of feeling the sense of urgency that everyone else felt.

McGarrity's hubris once again reminded me of Kenneth Livitski, and the reckless behaviour that landed him in a coma. I didn't want to see another kid get his life slashed to pieces because he lacked a grip on reality. Although when I saw McGarrity leap into action without hesitation, I wasn't frustrated with his behavior, and I wasn't angered by his recklessness – I was actually nostalgic for a time when I felt young and vital enough to be that careless myself, and that I never let loose and actually *embraced* it; those years were squandered as I immersed myself in fictional worlds, avoiding every possible outlet that could lead to some sort of adventure or personal growth.

I was a billionaire, and every cent I had couldn't buy back that time. I couldn't travel back and reclaim the moments that I should have experienced. Watching McGarrity live out his dream was my epiphany. I just didn't know it until now.

Brynja and Peyton came through the door just as McGarrity took his first swig. "Aww, did the boys hug and make up?" Brynja said with a condescending lilt, pouting her lower lip for effect.

"I refuse to dignify that with a response," I said flatly.

"We have some good news," Peyton replied with a beaming grin. She approached the bar and dropped a flat, circular device on the surface. It was a portable com – the first-gen design that projected a flat two-dimensional screen. "I already tried it out, and it works!"

I couldn't help but share her enthusiasm. We hadn't received any new information from the surface in quite some time, and the second London unit was lost in the flood on level two. Without access to holo-forums and simulcasts we were essentially in the dark. This was our chance to see who – if anyone – had reached the third level, and what type of opposition was being mounted at The Fortress.

Flipping open the com immediately triggered a faded ten-inch screen that flickered above the bar. I scrolled to the nearest news station and, as expected, helicopters were hovering around Fortress 23, affording us a bird's eye view of the entire surrounding area.

It had been abandoned.

Some supplies remained; tents, crates, a few Soviet flags jutting from the snowy landscape. But there wasn't a single soldier to be seen. Every single member of The Red Army was gone, along with their vehicles, weapons, and – I assumed – their leader, Valeriya Taktarov.

"I smell bullshit," Brynja snapped. "This is a Trojan Horse. They're hiding, trying to get us to return to the surface."

I scratched at the back of my hair, squinting at the low-resolution images flickering on the screen. "No, I don't think so. Valeriya had no way of knowing we'd be watching."

McGarrity leaned in to get a better look at the screen. "Maybe they just got spooked."

"Law enforcement?" Peyton guessed.

I shook my head. "They had enough firepower to take out every cop in the province. I think it was something bigger."

And as the words spilled from my lips a realization set in. There was only one way that I could suddenly become the proprietor of my own country in such a short span of time, with no intervention by my lawyers. And there was only one reason why it would be fast-tracked to today, of all days. It was no coincidence.

I stood so fast the chair flew out from beneath me. "They're going to nuke The Fortress."

"*Nuke*?" Brynja shouted? "Who's gonna do it – America? Won't Canada frown upon that? Being nuked?"

"They won't be bombing Canada," I explained. "The land being hit is now a sovereign nation – it's *my* country. No one gets their toes stepped on, and no treaties are violated."

"Why would they do that?" Peyton blurted out, wild and panicked. "This is insane!"

"Not really," McGarrity said as he flipped through the simulcast stations. Tokyo, Moscow, Cape Town, Berlin...one city after another was falling to looting and riots. The wildfire that began on America's East coast had spread throughout the world, and every major city was now engulfed in flames. "If Mox gets vaporized it might calm things down."

Valeriya's influence continued to embolden her followers, and their numbers were only growing; based on the simulcast footage, it was becoming apparent that law enforcement would be unable to contain the sheer number of protestors in most urban areas, leading to widespread chaos (and possibly a full-scale revolution in areas where the local population was especially well-armed – the ultimate doomsday scenario for any established government). The empty promise of Russia's Son rising from the ashes would remain unfulfilled in the event of my death, and the US government knew this as well as I did; angering Valeriya's followers was the best way to turn the tide.

It was a no-lose scenario: ridding the world of The God Slayer was their best chance at quelling the violence, and returning things to the status quo.

Brynja leaped to her feet and motioned towards the exit. "Isn't this usually the part where someone says 'Let's get the fuck out of here?'"

"We're almost at the tunnel," I said. "If we hurry we might be able to escape the blast zone."

With a few long strides I sailed across the bar and flung open the door. Peyton, Brynja and McGarrity followed closely behind as I sprinted into the street, where we were came face-to-face with a woman. A slender, serpentine figure with flowing raven hair and a matching dress. I caught a brief glimpse of her features, but they quickly faded from my memory...because everything I'd seen faded away when I glimpsed her eyes. Her dark, chaotic eyes that dragged me into an endless void.

And in that moment, the threat of a nuclear strike became the least of my concerns.

PART THREE
RECOMPENSE FOR TRANSGRESSIONS

CHAPTER TWENTY-SIX

"I would tell you my name," the woman said in a low, otherworldly voice, "but you already know it."

I nodded without averting my gaze. I couldn't have looked away if I'd wanted to.

Her eyes trailed over to my friends, who stood frozen behind me. "You may have a moment with them."

"A moment to what?" Peyton shouted.

I turned and placed my hands on her shoulders. "To say goodbye."

"No, no, no," she pleaded. "I need more time. I can't...it's too fast. This is too much..."

"You're the strongest person I know," I whispered. "And time is something I can't give you. But no matter what happens next, I know you'll make it out. Lead them to the tunnel. Don't wait for me."

Peyton was incredulous. "Don't wait? Have you lost your mind?"

The Nightmare had given me an ultimatum; she burned it into my mind with a single glance. "If I don't face her alone, right now, she'll take all of us. This way you can get a head start and find the exit. Before..." I trailed off, opting not to mention the volley of nuclear weapons that were probably en route to this location, poised to bury the entire Spiral under a billion tons of radioactive steel.

Peyton bit down on her lip and took a deep breath, exhaling through her nose. She blinked slowly. When her eyes opened they were infused with a new sense of resolve. "Fight her," she said. "With *everything* you have. You can do this."

Brynja gave me a reassuring nod and tugged gently on Peyton's arm. They both knew it was time, and precious moments were ticking away; moments we couldn't to squander.

"I won't make you say it," Peyton said, the words catching in her throat. "But, if you were *ever*—"

"Since the moment I met you," I interrupted. "and every moment afterwards."

The next few seconds were a blur, and my memories began to fragment. I remember a quick kiss from Peyton, and then swirling...I was tumbling through the vacuum of space, plummeting towards nowhere at incredible speed. I didn't realize until later that I had been standing completely still. My feet were planted on the ground while an egg formed around me, massive and expanding. It's shell was opaque, all-consuming...the darkness swarmed in and swallowed me whole.

And then, without the aid of any light source, she illuminated before me. The Nightmare – Grace Weaving. Whomever or whatever she was, her superhuman ability had never been fully revealed or explained; even those who witnessed her attacks were left with no clear memory of what she's done. Oddly, in that moment, it was my curiosity that filled my mind more than concern.

"You want to know how I do it," she asked. I didn't need to speak – she was intuiting every thought as it drifted in and out of my mind.

I nodded.

Weaving produced a paintbrush from thin air and swirled it, altering her physical appearance with an elegant looping stroke. "I am a creator," she explained. The Nightmare was no longer the raven-haired mistress of death that had first appeared before me. She was just a girl, like any young, auburn-haired girl you'd pass on the street, without any distinctive features that would stand out in your memory. "I design myself, and I design my surroundings. You see only what I want you to see."

"And how do you—"

"Kill people?" She interrupted. "I don't. I have never taken a single human life. It's not in my nature."

"Then what is?" I asked.

"Fear. It's what destroys people – eats away at them, stripping away everything their life might have been. I simply open the door. Once their fears take hold, the physical representation of their worst nightmare takes form. And," she added with a twitch of a smile, "it's usually quite painful. Let us begin."

With a swirl of her paintbrush she became my father, enormous and looming, towering above as if I were a five-year-old boy. He scolded me, his angry words slamming into my eardrums. I saw a vision of myself: crouched, cowering in the corner of my room as I always had, waiting for the storm to pass.

Another brushstroke created the vision of my best friend, Gavin. The young, accomplished man whom I'd always admired, but whose presence was a constant reminder of the potential I had wasted, and the years I would never get back. It was relief to see him, but my feelings of inadequacy quickly bubbled to the surface.

And then she became Cameron Frost. A walking, talking corpse, bleeding profusely from a gaping wound in his throat – the hole I'd blasted before winning Arena Mode.

All of the fears from my past, present, and future had been put on display. Every insecurity. Each regrettable moment. They were all manifesting before me, more vivid than my most horrific nightmares. Weaving had stripped away my armor, and struck me with the raw, unfiltered torment of each one, forcing me to absorb their full impact – though not for the first time. And in light of recent events, my fears seemed like trivialities.

"I think we might be at a stalemate," I said.

"I think not," she declared, brimming with confidence. With a swirl of mixing paint she resumed her previous form, dark and slender. "There is something deep within you...something that consumes you while you lie awake at night. What do you *fear*, Matthew Moxon? Let it wash over you, and choose the instrument of your death."

I just shook my head. "My fears won't manifest into anything. Stabbed, shot, burned, sitting through the Star Wars prequels for all eternity...none of it scares me. Because I know exactly how my story ends."

I began speaking in a mixture of thoughts and words, exposing my innermost secrets. "When they went in—"

Her eyes widened. "They didn't get it all."

I shrugged. "You'd think a billionaire could get better treatment."

"In Argentina...you wanted them to give you powers. Make you like us."

"That's right," I sighed. "The neurologists went in looking for whatever acts as a catalyst. They found something else."

"How long?" She asked.

"Months. Years. No one knows. The miracles of science, right? They can tell you the show is over, but not when the curtain is gonna fall."

"You truly don't fear it." It was a statement, not a question. She was intrigued, and genuinely fascinated.

"Not anymore. Because she's going to make it with or without me."

The Nightmare's black painted lips curled into a smile. "You don't deserve her."

I let out a short laugh. "My brain is dying but I'm not an idiot. I've known that all along."

"Without fear," she said plainly, "there is nothing more I can do. I have no power over you."

"Sorry to disappoint."

The Nightmare's hair, eyes and dress bled into the surrounding darkness, and the rest of her quickly followed. I heard the echo of her final words as soon as she'd disappeared. "I am not the one who will be disappointed."

The egg began to crack, allowing the lights from Times Square to penetrate the core, seeping through one ray at a time. With a pressurized pop the thin black shell burst from around me, raining down shards that dissipated as they fell.

CHAPTER TWENTY-SEVEN

They were frozen, locked into poses like eerily-lifelike replicas in a wax museum. Brynja's hand rested on Peyton's shoulder, and McGarrity looked on from behind.

And, somehow, when the egg shattered, I had resumed my previous position as well: I was face-to-face with Peyton, holding her in my arms, with our lips just inches apart. When I drew back we all blinked and shook our heads, suddenly refreshed and alert.

"Where is she?" Peyton asked, gazing curiously around the abandoned streetscape. The Nightmare was nowhere to be seen. At the mid-point of the intersection where she'd once stood was a flat, grey obelisk protruding from the asphalt, with the familiar glowing handprint, inviting us to register. The gateway to the fourth and final level was finally within our reach.

I wanted to tell them what had happened – how my confrontation with The Nightmare had ended – but there was no time. I raced towards the obelisk. When I placed my hand into the outline and spoke my name, Cameron Frost's booming digital voice congratulated me. I'd won. My name and face appeared in the sky, plastered across the rooftop like one of the garish advertisements that were a trademark of uptown Manhattan. As the first person to register on the third and final level, I was deemed the sole survivor, and would be granted access to the 'ultimate freedom' in the Hall of Victors as my reward.

A moment passed and nothing happened. No pods arrived, and no transportation to the lower level presented itself. I scanned the intersection until the double doors of a pizzeria across the street flew open, sending a shaft of golden light across the pavement.

We all approached cautiously. Once we reached the sidewalk, we realized the light source was emanating from an elevator; it was an ornately decorated lift with a metallic bronze interior. When we stepped aboard, I pressed the sole button on the dash, closing the doors and triggering our descent.

After a short freefall the elevator gradually lowered to a stop, and the doors slid open with a soft ping, revealing the bottom level of The Spiral. The hall, which was half-built, had a distinct Roman theme; towering columns, marble statues, and leveled seating that stretched in an oval around the perimeter. Hundreds of spectators would be able to watch the event from this area on towering holo-screens, and could greet the winner when he or she arrived at the Hall of Victors.

On a raised platform encircled by four towering white columns sat the 'ultimate freedom' that Cameron Frost had boasted about: it was a jet. A short, angular craft that shimmered like gold under the stadium lights. It was ultra-modern, like a concept drawing that had been realized in its early test phases. With short wings and no visible engines, I wasn't sure how the craft would even take flight; for all I knew it was a replica, and not even the finished prize. Much of the hall, beyond the seating and columns, was nothing more than unfinished scaffolding and piles of wood – most of it still strapped to skids that had been unloaded from abandoned forklifts.

"*Nice*," McGarrity said with a grin, mounting the podium. He walked alongside the jet and ran his hand over the smooth surface. "I don't know how I'm going to get this baby out of here, but I've always wanted my own private jet."

"You guys," Peyton said, craning her neck in every direction. "He's right – we can't get it out of here. Because there *is* no tunnel."

The schematic we were shown prior to entering The Spiral indicated an exit that led from the west side of the fortress, connecting to the surface. It was nowhere to be seen. A pile of boulders stretched from floor to ceiling on the far side of the hall, barricading what I assumed was the mouth of the tunnel. There must have been a million tons of rock sealing it off. It was likely a security precaution, built into the construction team's contract in the event of their dismissal – and unfortunately, the structural change was never logged into the fortress' database.

"We're sealed in," Brynja said gravely. "It's game over."

"There has to be another way out," Peyton shouted.

A shockwave reverberated through the room, sprinkling plaster and dust down around us. The entire foundation shook, cracking the concrete floor beneath our feet. The first bomb had made contact with the fortress. It was collapsing, one level at a time.

CHAPTER TWENTY-EIGHT

"It's no use," McGarrity shouted. He was hacking away like a lumberjack with a six-foot axe made of light, breaking chunks of rock away from the mouth of the collapsed tunnel. "This is taking too long. It'll take days to chop through this shit."

Another blast rocked The Spiral.

And then another.

More plaster fell from the unfinished ceiling, along with a lighting rig. The bulbs smashed into the levelled seating, and a length of metal scaffolding followed. The floor shook so violently that Peyton nearly fell over, holding my hand for balance as she stumbled.

"We're running out of time," Brynja screamed, kicking a pile of rocks across the hall.

"Wait," Peyton said, carefully studying the shimmering gold aircraft that sat atop the podium. "Frost kept calling the prize 'the ultimate freedom', right? Maybe there's more to this jet than we think."

McGarrity's axe faded away, and he joined us in the center of the hall where the jet was located. "Like what?" he asked between heavy breaths. "If it can shoot missiles, maybe we can blast our way out?"

I had my doubts that Cameron Frost would present the winner of Arena Mode with a jet that was armed with military grade weapons, but stranger things have happened. In my time living at Fortress 23 I learned to never underestimate him; when it came to ingenuity – no matter how twisted or immoral – Frost never ceased to amaze.

I pressed my palm into the side of the jet and a door slid open, completely seamless in its smooth golden exterior. We climbed aboard and into the cockpit. When I took the pilot's seat I was overwhelmed by the sheer number of buttons, levers and touch-screens that spread across the panel. Scanning the dashboard, I was deciding where to start when another blast rocked the fortress, toppling a number of marble columns around us.

The overhead lights flickered, and across the room I spotted water seeping through the elevator we had arrived in. The Spiral was on the verge of collapse, and the flooding we'd caused on the second level was now making its way downward. It occurred to me that the room we were in – The Hall of Victors – was by far the smallest in The Spiral; it could have fit inside of the lake on level one several times over. That much water would flood The Hall from top to bottom with plenty to spare.

We all exchanged a panicked glance. I immediately began pressing buttons and pulling levers, with no real understanding of what I was doing. I'd seen Mac do this in my own jet dozens of times, but this was a completely different configuration, and there wasn't a single label on the dash.

Another blast wave hit and Brynja had seen enough. *"Fuck this shit!"* She slammed her hand down on the controls, slapping her palm onto what must have been a touch-screen. The jet hummed with power and the cockpit lights burst to life, illuminating a golden glow all around us.

"Matthew Moxon," Frost's voice chimed from the dashboard. A small holo-screen materialized with an image of his disembodied head. "Congratulations, and welcome to your prize: the Ultimate Freedom. This is the prototype of my new jet, the TT-100. This machine will revolutionize the face of mass transportation, and within the next decade, will have a profound impact on the—"

"Enough with the infomercial!" I interrupted. "We *get* it – how does it *work*?"

"And does it fire missiles?" McGarrity added eagerly, leaning over my shoulder.

"I'm sorry," Frost's hologram said, "please rephrase the question."

"How do we get out of here?" Brynja said, impatiently rapping her fingers against the dash. As she asked the question, the Hall's overhead lights fizzled out, and the water began to rise around us. It was beginning to fill the room, and the tide was rocking the jet off of its podium.

"The TT-100," Frost explained calmly, "will transport the victor, Matthew Moxon, and any warriors he has aligned himself with to a destination of his choosing. But first, he must unlock the navigation by speaking the truth."

"The truth is that I'm pissed off," I shouted. "Let's go!"

"I'm detecting three additional competitors aboard the jet with you," Frost continued in a frustratingly slow cadence. It might have been the ceiling caving in around us or the rising water level that threatened to drown us in a cavernous tomb, but Frost seemed to be really taking his time – even more so than usual. "Your journey will begin once you've revealed a truth that you've been concealing from your allies."

I clasped my hand over Peyton's and looked into her eyes. For a split second I considered my answer – the secret I'd buried for months was like a drop of acid burning the tip of my tongue. There was no better time to spit it out. "The truth," I said, "is that I never completely trusted McGarrity...but as it turns out he's not a complete asshole."

The lie detector required a truthful statement, but didn't specify how personal it needed to be. Thankfully my response was acceptable and triggered the jet: a three-dimensional map of the world appeared, which replaced Frost's hologram. It was dotted with twenty-four red markers scattered across the globe in random locations.

"What now?" McGarrity said, squinting at the map.

I chose at random, pressing my fingertip into one of the glowing dots that floated above the South China Sea. The map disappeared with a high-pitched chime, and the cockpit lights darkened as if I'd powered down the jet. The faint hum of energy vibrated throughout the craft, but there was no indication it was going to take off (or blast its way through the collapsed tunnel, if that was even an option).

"What did you do?" Peyton asked, frantically flicking switches on the dash.

"Nothing!" I shouted. "What the hell was I *supposed* to do?"

A hole burst through the ceiling above the tunnel, pouring a fountain into the Hall. The sudden rush of water jerked the ship off its axis, sending us all crashing into the side of the cockpit. The jet was submerged within seconds, and the darkness closed in around us.

When I thought we were finished – just at the moment when I'd lost hope that we'd somehow escape The Spiral – something strange happened: a dizzying kaleidoscope of flashbulbs and violet streaks entwined our jet, blinding everyone in the cockpit. There was no sound, or even the faintest indication that we'd moved. When the light show faded we blinked the sting from our eyes and gazed out the cockpit window, stunned by the glittering orange vista.

We were hovering above the ocean, staring out at a sunset.

CHAPTER TWENTY-NINE

I don't often have thoughts that could be labeled as religious, though I have to admit, there was a moment when I considered we had died in The Spiral. That this was the afterlife, and we were about to be reunited with our loved ones in a celestial paradise. For just a millisecond I entertained that fanciful notion, and my soul-crushing cynicism melted away. Then I glanced over my shoulder and realized McGarrity was still here...it became painfully obvious that if a Heaven existed, I wasn't there.

The jet's autopilot system banked hard and descended, allowing us a view of our destination. The fading amber daylight spilled between a pair of towering rock formations, illuminating the water in a crystal blue cove. As we made our approach I noticed that the sun-bleached peaks, over-grown with lush vegetation, were not only part of the stunning landscape – they were part of a fortress. Like Fortress 23 in Northern Alberta, there was a small city built directly into the sides of the mountain range, spanning across the top of the entire chain.

A pair of three-winged aircrafts (likely drones, judging by their diminutive size) buzzed around the jet as we made our descent. Whomever this fortress belonged to, they were well aware of our presence.

We continued our gentle, downward path towards what was now a clearly visible hoverpad, which was encircled by a series of flat, dome shaped buildings, each with a bronze-colored rooftop that was serrated like a shell. The craft's landing gear extended beneath us and we touched down with a soft bounce, triggering the engine to power itself off.

The door slid open behind us, and a staircase invited us to step onto the tarmac.

I was the first to make my exit, followed by Peyton, McGarrity and Brynja. As we gazed at the bizarre architecture that surrounded us, we were approached by a cheerful young blond woman; she was shrink-wrapped into a gaudy yellow dress, with her matching yellow hair pulled back in a tight braid. She looked exactly how I remembered her.

"Welcome to Fortress Eighteen," she said with a song in her voice, wobbling towards us in her six-inch heels. "I'm Bethany Price. We don't get many visitors out here so this is *quite* a treat. Can I interest any of you in a refreshment? Teleportation can be very dehydrating from what I hear." She glanced down at her digital clipboard and poised her finger over the touch-screen, eagerly awaiting our drink selection.

"We've met," I said flatly.

"Really?" she replied, tilting her head slightly as she studied my features. "Well, that's a surprise. I never forget a face...and I'm sure I'd remember yours, cutie."

From behind me, I could almost hear the sound of Peyton's face creasing into a disapproving frown.

As if the moment couldn't get any more awkward, I decided to re-introduce myself. "Matthew Moxon. We met right before Arena Mode last year...you were producing the event." Her eyes remained vacant. "My *eyebrows*..." I explained, pointing towards them with both hands. "You told me I needed them 'shaped' before I went on the air – whatever that meant?"

"Oh, right!" she exclaimed, her smile brightening. "I got a promotion the week before, so that was my last day in the media department. I was transitioning into my new role here at Eighteen, and I flew out of New York just after the event kicked off." She trailed her eyes across the confused faces of my friends, anticipating some kind of a response. "So, don't keep me in suspense, you guys...Arena Mode – how'd you do?"

"I'm alive," I said with a shrug.

"I can see that!" she exclaimed, playfully cuffing my shoulder with the back of her hand. "Congratulations." Bethany scanned us once again, this time trailing here eyes from our feet up to our shoulders – no doubt perplexed by our body armor. "You're here to shoot a sequel to Tron, I'm assuming? Mister Frost never sent a memo about the fortress being used for filming, but I know he's been trying to acquire the rights to that franchise for quite some time."

"No, we're...it's actually a long story."

"*Well*," Bethany said, gesturing towards our shimmering gold jet, "Mister Frost *must* trust you all implicitly to let you take the prototype for a spin. We manufactured the TT-100 right here, you know. *Very* exciting. This is the only jet in the world that can teleport. Well, until next year when they go into regular production."

It occurred to me that Bethany was continually referring to Cameron Frost in the present tense, which meant that she hadn't seen the news in a *very* long time. "You didn't catch Arena Mode last summer," I said delicately.

She shook her head. "I've been here with the rest of the team for eight months, completely off the grid. Mister Frost feels that simulcasts distract his employees from their responsibilities."

I nodded and bit my tongue. Denying his employees even basic access to communications didn't seem out of character for Frost, but considering what I was about to explain, I figured it was better to keep that sentiment to myself.

"So how is he doing," Bethany asked cheerfully. "It's been so long since I've seen the big lug!"

"He's dead," I blurted out. *Shit.* Being delicate clearly wasn't my strong suit.

"Oh...okay." Her smile faded and she winced awkwardly. It was almost painful to watch. I had a feeling that Bethany's mouth was so used to being stretched into an artificial smile that it contorted like this as a default reaction. "Was it like...an accident?"

"No," I said casually, staring off into the distance. "I was sort of the one who killed him."

"Sort of?" she asked innocently. "Like...you didn't *mean* to?"

"Oh no, I meant to. It was pretty intentional, actually." She recoiled slightly, so I added, "But he was trying to kill *me* when it happened, so...you know. It's all good."

Brynja patted me on the shoulder. "Nice save."

"Oh...okay," Bethany repeated, now chewing on her lower lip. She wrapped both arms around her digital clipboard, hugging it against her chest. "So...that makes this a little weird."

"You don't know the half of it. Does anyone know we're here?"

"As in..."

"As in several million people and at least two governments want me dead, so the fewer people that know my location, the better."

Bethany shook her head. "No one knows about Fortress Eighteen. In fact, the location of *every* fortress is confidential, even to other employees. Our fortress is R and D."

"So aside from research and development, what else does...*did*, Cameron Frost have his fingers in?"

"Oh, a bunch of different things," she said with an awkward shrug, still clutching her tablet like a security blanket. "Fortress One is agriculture, Fortress Two is connectivity, Three is artificial intelligence, Four is space exploration...it goes on and on." She paused for a moment and took a breath, seemingly to re-focus her attention. "So, why are you all here again?"

As I spoke with Bethany, I wasn't aware that Peyton had wandered off in search of better reception for her com. She opened the small round device she'd located on level three of The Spiral, and had acquired a signal for a local simulcast. "Matty," she shouted, "you need to see this."

I jogged to the edge of the hoverpad where Brynja and McGarrity were already gathered, cupping a hand over their eyes to make out the images on the screen. Even though it was two-dimensional, and the colors were washed out against the setting sun, a picture was beginning to snap into focus. A crowd was gathering – hundreds, maybe thousands – outside of a hospital, surrounded by snow-capped evergreens.

The reporter was speaking Thai as the camera panned over the screaming mob, which was of little help – but I was able to discern a few of her words that were said in broken English: "Thunder Bay."

CHAPTER THIRTY

"We can't just rush back there without a plan," Peyton said, clutching my upper arm with both hands. "You know Valeriya will be expecting that."

"She's right," Brynja added. "We have no weapons and no strategy. She has an army."

We were finally safe, apparently beyond her reach. Valeriya Taktarov had no way to retaliate after being forced to flee Fortress 23, so she was making her final play – the only move she had left. She promised to make the people I love suffer, and that I'd be forced to watch them die; I had Peyton and Brynja with me, Gavin was nowhere to be found, and my sister and her kids were under police protection; the last person she could get to was Kenneth Livitski, who was clinging to life in a coma. I hated myself for not considering this option. With Valeriya's resources it was just a matter of time before she'd locate Kenneth, and in her mindset, she'd have no misgivings about executing a man who was lying defenceless in a hospital bed.

It was no secret that I betrayed Kenneth back in Arena Mode; ending his life before I could make it up to him would be the ultimate act of revenge. And threatening him, Valeriya was well aware, would be the most effective way to draw me out in the open.

"We can't expose you like this," Brynja said. "Think this through: as far as we know, the Canadian *and* American governments sanctioned your execution. You can't just waltz back there *now* – the cops might execute you before the Red Army does."

I was so incensed that I trembled. Part of it was rage, because I knew Brynja's assessment was dead-on. And part of it was teeth-grinding frustration, because there is nothing that I hate more than this kind of paralysis – knowing that something *has* to be done, and not having a logical solution to see it through. Raking my fingers through my hair, I considered every possible course of action. "Bethany," I said, "what kind of weapons do you have here?"

"N-nothing," she stuttered. "I mean, we're research and development, but nothing military-grade. Everything we're working on at the moment is for transit."

"There has to be security protocols," I snapped, throwing my hands apart. "Come on, *think* – there's nothing? Not even a guard with a sidearm?"

"Look at this place!" she said, her eyes darting around the perimeter of the hoverpad. "We're in the middle of an *ocean*. No one even knows we're here, and if any suspicious aircraft approach we cloak and go into lockdown."

I let out a frustrated groan and turned to my friends. "We've lost too many people today. People who didn't deserve to die. Kenneth, he's..." I trailed off, letting my head sag. The thought of losing him – especially like this – was twisting my stomach into a painful knot.

"I know," Brynja whispered, running her hand along my shoulder. She had forged an alliance with Kenneth inside The Arena as well, and knew better than anyone about the pain of letting someone go. She could be jaded when it came to losing acquaintances – almost to the point of being callous – but her armor was stripped away when it came to Kenneth. She'd be as devastated about his loss as I would.

McGarrity used the light from the setting sun to produce a glowing broadsword. "I can't let you go alone and hog all the glory. This shit is gonna be seen worldwide, so when you come out on top I wanna be there."

Whether he was doing it for my benefit or for his ever-expanding ego, I didn't care. Brynja and I desperately needed backup, and McGarrity was the cavalry. "Thank you," I said with a small nod.

"*And*," he added without missing a beat, "let's face it, Mox – without me you're kinda fucked."

I nodded again. "I appreciate your candor."

"Let me guess," Peyton interjected, "'You're a delicate tulip – stay behind and out of danger'?"

Pulling Peyton aside, I left Brynja and McGarrity to board the jet. "I was *going* to say that I need you to carry on here – just in case something happens to me."

"Carry on what?"

"This," I said, motioning around me. "The Frost Corporation...or whatever you want to re-name it."

"You want me to run your business?"

"No matter what happens in Thunder Bay, it's all yours now. Most of my assets will be in your name by the end of the week."

Peyton wrapped her hands around the back of my neck and leaned in, resting her forehead against mine. "This is *crazy*, Matty – what am I going to do with billions of dollars?"

I replied with a tiny smile. "What you *always* do: make a difference."

Her tired eyes fell shut. "I don't want this much responsibility," she whispered.

"And I don't want to be this chiseled and handsome, but—"

"We all have our crosses to bear," she said with a weak smile.

I glanced over Peyton's shoulder and spotted McGarrity, standing at the top of the jet's entrance ramp, frantically waving me in.

"You're the one," I said, brushing my lips against her cheek for what might have been the last time.

"And you're late," she replied. "We'll finish this discussion when you get back – now go save the day."

CHAPTER THIRTY-ONE

The trip from one side of the planet to the other took only seconds. The brilliant sunset over the South China Sea blinked away, replaced by a dull grey sky that blanketed Western Ontario.

Teleporting was not an exact science, according to Bethany – at least not yet. The TT-100 got us in the general vicinity of our destination, but we'd have to manually land the craft once we made our approach. The early morning sunlight that filtered through dense clouds and flurrying snow made visibility an issue, but fortunately we were able to borrow an experienced pilot from Fortress Eighteen. He agreed to stay aboard and hover back into the clouds, waiting until we signaled for an extraction. It was essential for our jet to avoid gunfire and superhuman entanglements. Without a functioning aircraft we'd have no way to escape, and I had no intention of making this a one-way trip.

We touched down on the hospital's rooftop hoverpad. The door slid open, and before the ramp could extend into place I leapt into the knee-deep snow and hurtled towards the staircase. I ran faster than I'd ever run before. Brynja was at my side and McGarrity followed closely behind, sword illuminated, screaming like a Viking prepared to sack a village. Within moments we were in the hall, sprinting towards Kenneth's room. A janitor – the same one I passed three months ago – mopped the floor in roughly the same location, this time with a pair of oversized headphones engulfing his narrow head. He didn't even look up as we flew by.

We rounded the corner and spotted Kenneth's room. Without thinking I threw open the door, and had stumbled several paces inside before I spotted them: Valeriya flanked by a pair of her henchmen, with assault rifles in-hand.

I didn't have time to react. The following events happened before I could draw a single breath. Shots rang out and my eardrums nearly burst; confined in a small room, the gunfire sounded like grenades going off inside my skull. The ringing in my ears was shot through with a frantic scream at my back. I spun to see McGarrity laying just outside of the room; his reddened t-shirt obscured his wounds, and a dark puddle expanded around him. Brynja was crouched at his side, shaking his motionless body.

With a twitch of her finger Valeriya invited Brynja to approach. She stood and paced slowly into the room, leaving a trail of crimson footprints behind.

"Close the door," Valeriya hissed.

Her henchmen leveled their guns, pressing the stocks into their shoulders.

I froze. My eyes flicked to Kenneth's hospital bed, and thankfully he was still breathing. The electronic device tethered to his comatose body was blipping quietly, and the pulsing red line on the wall monitor jumped with each heartbeat.

Valeriya, angered by Brynja's hesitation, snapped her finger towards the entrance. "Close. The. Door." She was biting off each word, grinding them between her teeth.

Brynja raised her hands and inched backwards, using a single digit to push the door closed until it latched. The guards looked twitchy, so she was careful not to make any sudden movements. As it swung shut I spotted McGarrity in my peripheral vision, and hoped that someone would tend to him – although after the sound of gunfire erupted down the hallways I doubted that any staff remained in the area. Either way, he wasn't coming to our rescue.

"Think this through," I said softly. "This is over. At the fortress you had immunity, but this is the real world. There'll be consequences."

"But not for you," Valeriya scoffed. "For the God Slayer there is only celebration and the spoils of victory."

I shook my head. "You think that's what I've been doing since Arena Mode? Partying like a rock star? That freak show ruined my life."

"Ruined *your* life?" she shouted.

"Yes," I fired back. "Since last summer I barely sleep. And when I do I see Frost, and your brother, and everyone else who died that day...I didn't want *any* of them to die, but there was no choice."

"You always have a choice, Matthew Moxon. That is what life is: a series of choices. They are a painful necessity of being a human."

"And of being a superhuman. Your brother went into Arena Mode knowing he might not come out." I took a small step forward and Valeriya's henchmen readjusted their firearms, just enough to let me know they hadn't fallen asleep at their posts. I locked my feet in place, careful not to move another muscle. "This is *over*," I repeated. "Walk away, and we'll do the same."

Valeriya shook her head with disgust. "If the two of you think I have come this far to let you walk away now, you do not understand my commitment. I would rather die than watch either of you experience one more second of happiness."

Her eyes were weary, but still burned with determination. I knew what she was about to do; it was the mission Valeriya could have carried out before we had arrived, but she'd patiently awaited the audience that she needed for the show to fully resonate.

"Don't..." was the only word Brynja could produce, her eyes darting towards Kenneth.

"You will have your executions," Valeriya promised, "but not yet. You need to feel what I felt before leaving this world." She marched to Kenneth's bedside and gathered his life support cables in her tiny hands. She paused and we made eye contact; her gaze lingered for a just moment, ensuring I knew exactly what was about to transpire – as if there would be any doubt. With a downward jerk she ripped the cords from his body.

She left only his heart monitor attached. The bouncing red line on Kenneth's wall monitor persisted, gradually weakening with every beat. We had no weapons, no back-up, and no plan...there was nothing left to do but stand witness, watching our friend slowly expire.

I dropped to my knees, and Brynja crouched at my side. The soldiers stepped forward and pressed the barrels of their guns to our temples. I didn't even flinch. I was still fixated on the dying pulse, watching the blips as they gradually came in longer intervals...and then, before long, the remaining heartbeats faded away. The red line flattened, and a continuous droning beep cut through the silence.

Watching Kenneth's chest rise and fall for the last time ripped out my heart. Tears rolled down my face and I silently begged him for forgiveness. It was my lie that put him here, and it was my fault this was happening; I could only imagine the pain his family would suffer knowing how he came to an end – it was almost too much to process. My only solace was that he wanted this; when Brynja read his thoughts, he asked for the plug to be pulled. I had no idea what kind of pain he was enduring in his comatose state, but at least it was over.

Valeriya smiled as I broke down. It may have been her age, but her expression didn't seem vindictive or malicious – it was almost a smile of relief. "This is it," she said, kneeling at my side. "This is what I have been waiting for. You believed you could save him, did you not? That one day he would walk again, and live a normal life. Now, you can die knowing you are a failure, and that the rest of your loved ones will suffer the same fate."

Police sirens blared outside the hospital, followed by a hail of gunfire. The authorities were no doubt responding to the shots inside the building, and were being held at bay by the Red Army. Valeriya was leaving nothing to chance – no one was getting inside.

The guards ordered us to stand, and I glanced out the window. The parking lot was overrun with Taktarov's followers, and a lone, bullet-riddled police car smoked in the distance.

"They await your trial," Valeriya said. "It is time to pay for your transgressions. Both you and the ghost."

I turned and began trudging towards the door, slow and resigned. Brynja followed, and remained silent; I expected her to say something telepathically – to convey some sort of emotion, or possibly formulate a plan for our escape. If she had an idea, she wasn't sharing it.

I locked my feet for just a moment, contemplating if I'd give Valeriya and the Red Army the satisfaction of a public execution. A gun barrel jammed my spine, pushing me towards the exit.

"*Move*," the guard instructed in a thick Russian accent.

Screw it. If I was going down, I'd go down swinging.

I spun and knocked the barrel aside. I pressed my gauntlet into the henchman's throat, shouting for the stun gun to activate. He convulsed and crumpled to the floor as electricity filled his body, dropping his AK-47. I snatched it off the floor just as the stock of the second guard's rifle slammed into my temple. James Bond always made disarming two people simultaneously look easy...I clearly hadn't earned my double-oh status.

I lost track of the following few seconds. My next memory was the sight of the hospital room's fluorescent bulbs spinning overhead. The concussive blow to my skull had blurred my vision and rattled my hearing. The guard who floored me drifted into focus; he was struggling to detain Brynja as he shouted instructions. His mouth was moving, but he wasn't producing any sound – his voice was being drowned out by a piercing chime. The ringing in my ears became a pulse; a powerful series of beeps that grew louder and closer together, like a rapid-fire heartbeat that shook the room.

I felt a rush of cold wind and the guard disappeared from behind Brynja, sailing out of view. The other henchman followed. Then I was yanked to my feet, stumbling to keep my rubbery legs beneath me, eyes transfixed on the snow drifting into the room. The guards had been tossed through the fourth-story window, and had landed somewhere in the parking lot.

My hearing snapped back like a volume knob being twisted from zero to ten. I spun to see Valeriya crouched against the wall, screaming that this was impossible, followed by something in Russian.

And standing above her was Kenneth Livitski.

Kenneth was wrapped in an electric blue body suit that glowed and pulsed with a life all its own. It was his homemade Living Eye costume on steroids: his gloves, boots, wrap-around mask, and the all-seeing eye logo emblazoned on his chest all radiated with an energy source that seemed otherworldly – if I'd seen it on film I would have sworn it was a digital effect.

It wasn't just Kenneth's new costume that was on steroids; his body had completely transformed. His physique was no longer frail and drawn out from months spent in a coma – he now was packed with lean muscle, healthy and vibrant. His posture even suggested a newfound confidence that I'd never seen in him before.

Kenneth extended his hand towards Valeriya, and her body shot upright. A glowing blue straightjacket materialized and latched around her, buckling its straps into place. She struggled for a moment before slipping and falling to her side with a painful thud.

As I regained my footing I teetered and swayed, still woozy from the blow to my head. Kenneth reached out and gripped my arm, steadying me. "You should have listened," he said bluntly, glancing down at the discarded pile of cords. His eyes flicked towards Brynja. "You both should have."

The energy from the sensors connected to Kenneth's body were disrupting his brainwaves, preventing him from escaping the coma – it was the only explanation. Like the Cerebral Dampening Units that the government used to limit superhuman abilities, the medical devices that kept him alive were simultaneously sapping his powers. He'd been imprisoned inside of his own mind with no way to escape.

"I—I didn't *know*," I stuttered. "I thought you wanted me to kill you."

"I'm *so* sorry," Brynja added softly. "We both are."

"That doesn't matter now," Kenneth said, glancing out the broken window. "Millions are waiting for your execution."

"So what are you going to do?" I asked.

"I'm going to change their minds." As he said the words it seemed impossible. But I knew, without any reservations, that he would pull it off. After everything I'd done to Kenneth and his family, he was still willing to do what he felt was right.

"I know I don't deserve your help," I admitted.

"You're right," he said. "And I'm not doing this to help you. I'm doing it for her." His eyes trailed over to Brynja. "She's finally stable, and she deserves a second chance. As far as the Red Army is concerned, she's as much a god slayer as you are. As long as they believe they're on a crusade to avenge Sergei Taktarov, she'll never be safe either."

"I'm just glad to have you back," I said. "And Kenneth, I will do anything to make this up to you. Just name it."

My words were immediately followed by a second hail of gunfire, this time coming from multiple shooters. Additional police patrols were arriving, and the death toll was rising.

With a burst of blue energy he exploded out the window, knocking Brynja and I off of our feet.

CHAPTER THIRTY-TWO

Media helicopters swarmed the skies while rioters, now in the thousands, rumbled below. The dissidents were undeterred by the increasing police presence: a SWAT team formed a wide perimeter around the parking lot, and reinforcements were pouring in.

Chants of "Avenge, Destroy, Rebuild" roared throughout the ever-expanding mob; fists pumping, flags waving, guns brandished openly in an act of defiance. They wanted blood. The first phase of their credo was about to reach its completion, and the promise of a new savior was moments away from being realized.

They no doubt expected Valeriya's henchmen to drag me from the hospital to face justice. I would probably have been expected to appear remorseful and penitent, or possibly ashamed that I was responsible for the death of the second coming.

I tried to imagine their surprise when Sergei Taktarov appeared instead; a glimmering spectral figure hovering high above, pulsing with raw energy. A vibrant blue light surrounded him, but that small detail was the only give-away. Kenneth's re-creation was pitch-perfect, right down to the last detail. As far as the live crowd and the millions watching around the world were concerned, this was their savior: Russia's Son had risen from the dead, just as his sister had prophesized, and he was about to launch a revolution.

"I have returned," Taktarov boomed. His voice was a thunderclap that resonated across the city, as if amplified by a thousand speakers. "Although I can remain on this plane of existence for only a short time."

The screaming mob fell silent. Guns clanked to the pavement, flags lowered; every eye was transfixed on the floating apparition. Some were recording the event on their wrist coms, but no one spoke a word. Even the SWAT team had discarded their shields and batons, awestruck by Taktarov's presence.

"My sister," he began, "promised you an age of renewal, and that my presence would be the catalyst. She was mistaken. Saddened by my passing, Valeriya gathered an army – all of you – in the hopes of avenging my death. She had no plans or desire for a revolution to follow. She was grief-stricken, unable to cope with my death. Please do not blame her...those with the purest intentions are often the ones whose judgement is most clouded.

"Do not blame Matthew Moxon or Brynja for my death. They are not 'god slayers' any more than I am a god. And do not mourn me, or seek retribution. Vengeance leads to darkness, which will further decay a world that can ill-afford any further corrosion. I died of my own arrogance...I know that now.

"I have not returned to lead you; I am here to deliver a message – nothing more: do not carry out acts of violence in my name. Do not lash out with hatred, bigotry and anger, passing the responsibility of your own thoughts and actions onto a man who wishes for nothing more than unity.

"I have made mistakes. I revelled in my own youthful arrogance, and I took lives with impunity; if I truly did possess the powers of a god, I would go back and change it all. But the past is the past.

"Let this be the advent of a greater future. Not of a revolution, but of an era where wealth and material gain are no longer the sole benchmarks in human achievement. This way of thinking has bankrupted our world in every way possible.

"I will not be returning. My time has come to an end, and my presence is not required. You have no need for a leader – only each other."

A blinding flash appeared like a lightning strike above the stunned crowd. When my vision cleared Taktarov was gone, and The Living Eye was back in the hospital room, standing at our side. Brynja and I felt the rush of wind as he returned through the shattered window, but never saw his entrance.

Valeriya was in the fetal position, tucked tightly into the corner. Her arms were bound at her back by Kenneth's straightjacket, knees pulled into her chest. A wave of golden hair blanketed her face, but couldn't conceal her tears. They flowed freely down her cheeks and dripped to the floor. She was broken. The sound of her brother's voice – even though it wasn't truly his – had opened a floodgate in a way that she couldn't have anticipated.

"What happens to her now?"Brynja asked.

The straightjacket dissipated into sparkling blue dust. She stood on shaky legs and wobbled to the window, resting her shoulder on the sill. She stared listlessly at the crowd dispersing below.

"I'll take care of her," Kenneth replied, gently stroking her hair with a gloved hand. "She's just a child. She needs help."

"Where will you go from here?" I asked.

"Away." Kenneth turned towards me, and his mask disappeared as our eyes met. "I don't hate you, Mox. But I can't forgive you. Don't try to find me, and never ask me for anything else."

A million words lodged painfully in the back of my throat. I wanted to thank him for saving me, for saving Brynja; for freeing us from a lifetime of running and isolation. And I wanted to ask – no, to *beg* – for his forgiveness. To say something so pure and genuine that Kenneth would have no choice but to stop and consider my words for even a moment. And possibly, one day, reach a point where forgiveness was an option.

I remained silent.

My unspoken words turned to cinder in my mouth as Kenneth sailed from the window with Valeriya in tow, disappearing into the ashen sky.

CHAPTER THIRTY-THREE

It was nightfall when the TT-100 blinked back to the sky above the South China Sea. We were guided down to Fortress 18 by a pattern of lights that bordered the hoverpad, where Bethany and Peyton nervously awaited our arrival.

McGarrity was rushed to the infirmary by a team of medics. Brynja and I gave him a cursory examination before loading him onto the jet in Thunder Bay; tearing away his blood-soaked shirt, we discovered that one of the bullets fired by Valeriya's henchmen grazed his ribcage, apparently missing every major vein and artery (an educated guess, based on the fact that he didn't bleed out). And the second round struck his left shoulder, leaving a small opening in the soft tissue, but causing no permanent damage. Despite the gruesome appearance of Steve's wounds, we were assured he was in no real danger.

Peyton threw her arms around my neck as soon as I stepped off the ramp, and even offered Brynja a quick hug. I'm sure it was a reflex – Peyton was a hugger. To my surprise Brynja responded with a warm smile, and offered a little squeeze of her own. It's amazing what happens when someone steps off of an aircraft: whether you're returning from a sun-drenched paradise or a blood-soaked battlefield, all is forgiven the moment you're reunited.

Bethany escorted us into the primary building, which featured the same stark color palettes and minimalistic design as Fortress 23. We followed her down a long narrow corridor to the media center, and collapsed onto a circular couch. After consuming the snacks and refreshments that Bethany insisted on serving, we dimmed the room and illuminated a holo-screen in search of information about the events that took place in Thunder Bay.

There was no shortage of media coverage. Every simulcast feed, in every language, was covering the 'resurrection' that took place less than an hour ago. Although news anchors and commentators discussed the same event, there was no clear consensus as to what actually occurred, or what it would mean to the world.

Some believed it'd been a religious experience; that there truly had been a resurrection of biblical proportions, and the message Kenneth had delivered under the guise of Russia's Son was now tantamount to scripture.

Skeptics blew off the display as nothing more than an elaborate hoax, like the cleverly-edited viral videos that have been annoying viewers for decades. One particularly annoyed commentator claimed that he'd been able to spot wires attached to Taktarov's shoulders where he was elevated, creating the illusion of flight.

New age physicists debated the prospect of an afterlife that, for the first time, could be quantified and measured. More traditional scientists simply noted that in light of recent discoveries about superhuman abilities, we had a great deal to learn about the universe and its laws. Rules that were once thought of as rigid were becoming infinitely more elastic as new discoveries surfaced. If there is a life after death, we hadn't yet seen any proof, but several experts wouldn't dismiss the possibility that evidence could be gleaned from studying Taktarov's reappearance.

And some even mused that the entire event was staged by the government, all in an attempt to quell the rising tide of violence; and that if this *was* a pre-meditated, scripted event, it was a brilliant one. Thanks to Taktarov's rousing speech, the looting, riots and worldwide backlash was beginning to dissipate. Rotating through one simulcast after another, from Moscow to Tokyo, Auckland to London, we noticed that every city shared a common theme: massive crowds dispersing without incident, just as they had in Thunder Bay. We never witnessed a single act of brutality carried out by peacekeepers or riot police – there was no need. Everyone was leaving of their own accord. People returned to their homes, leaving the streets littered with protest signs and makeshift weapons. Even firearms were discarded, left for local law enforcement to collect.

The flickering embers of the Red Army were fading to black before our eyes, and peace had been restored. Even if a spark of the movement remained, it was clear that the raging wildfire had been extinguished.

The next morning came quickly. A brilliant yellow sunrise spilled into the media room through wide-open skylights, warming my face. I'd fallen asleep in a lounge chair, and Brynja had passed out on the couch, sprawled haphazardly across Peyton's lap. But it wasn't the sun that woke us: it was the painfully cheerful sound of Bethany shouting, "Rise and shine, people!" before asking how we preferred our eggs, and if we'd like milk, tea or juice with our meal. I'd been awake for exactly six seconds and I was already exhausted. Bethany had that effect on me – it was like being followed around by the world's most enthusiastic flight attendant.

By the time we'd eaten and stepped onto the hoverpad, McGarrity was already there. He was dressed in a crisp new t-shirt, runners and jeans, and was freshly showered and shaved. Seemingly no worse for wear, he polished the glimmering TT-100 with a rag, whistling a tune as he buffed the hull. I had no idea what kind of painkillers the EMTs had given him after they stitched his wounds and operated on his shoulder, but they must have been amazing. I made a mental note to ask for a bottle of whatever he was on the next time I stopped by the infirmary.

"How are you feeling?" I shouted, strolling across the tarmac.

"Pretty awesome," he replied without turning around. "I saw you three catching up on your beauty sleep, but I didn't want to wake you."

"I appreciate the gesture," I said with a smile, motioning towards the TT-100, "but you don't have to polish my jet. I'm rich – I can pay someone to do it for me."

"I'm not polishing your jet." McGarrity turned towards me, tucking the rag into his back pocket. "I'm polishing *my* jet. I won it in The Spiral, remember?"

"You did offer it to him," Brynja was quick to remind me.

Before I could protest I remembered that the TT-100 could teleport, meaning McGarrity could be far, far away from me in just a matter of minutes. Possibly all the way on the other side of the planet. "Well, I hate to see the old girl go," I said, patting the freshly-polished hull, "but she's all yours."

"Hey, hey, hey," he said hastily, swatting my hand away as he yanked the rag from his pocket. "Fingerprints!"

"So where do you go from here?" Peyton asked.

"Wherever I'm needed," McGarrity stated proudly, straightening his posture. "As a superhuman I have a duty to protect the innocent, and fight crime wherever it may be."

We all stared at him for a moment, unconvinced.

"Or I'll take a long vacation and get drunk on a beach," he conceded. "This is what – January? I hear the Bahamas are pretty sick this time of year."

"Well, you'll need someone to help try and pilot this thing," Brynja added. "And if anyone could use a tan, it's me."

"You're leaving?" I asked. This was the first she'd mentioned her plans – although it's not like we'd been afforded much time to discuss our futures since battling our way through The Spiral.

"I figure with this much cosplay talent," she said, gesturing towards herself, "it'll go to waste hidden inside one of your fortresses. I need to hit the convention circuit and share my gift." Brynja smiled and glanced towards Peyton. "And besides, if I stick around here, the princess will just keep hugging me."

"I might," Peyton said flatly. "I have a hard time controlling it."

Brynja wrapped her arms around me and her lips brushed my ear. "I have to leave," she whispered, her voice laced with a thread of sadness. "You know it has to be this way."

"This isn't the end," I thought, staring into her eyes as she drew back. *"I'll see you again soon."*

Her lips curled at the corners. *"You've always been a shitty liar."*

I shook McGarrity's hand, gave Brynja one last hug and sent them on their way. I stepped back and wrapped an arm around Peyton's shoulder as the jet hovered into the sky, blinking away in a swirling thunderstorm of purple streaks.

We had a million things to do. My sister, niece and nephew needed me in Canada. Gavin was still lost somewhere in the Dark Zone. And with the discovery of more fortresses scattered around the world, I had a lot of investigating to do, and multiple loose ends to tie up. But before we got started, I had to tell Peyton something that had been burning in my mind for months.

She turned to me and flashed a knowing smile. "Whatever you have to say, it can wait."

"What?"

"You're afraid to tell me something," she said, pulling me close. "I know when your big fat brain is working overtime. I can practically see the steam coming out of your ears. It's okay, really. We have people who need us now...you can tell me later."

I shook my head and averted my eyes. "No, I really can't."

She placed her hands on the sides of my face, gently tilting my head until our eyes met. "*Say it*, then." She gazed at me with a sense of hope and optimism that penetrated right to my heart. It was a brilliant light that shone through the darkest moments, never dimming, no matter what the circumstance.

"Even though I'm here, I just..." I took a deep breath, t to summon the right combination of words. How do you explain to someone that you have only a short time left? "I don't know if I can give you the kind of future you deserve."

"I don't need you to 'give' me anything," she replied with complete confidence. "Don't get me wrong – I love you. And in your own idiotic way I know that you love me too. But I'm my own person. I was doing fine for a couple decades before I met you, and I'd be doing fine even if we never met."

"I don't know what's going to happen..." I sighed heavily and trailed off. The words never spilled out...I tried to force them, but they never came.

"No one does," she said. "But we don't give up on the things we want. We just keep moving forward."

One level after another we fought through The Spiral, never knowing what awaited us below. We didn't know how it would end, or how we'd escape when the water rose and the darkness swarmed in around us – we just kept fighting until we found a way.

Five years, five months, five weeks – I had no idea how much time I had left. But having a brain tumor or not, it didn't really matter – because in reality, *no one* knew. Everyone who died in The Spiral had woken up that morning thinking – *knowing* – that they had the rest of their lives to look forward to, and just a few short hours later their futures were torn away. My mind drifted to Doug, Chandler, Mac, and everyone else who'd died in The Fringe. They'd all lost their lives without a moment's notice.

I wasn't going to spend my final days worrying about how many of them I had left – I was going spend each one filling it with as much life as I could.

End of Volume Two

Partial transcript from the BBC News Simulcast 'The Daily Express'
Hosted by Liam Beckett, April 2042

Liam Beckett: "Devastation in Moscow as an explosion rocked the Kremlin just moments ago. Three of the palaces and one of the cathedrals have been completely destroyed, and the death toll is expected to be in the hundreds. We are being told that the President and his staff have been safely evacuated amidst the chaos.

"No one has claimed responsibility, although with Russia currently embroiled in three different wars throughout Eurasia, there are a number of possibilities as to who could be behind this deadly attack.

"As fires blazed and buildings collapsed, security footage confirms that a small group of masked assailants entered the Kremlin's lower levels. They emerged with a large casket, which they loaded onto an aircraft before fleeing. Russian Intelligence has declined to comment at this point, but speculation abounds that the casket contained the body of superhuman Sergei Taktarov.

"More on this harrowing story as details become available."

Character Profiles (spoiler alert)

Warning.

No, seriously, this is a *real* warning. It's not like one of those meaningless signs that says 'wear a hardhat', or 'don't combine alcohol with this medication' – this is for realsies.

There is a possibility of being slightly spoiled – just the *teensiest* bit – if you read these profiles, or even see the artwork. Not a lot, but if you're one of those people who hates to see the trailer before a movie comes out, then you might want to wait until:

a) you've already read the entire book, or
b) the character you want to check out has already made their appearance

I've done my due diligence, and the spoiler alert siren has been activated.

Carry on.

Mox

Matthew Moxon

Gender: Male   **Height:** 5'11" (180 cm)
Nationality: American   **Weight:** 185 lbs. (84 kg)
Born: April 13, 2012   **Build:** Average
Age: 29 (as of January, 2042)   **Hair:** Brown, short
Hometown: Buffalo, NY   **Eyes:** Blue

Powers and Abilities

Super-genius level intelligence

Moxon's IQ is among the highest in the world (most recently tested with a score of 220.) He also possesses a photographic memory, and can perform advanced mathematical calculations in his head.

By the age of 24 he could calculate cube roots faster than a calculator, and recall pi up to 23,800 decimal places.

See Mox's full profile at www.arenamode.com/wiki

Art by John 'Roc' Upchurch
Twitter @ JohnnyRocwell
johnnyrocwell.deviantart.com

Russia's Son

Sergei Taktarov

Gender: Male

Nationality: Russian

Born: December 25, 2020

Died: July, 2041

Hometown: Stary Oskol, Russia

Height: 5'9" (175 cm)

Weight: 190 lbs. (86 kg)

Build: Muscular/slim

Hair: Blond, parted

Eyes: Blue

Powers and Abilities

Flight

Taktarov can fly for limited periods of time. His maximum range is unknown, but he has been seen traveling as far as the ozone layer.

Laser Vision

The ability to produce a beam of light from both eyes, with a range of over 500 feet. The lasers can cut through virtually any substance, including metal and stone.

See Taktarov's full profile at www.arenamode.com/wiki

Pencils by Steve McNiven
Inks by Mark McKenna, Colors by Roc Upchurch

Brynja
Brynja Guðmundsdóttir

Gender: Female
Nationality: Icelandic
Born: Unknown
Age: Appears early 20s
Hometown: Reykjavík, Iceland

Height: Abstract
Weight: Abstract
Build: Slim
Hair: Appears blue
Eyes: Appear blue

Powers and Abilities

Limited Psychic Abilities

Brynja can read 'surface' thoughts, but doesn't have the ability to dig deeper into someone's memories unless she's invited in by the person she's attempting to read.

See Brynja's full profile at www.arenamode.com/wiki

Art by Comic Book Girl 19
youtube.com/comicbookgirl19
www.comicbookgirl19.com
Twitter @ cbgirl19

The Living Eye

Kenneth Livitski

Gender: Male

Nationality: Canadian

Born: August 15, 2018

Age: 23 (as of January, 2042)

Hometown: Thunder Bay, Ontario

Height: 5'10" (178 cm)

Weight: 210 lbs. (95 kg)

Build: Average/non-athletic

Hair: Brown

Eyes: Brown

Powers and Abilities

Solid Energy Constructs

By focusing his intention, The Living Eye can create any object or living creature, and control them indefinitely. He claims that these constructs can be nearly infinite in size and mass, and are limited only by his imagination.

See The Living Eye's full profile at www.arenamode.com/wiki

Art by John Broglia
Twitter @ JohnBroglia
fb.com/jpbroglia

Peyton Lockridge

Gender: Female

Nationality: American

Born: September 1, 2020

Age: 22 (as of January, 2042)

Hometown: New York City

Height: 5′6″ (168 cm)

Weight: 130 lbs. (58.9 kg)

Build: Average/Curvy

Hair: Pink

Eyes: Blue

Powers and Abilities

None.

eve McGarrity

aka: 'Braveheart', aka: Murder_Lion_14

Gender: Male
Nationality: American
Born: November 24, 2021
Age: 21 (as of January, 2042)
Hometown: Austin, Texas

Height: 6'0" (183 cm)
Weight: 190 lbs. (86 kg)
Build: Average
Hair: Blond
Eyes: Green

Powers and Abilities

Light Bending

Can use any significant light source to create weapons – typically a broadsword.

Art by Derek Laufman
dereklaufman.deviantart.com
Twitter @ laufman

ᴚltan Saeed Al Darmaki

Gender: Male

Nationality: Emarati

Born: August 24, 2010

Age: 32 (as of January, 2042)

Hometown: Abu Dhabi, U.A.E.

Height: 6'0" (183 cm)

Weight: 210 lbs. (95 kg)

Build: Average

Hair: Black

Eyes: Brown

Powers and Abilities

Elemental Control

Can harness the power of all four elements – wind, earth, fire and water – and use them as weapons or constructs.

Art by Derek Laufman

dereklaufman.deviantart.com

Twitter @ laufman

.ıentina

Gender: Female

Nationality: American

Born: March 9, 2015

Age: 27 (as of January, 2042)

Hometown: Liberty, KY

Height: 5′3″ (160 cm)

Weight: 120 lbs. (54.5 kg)

Build: Athletic

Hair: Red

Eyes: Green

Powers and Abilities

Hydrokinesis

Can manipulate water and use it as a weapon, or to create partially-solid objects.

Art by John Broglia
Twitter @ JohnBroglia
fb.com/jpbroglia

Colors by Jasen Smith
Twitter @ Jasen_Smith
jasen-smith.deviantart.com

e Nightmare

race Teach Weaving

Gender: Female
Nationality: Unknown
Born: Unknown
Age: Unknown
Hometown: Unknown

Height: Unknown
Weight: Unknown
Build: Varies
Hair: Brown (natural)
Eyes: Hazel (natural)

Powers and Abilities

Shape-Shifting

Can assume any physical form by 'painting' herself into a new version of herself. Weaving often embodies the form of 'The Nightmare': a slender, black-haired woman who can bleed in and out of shadows.

Fear Manipulation

Uses her opponent's fears against them, causing their worst nightmares to manifest into reality.

Art by Dave Johnson
Twitter @ Devilpig666
devilpig.deviantart.com

Jason Baroody
aroody.deviantart.com
ebook.com/jasonbaroody

and Mark McKenna
markmckennaart.com
facebook.com/markinker

Colors by Jasen Smith
Twitter @ Jasen_Smith
jasen-smith.deviantart.com

About the Author

Blake Northcott is an author, Twitter-er, and Slayer of Vampires (only the ones that sparkle).

She enjoys comic books, novels, movies, travel, and the occasional rum & Coke. Turn-offs include Wheel of Fortune and Ke$ha.

Blake lives just outside of Toronto, Ontario, Canada with her family.

If you want to know more about Blake, visit her on one of those social media thingies. Or her website ... she has one of those too.

BlakeNorthcott.com

BlakeNorthcott.com
facebook.com/BlakeNorthcott
twitter.com/ComicBookGrrl

25700313R00224

Printed in Great Britain
by Amazon